T0374306

THE LAST MESSAGE

THE LAST MESSAGE

A NOVEL

KEN BEARIE

iUniverse, Inc.
New York   Bloomington

The Last Message
A Novel

iUniverse books may be ordered through booksellers or by contacting:

iUniverse
1663 Liberty Drive
Bloomington, IN 47403
www.iuniverse.com
1-800-Authors (1-800-288-4677)

Because of the dynamic nature of the Internet, any Web addresses or links contained in this book may have changed since publication and may no longer be valid. The views expressed in this work are solely those of the author and do not necessarily reflect the views of the publisher, and the publisher hereby disclaims any responsibility for them.

ISBN: 978-1-4502-3428-3 (sc)
ISBN: 978-1-4502-3429-0 (ebook)

Printed in the United States of America

iUniverse rev. date: 6/2/2010

"Civilization is a race between
education and catastrophe."

H.G.Wells

"In my dream, the angel shrugged and said, 'If we fail this time, it will be a failure of imagination' and then she placed the world gently in the palm of my hand."

Brian Andreas

ACKNOWLEDGMENTS

I would like to thank my family and friends for their support, especially my wife and soul mate Linda for encouraging me in this quest. I am also much indebted to Tom Bearie, who diligently functioned as reviewer, critic and editor extraordinaire.

Chapter 1
June 9, 2:00 PM

"This can't be possible! We've been examining this damn thing for days, and we still can't make any sense of it!" The exasperation and agitation were evident in Randolph's voice as he addressed the gathered team members. For the past four days, the optimism of everyone in this elite group had been steadily declining—along with their physical stamina. The team had spent virtually all of their waking hours confined in this tightly secured facility less than fifty miles from Manhattan. Could the world's future really depend on this small team's efforts? Could the bizarre object they were examining actually cause the end of civilization? The emotional breaking point was painfully close for many of the exhausted researchers.

Randolph Schiller was the nominal head of the research team, personally selected by President Arbust. Randy, as his politically connected friends in Washington knew him, had an impressive background. He had advanced steadily through the academic world and had attained wide recognition for his research in elementary physics. With dark brown hair and even darker brown eyes, Randy personified several traits of a typical leader. A physically imposing figure at six feet four inches and 210 pounds, Randy was in excellent shape despite his age of fifty-six. He was quite self-satisfied about having maintained a daily six-mile jogging regimen throughout his adult life. Regardless of the weather or his frequent business trips, maintaining a rigorous exercise regimen was a key part of how Randy lived. It always amazed him that so many associates had failed in life by not controlling their desires and actions. To perpetuate his string of career successes, he knew it would also be essential to control the researchers assigned to this project.

Randy had a style of dealing with people that made their conversations with him seem more like being on the receiving end of a lecture. Everyone was aware of his sharp intellect, but he was even more aware of it, so he routinely expected others to defer to his superior thinking. If they would not, Randy could always replace them with others who were more appreciative of his capabilities.

Most of the team had gathered in the lab's impressive conference room to update each other with their respective progress, or more accurately that day, their lack of progress. Under normal circumstances, this advanced research site would have been a highly desired assignment for the selected team members. The spacious office and laboratory areas were outfitted with the most sophisticated test equipment available. The rolling, park-like grounds and highly secured entrances to the complex heightened both the attractiveness and the prestige of the facility. All the accoutrements affirmed that those chosen to work here were regarded as being among the most successful in their respective fields. Unfortunately, any current appreciation for the beauty and prestige of the setting was totally overshadowed by the dire task at hand.

"All of us know the dwindling time frame to solve this dilemma." Randy addressed the group in his usual grim manner, omitting unnecessary civilities. This was the first team meeting where fatigue had become apparent in his usually robust voice and appearance.

"I'm not trying to add to everyone's stress, but we're rapidly running out of time. I'm providing a briefing to President Arbust at 5 PM. That gives us three more hours. Let's at least put together a better guess at what we're dealing with!" Randy had not reached his level of accomplishment in the academic world by failing at tasks—this was a new and exasperating feeling for him. He also knew that not everyone was hoping the team would be successful.

When the pending catastrophe was first recognized, the research team had been hastily assembled, with the unavoidable political mishaps from recruiting many individuals within only a few days. A number of notable and highly visible candidates were left outside the team, several of which elected to cavil among themselves and to any media journalists willing to listen. How could the selection team have overlooked their publicized Nobel Prize achievements, their stellar academic reputations or their innovative inventions? Too many outsiders with a vested interest in the breakdown of the selected group were waiting and hoping for an opportunity to nudge the team toward failure. A number of these arrogant leaders in science and business would jump at the first chance to take charge of such a crucial project.

Among all the investigation team members, Rob Thornton had quickly risen to become the real team leader, solely due to his unequaled competence in attacking the problem. His even-tempered method of synthesizing all the research data was not rare in the scientific community, but it was definitely impressive when applied in this unique and extraordinarily stressful situation.

Rob was well aware of the respect the others had for him, but he also knew they considered him an outsider to their established Washington network. The fact that he was still in his thirties was an obvious variance from the older age of most of the team members. He had an athletic build, kept lean by his frequent tennis matches and generally active lifestyle. His dedication to his work precluded much of a social life, which was always something he intended to remedy but never quite got around to. Since most women found his deep blue eyes and his dry humor very appealing, he always figured there would be plenty of time for a long-term relationship, perhaps when his career wasn't consuming so much of his time.

The selection committee had chosen Rob primarily because of his recent near-celebrity status achieved by solving a decades-old engineering challenge. Scientists had long dreamed of a device that could efficiently transport objects between Earth and an orbiting space station. Rob's background in physics and his experience in structural engineering enabled him to creatively employ a laser beam as a power source for a space elevator. The working model of the elevator was capable of rapidly ascending and descending a thin carbon nanotube to a height of over six hundred feet, laying the groundwork for future enhanced versions. The attendant publicity marked him as an extremely bright scientist who was equally adept with both traditional research techniques and with innovative outside-the-box thinking.

As the team members moved out of the conference room to continue struggling with the dilemma, Rob returned directly to C Lab, the building that contained the bizarre object. C Lab was located only a few hundred yards away from the team's conference room. As he quickly walked by himself along the paved path between the buildings, he was oblivious to the manicured landscape and the balmy spring weather. Focused on the pressing crisis, he couldn't help but wonder how many more days they might survive. They had to figure out how this object seemingly defied the laws of physics.

As Rob reached the lab building, he quickly passed through an outer door and placed his clearance badge on a glass scanner. All building accesses were monitored 24/7 by surveillance cameras scattered throughout the complex. Entrances to the most secured buildings in the complex were constructed with two electronically controlled doors. Anyone attempting to enter these secured buildings required passing two identification tests.

The first test required the employee or visitor to place their personally assigned clearance badge on the scanner mounted within the dual entrance doors. A computerized system instantly determined if the owner of the badge was authorized to enter that specific building. From a remotely located room filled with monitors, the security staff then visually verified a live camera image of the person attempting to enter. If the individual entering the facility was not the assigned owner of the badge, the inner entrance door would remain locked. Since anything out of order also resulted in the system electronically locking the outer door, this process trapped the individual in the entrance area until the discrepancy was resolved.

As the remotely controlled inner door was opening, Rob was immediately surprised to see a stocky, middle-aged person standing next to the object. As the individual turned toward the opened door, Rob easily recognized Taylor McCracken, one of the senior physicists on the team. "Taylor must have left the briefing early, or maybe skipped it entirely," Rob speculated to himself. Recalling the conference room that he had left only a few minutes earlier, Rob could not remember seeing Taylor at the team meeting. Quickly passing through the inner glass door, he was shocked at what he saw.

"Don't touch that!" Rob shouted, from just inside C Lab's secured entrance.

Taylor jerked back his outstretched arm, caught in the act of intentionally violating the strict controls in effect since the mysterious object had first been brought into the lab. He apparently was trying to excise a small sample from the object's exterior.

"We're running out of time!" shouted Taylor without the least bit of embarrassment at being caught. "We have to get a sample to Livermore's TEM."

The world's most powerful transmission electron microscope, called a TEM, was available for their use, although its location was problematic—almost three thousand miles away at the Lawrence Livermore Laboratory in California. For the TEM to analyze the object's material, the team would have to excise a minute sample from the object's surface and deliver it to the California lab. The TEM technicians could then cut and polish the sample until it was transparent to high-energy electrons for imaging. Unlike most electron microscopes that image the surface of materials, this state-of-the-art machine actually probed the internal structure.

"We can't risk it! As far as we know, any damage to the surface could cause it to explode." Rob Thornton was seemingly the only voice on the team still pushing for continuing their cautious approach. Most of the team members had run out of ideas. Under the strain of physical exhaustion, they were desperate to try approaches that were more radical.

"Hell, it could explode regardless of anything we do," retorted Taylor as he reluctantly backed away from the object. "We have to know what it's made of!"

The exhaustive spectroscopic scans conducted locally had already determined the object contained a totally unknown element, at least on the outer shell. What lay within was the ominous question of the hour. And of course, the bizarre fact that its phenomenal weight was somehow doubling every day.

Chapter 2
June 9, 3:30 PM

The worldwide media had pounced on the story as soon as the initial discovery occurred. Not since the World Wars of the twentieth century had a single topic so riveted the entire planet. Calamities had always made great news stories, but for the majority of the world's citizens, such disasters were usually in far-off locales. As long as it did not affect one's daily life, where was the urgency in dealing with yet another crisis in a far-away country? Calamities were always affecting people somewhere in the world.

Doomsday forecasters have existed throughout history, foretelling imminent destruction for countless reasons. This situation, however, was quite different from any previous threat to a country or group—this calamity would soon affect every single person on the planet. The crisis was providing ample fuel for doomsday cynics as well as pushing anyone with the slightest tendency toward depression closer to their personal abyss.

What the team had discovered over the past week was very limited—studying the mysterious object had generated far more questions than answers. All their efforts focused on understanding a metallic-appearing cube slightly less than six inches on each side. No seams were visible anywhere on the surface, which was a solid, light grey color. All six sides contained a number of markings, different on all sides, yet similarly centered on each surface. The investigators were trying to determine if they were random marks left by a metal milling operation or alternatively, a type of writing inscribed on the exterior. The team had optically scanned all six sides of the cube when it first arrived at the lab, but despite all their efforts, they could not match the odd markings to characters in any known language.

The initial chemical scans detected absolutely no traces of explosives or radiation. In fact, unlike all known substances, no chemical traces of any kind emanated from the object—at least none that they could detect. It exhibited no magnetic qualities and its temperature, which they could only measure on its surface, was exactly that of the ambient room temperature. The exterior was smooth and extremely hard, although by touch, it appeared no different from any other hard metal.

Spectrographic analysis confirmed the exterior was composed entirely of an unknown element. It had been several decades since anyone had identified a new stable element. The periodic table taught to every schoolchild expanded infrequently, but the only additions in recent years had been for transitory elements that do not occur naturally and generally devolve rapidly to more stable forms.

How could a small object possibly have such extraordinary weight? Incredibly, it now weighed over 140,000 pounds. Furthermore, how could the weight possibly be increasing? It was exactly doubling in weight every cycle, which was occurring daily. So far, the team was at a total loss to explain either its extraordinary weight or how that weight could possibly be increasing.

It had not taken the scientific community long to realize the potential impact of this object. Any item with its weight increasing without any increase in size was not just a bizarre oddity. If this inexplicable phenomenon continued, as it appeared to be doing, it would soon crush through the floor of the laboratory and begin descending through the Earth's crust. The extreme weight had already started to deform the surface directly underlying the object. The opportunity to directly observe and hopefully to somehow alter this object would soon be lost if it descended out of sight.

The fact that the object might soon sink through the lab floor was not the reason for the escalating worldwide concern. If the object continued growing in weight within the Earth's interior, the planet itself would eventually be at risk. Geophysicists across the world were debating the eventual effect of such an object, producing wide speculation and different predictions. But all of the predictions were dismal, and everyone involved with studying the object was aware of the dire forecasts.

Seismologists had only recently established that manmade objects could actually cause devastating earthquakes. The construction of large dams causes millions of tons of water to press down on any nearby fault lines, potentially forcing them to either slip apart or press together.

In 2003, the Chinese government built the Zipingpu dam less than a mile from a known major fault. Although a large earthquake had not occurred in that area of China for thousands of years, a devastating quake happened in 2008. The 7.9 quake cracked the 511-foot high dam, causing one of the biggest disasters in recent history— seventy thousand people were killed and five million were left homeless. Geoscientists estimated the weight of the water in the reservoir created twenty-five times the natural stress that tectonic movements exerted in a year.

At the current rate of doubling in weight, it would only be a matter of weeks before this strange object could cause cataclysmic events. If this increased mass descended into the Earth's interior and continued its growth, seismic waves would soon propagate throughout the entire world. Any greatly enlarged mass at a single point within the Earth's crust or mantle would radically disrupt the overall equilibrium of the planet. The imbalance would soon affect the structurally weakest points between the Earth's tectonic plates, causing massive earthquakes with increasing frequency and strength. Geoscientists predicted earthquake damage, volcanic eruptions and tsunamis would eventually affect every location and every person on the planet.

The threat of tsunamis particularly evoked feelings of terror. Most people still vividly recalled the earthquake spawned tsunami of December 2004 when just one seismic shift off Malaysia claimed over two hundred thousand lives. With 10 percent of the globe's inhabitants living in coastal areas less than thirty-three feet above sea level, there were valid reasons for the growing panic.

CHAPTER 3
JUNE 10, 1:46 PM

"286,720 pounds! Damn! Exactly the same doubling in weight!" Sharon Catwold, one of the key investigators, read the chilling measurement from the meter. It was hardly a surprise to Rob and the others who gathered by the monitors—the same rate of increase had occurred at every past cycle. It occurred again precisely at 1:46 PM. The hope had been almost palpable that the inexorable growth would cease, or at least slow down. But not today.

The selection committee had solicited Sharon to join the team because of her exemplary work in molecular biology. Her theories on the similarities between organic and inorganic molecules significantly blurred the historic definition of what constituted a living thing. She was actually the last person assigned to the team, almost as an afterthought by Randy and the selection committee.

Randy Schiller had initially selected members with whom he had worked over the years. He was not inclined to recruit anyone who might usurp his authority, or more importantly, who might detract from his central role in leading the project. The Administration's selection committee had previously solicited Rob Thornton and other notables, but Randy was certain he could control who the media would be interviewing.

Another key condition for prospective team members was a willingness to join an evidently dangerous assignment. Since the object was made of an unidentified material, anyone in close proximity to the device could be exposed to unknown dangers. Those electing to join the project risked themselves for a variety of reasons, most viewing it as a unique lifetime opportunity for global recognition in their particular field of science.

Randy was unconcerned that no one on the team represented the biological sciences, an area he had considered of little value in this problem. However, the selection committee kept emphasizing that the synergy of having all disciplines attacking the problem from different angles should help. Randy eventually agreed, knowing he could always steer the team's direction by allocating the resources himself.

In most mixed team settings, anyone as attractive and vibrant as Sharon would have generated lots of interest from the other team members. Just past her thirty-eighth birthday, she was in great shape and well proportioned. Her auburn shoulder-length hair gracefully framed an alluring face. Sharon's green eyes were easily her most distinctive feature—they flashed with intensity whenever she discussed a favorite topic. Despite the frantic work pace of the past several days, Sharon remained upbeat and even managed to joke with her associates.

As most team members who agreed to join this potentially hazardous project, Sharon was single— her intense career path had left little time for serious relationships. Although the women were outnumbered three to one on the team, the sexual tension among the team members had so far been fairly latent. Knowing they were facing a possible life-or-death situation, Sharon and the rest of the team members were trying to focus single-mindedly on their task.

Outside the team, people reacted in vastly different ways depending on their personal worldview, their religious beliefs and their emotional state. As terrified people across the entire world watched, with no way of influencing the investigation or the planet's fate, denial of reality was a common response. Surely, someone would find a solution.

Of those who viewed these events as the approaching end of the world, many sought solace in their respective religions. The concept of an afterlife undoubtedly helped many individuals confront their potential death, but it was difficult for them to reconcile the object's presence with the theology and prophesies of their respective religion. It was especially difficult for those who had very specific beliefs and expectations of what would occur in their anticipated end-times. Based on their interpretation of the biblical book of Revelation, the expectations of the "Left-Behinders" were definitely not going to be met, nor were prophesies in the Qur'an as interpreted by many Muslims. Whether an individual was religiously inclined or not, many found themselves drawing closer to their loved ones and attempting to make the most of what they feared was their remaining time.

Buffered from the worldwide reactions to the crisis, the research team focused on finding a means to halt the object's doubling in weight every day. At the moment, Sharon was investigating the timing of the cycles and was about to brief the rest of the team on her findings. With the sophisticated equipment in the lab, the team now had much more accurate measurements, including the exact interval between each cycle.

Although there were a number of researchers present in the room, Sharon found herself directing her comments primarily to Rob. She had discovered earlier that her conversations with Rob were far more useful than those she had with other team members. Rob always seemed completely open to discussing potential explanations for the device, even the most extreme possibilities. She was intrigued by how he sometimes seemed to know where she was headed in a dialog even before she realized it herself.

"There's absolutely no variation. A growth cycle lasts exactly 23 hours, 59 minutes and 55.385 seconds," Sharon informed the group, pointing to the figure she had scribbled earlier on the whiteboard at the front of the room. "Can this extremely precise interval be a clue to its nature?"

The investigators first thought the cycles were exactly on a 24-hour basis, leading to speculation that a simple timing device controlled the growth process. After the scientists monitored it closely with the lab's sophisticated equipment, the slight deviation from a 24-hour cycle became apparent. They also discovered the frequency never varied by even a millisecond.

Sharon asked Rob directly, "Could there be a correlation with Earth's solar day?" She wondered if it might be a type of circadian rhythm, based on the Earth's rotation or axis to the sun.

"I doubt it," Rob responded. "The solar day varies slightly all through the year, so early astronomers established an artificial average solar day at 24 hours. We now know it's actually a few milliseconds longer, so we add a leap second every so many years. This object's doubling cycle doesn't match the average or the adjusted solar day. As for the Earth's rotation, due to our orbit around the sun, the Earth actually takes four minutes less time to complete one revolution—23 hours 56 minutes. The weight doubling cycle doesn't match the rotation time from the sun's axis either."

"I'm not so sure." Sharon wondered if there might still be some significance. "Even though it seems constant to us, the Earth's revolution time has varied over our planet's history. Did you know that when the Earth first formed, a day only lasted ten hours?" A few of the team members seemed surprised by this fact, like they had just been told the sun hadn't always risen in the East.

Sharon continued, "Natural events like ice ages and hurricanes have a small impact that slows the planet's revolution. But the largest affect has always been from tidal friction—the constant gravitational drag between the moon and the Earth."

"That's true," Rob responded. "It's a long shot, but we should contact the Astrophysics Institute in Palo Alto. They recently published an article on how climate has affected the Earth's revolution time. Let's see just when the Earth had a solar day that matches this weight doubling cycle." Sharon agreed it was worth checking out—the information might be useful.

Rob continued brainstorming with Sharon and the other team members present. "It's definitely consistent. Whatever this object is, its weight is exactly doubling every cycle. But ever since the object was first discovered, the size of the object has remained constant. The cube still measures exactly 14.92 centimeters. This bizarre increase in weight has to have an explanation."

Yet both Rob and Sharon realized it defied known laws of physics. Mass just did not increase without an offset to mass elsewhere, or to a reduction of energy. $E = mc^2$ was considered inviolate, at least in the world above the molecular level. The entire team was baffled as to how this general law could not apply.

"Could the precise timing be due to an internal rhythm from nuclear forces—oscillating frequencies, similar to the quartz-timing element used in watches?" Seeing the glazed look of a few of the team members, Sharon further explained her idea. "Like a small current in a watch excites the nuclear elements of a quartz crystal to vibrate in a consistent timely manner."

After a few moments of thought, Rob speculated to the gathered group, "There might be significance to this exact regularity of cycles. If we could relate it to any natural phenomena, maybe we could better understand the process."

As a molecular biologist, Sharon was the first to highlight the similarity to mitosis in all organic molecules. "When cells divide, either animal or plant, they effectively double their number in a fairly regular time pattern. But this pattern in cells is never precise—there are always huge variations in environmental and chemical components."

Sharon offered an intriguing suggestion, "Could the doubling be driven by nuclear mitosis? If so, then why isn't it doubling at a phenomenally rapid rate like most nuclear reactions?"

Building on the idea, Rob immediately suggested another thought. "Maybe it's related to the half-lives of elements, which can span from nanoseconds to millennia. Perhaps this is the rate for an element never before detected on Earth."

Then again, a few of the researchers wondered if it could actually be mitosis of organic molecules, or, as the sensational six-inch headlines had displayed on that morning's Los Angeles Times, could it be: "A L I V E ?"

CHAPTER 4
JUNE 10, 3:00 PM

286,720 pounds

As all the major media outlets continued to spread reports of the object, the bizarre news mesmerized people across the entire world. When the team first realized the extreme threat from the object, they readily provided their research data to the global news media. They recognized they had a limited amount of time to study the object, and so far, there was no solution in sight. The team hoped the wide news coverage would quickly stimulate leading scientists around the world to assist in solving the puzzle.

A number of the world's most esteemed scientists offered their services and joined the research team. Their participation greatly expanded the scope of the investigation, and provided a challenge for Randy Schiller to coordinate the diverse group. Although a variety of nations were represented, English was the predominant language used in team sessions and communications with scientists in distant locations. Video conferencing brought even more participants into the brainstorming sessions, as research labs and academic centers across the world provided suggestions.

Besides addressing the dire threat to the planet, the challenge to established rules of physics was a key incentive for scientists around the world to participate. The science world was puzzled with this unusual discovery—being the first to unravel this mystery, or even to be the first to debunk it as a hoax, provided strong motivation in every physics community.

The research effort was becoming more global every day. The International Geosciences Institute was one of the first organizations to forecast how the object could cause horrendous seismic activity. The International Union of Pure and Applied Physics coordinated communications between its own members and the research team in New York. Numerous academic institutions were providing liaisons to the research team, which brought in several of the most leading edge thinkers in theoretical physics.

Despite the high visibility and daily press releases, the citizens of many developing nations still viewed the dilemma as a hoax perpetrated for the purposes of furthering Western political and economic ambitions. Lack of trust in the veracity of reported events was nothing new. Even with overwhelming evidence and testimony surrounding the first lunar landing in 1969, a few individuals continued to believe it was all a carefully orchestrated hoax. Likewise, a number of factions flatly denied the reported details and the potential impact of this crisis.

Conspiracy theories had frequently emerged to explain international incidents, particularly unexpected deaths of political leaders. With an infinite number of possible explanations, and the common tendency to obscure political and economic motives, there was always room to postulate a sinister force behind any event.

Although they found it puzzling, most individuals exposed to the media reports accepted the news as truthful. Attempting to calm the growing panic, politicians and respected leaders provided frequent media interviews to describe how the government was dealing with the dilemma. In the United States, the Secretary of the Treasury joined Federal Reserve Board officials in efforts to calm financial markets and halt the growing turmoil in the world's stock exchanges. Global banking groups were similarly trying to quell the emotional sell-offs by investors who feared the uncertainty of halting the object's growth.

As in most perilous situations, many people turned to their religious leaders for solace and hope, but the frightening development provided a major dilemma for members of many religious organizations. Representatives of virtually all the world's major religions attempted to explain the phenomena, but all came up painfully short. It just did not make sense—not just the puzzle of how this was happening, but why God would allow such a doomsday object to exist.

Most religions offered explanations as to the vagaries of man's existence, often describing them as trials meant to test one's faith. Many religious associations regularly pronounced misfortunes and catastrophes to be divine retribution for humankind's actions. A few spiritual leaders even claimed God directed disasters to entire groups of people because of a single individual's actions, serving as both punishment and as an example to others.

When the tools of modern science failed to provide any reasonable explanation, a number of people of various faiths were content to believe it was not essential to really understand the object. As with intangible concepts like the soul or heaven, perhaps this was also too complex or mysterious for humans to comprehend. Many of these believers found comfort in the premise that even if this strange object's existence could not be explained, everything still had a specific reason, pre-determined by a creator or designer.

Even those who believed in a god who did not interact with the world could not find an adequate explanation as to why such a god would allow all life on Earth to end. What was the point in creating a world that would come to an abrupt and inglorious end? Throughout human evolution and the growth of civilization, setbacks and disasters had been commonplace, yet the overall advance of life forms continued. This mysterious object, if it continued in its current development, would cause the total destruction of the planet.

There had to be an explanation. There had to be some way of preventing the end of the Earth.

Chapter 5
June 10, 4:00 PM

286,720 pounds

"Get the facilities manager here as soon as possible," Rob hurriedly instructed the team's liaison with the permanent lab complex staff. "Tell him to bring the construction specs that include the lab's floor and whatever lies beneath it. Also, have him bring whatever engineering data they've got on the entire site—soil composition and density, depth to underlying rock layers, and known fault lines. If we're lucky, all of that detail was collected before this complex was built." As usual, Rob was way ahead of his teammates in identifying the critical path to pursue.

The facilities manager entered the conference room about an hour later, accompanied by his senior engineer who was struggling to carry five large blueprints, each tightly rolled and about four feet long. The engineer also had an oversized briefcase stuffed with reports and file folders. While the engineer organized the various documents on the conference room table, the facilities manager introduced himself to Rob and the other researchers in the room.

"Dr. Thornton, I'm Brad Collins. I've been responsible for construction at this complex for the past twelve years, and I think we have what you need." The short, stocky facilities manager was in his early forties and appeared surprisingly cheerful despite the desperate situation faced by the team. His good mood was apparently based on pride in the level of detail he had been able to collect so quickly. He addressed the researchers that had gathered around a large table.

"We're in luck. Environmental Impact Reports were required for this area several years before the first building in this complex was constructed. So we've got an accurate picture of the underlying soil layers, and there are no signs of any fault lines within fifteen miles of this site." He unrolled a large blueprint titled "Bldg 401" and quickly spread it on the oversized conference room table.

"C Lab, the building we're now in, was identified in the original specs as 401. You can see on this chart how the floor was constructed. We're looking at a six-inch concrete floor, reinforced with #4 rebar, placed directly over two feet of compacted topsoil. Beneath this is the natural soil and rock terrain."

The facilities manager leaned over the table and pointed to an odd shaped symbol on the drawing. "You can see from these marked points on the chart that they probed the soil at a number of locations. By hydraulically pushing a probe into the soil, they measured the resistance on the probe. Matching these measurements with known resistance from various types of soil, they determined the underlying soil composition, at least as to moisture, air and compressibility."

"But what about the floor itself?" queried Rob.

"This type of reinforced concrete has a compression strength rating of forty-five hundred pounds per square inch." Brad Collins was very thorough as he continued the briefing. "The inspection reports show spot testing of the concrete in three separate locations in the building complex, all of which exceeded this average strength by 5 percent or more. Incidentally, these ratings are far in excess of building code requirements. The building inspectors actually excised three core samples and subjected them to standard compressive strength testing. This involves increasing pressure on a sample until its compressive strength is reached and the concrete is compacted into a smaller volume."

Impressed with the detail available and the obvious competency of the facilities manager, Rob was confident that the critical estimate they needed could be provided. There was only one layer between the object and the concrete floor—a steel sheet that had been used to support the object during its transport to the lab.

"That's great. But we also need to know how the increasing weight of the object will deform the underlying metal panel. Likewise, what effect will the size of the metal section have on the surrounding concrete?" The senior engineer and several of the other researchers began calculating various scenarios, using one of the computer terminals located in the back of the room.

The engineers would soon have the data to predict how much weight would be required before the object crushed the concrete floor and started its descent through the underlying soil. Once that occurred, there would be minimal opportunity to either study or affect the object.

If the object actually descended into or even through the Earth's crust, the team would have to consider entirely different factors. How would the increasing temperature of the Earth's interior affect the object? What would the extreme pressure inside the Earth do to it? If the object continued to descend, would it be possible to estimate how long it would take to reach the Earth's center? Would all life have been destroyed by that time?

It took less than ten minutes for Brad and the senior facility engineer to return to Rob, who was still working at the conference table. The engineers had finished the calculations for the immediate problem and lost no time in presenting the results. Brad pointed to the center of the floor plan depicted on the unrolled blueprint and announced to the gathered team members, "Here's what we've got. The rebar that reinforces the entire floor doesn't add to the compression strength of the concrete, but it will spread the stress over a much larger area and likely cause most of the building to collapse. Likewise with the steel panel that's underneath the object. The panel will also spread the stress over an area wider than the base of the six inch cube, and the steel panel will eventually fold around the object as the weight increases."

Rob immediately responded, "If the building collapses, that ends our monitoring. If it turns out we can't halt its weight expansion, at least we need to preserve our equipment. We'll need it to continue monitoring the object after it descends through the floor."

The senior engineer agreed, and had already considered that in his calculations. He continued, "We can isolate the stressed area by sawing the concrete floor and steel panel in a three-foot diameter circle around the object. We've estimated the amount of pressure before this round segment is driven through the concrete and into the underlying layers of soil.

"The three-foot circular section should support about 4,578,000 pounds of pressure. If the object exceeds this weight, it will crash right through the floor. For planning purposes, I'd say anything over four million pounds could drive it right through the Earth's surface."

The engineer continued describing possible variables, limits to modeling techniques and typical disclaimers for these types of estimates. But whether it took an additional one or two cycles to reach the critical point was not the essential issue. What was crucial was how little time was left to study the object.

"That's only four more cycles!" Rob exclaimed. He had previously calculated the projected weight of the object if the weight doubling cycles continued on the same schedule.

"Since it was first measured at 280 pounds, the object has doubled in weight at each of the last ten cycles to reach its current weight of 286,720 pounds. If it continues increasing at this rate, at 1:46 PM this Saturday, it will double in weight from about 2.3 million pounds to over 4.5 million pounds. We've got less than four days to figure this damn thing out."

CHAPTER 6
JUNE 1, 7:15 AM

Nine days earlier, Frank Whippert had started his shift at the mail facility of the United Nations complex in Manhattan. The job was not too demanding, which matched Frank's level of interest in his career. Hired right out of high school, he had been performing essentially the same function for the past eleven years. Frank's real interests had always been focused outside of his work, centered on his young family and his close network of friends. He was looking forward to seeing his son's soccer game that afternoon, so had planned to both begin and end his day an hour earlier than usual.

After finishing his usual venti coffee from the ubiquitous neighborhood Starbucks, he began his regular morning task of moving the recent deliveries into the mail sorting room. Since it was a Monday morning, he anticipated a higher volume due to multiple deliveries over the weekend.

For the past ten or so years, the AutoClear had automatically scanned all packages before they were transferred out of the basement receiving area. This efficient machine was a conveyor belt driven x-ray device similar to those used for scanning checked luggage in many modern airport facilities. It scanned the packages in the facility's support wing, safely separated from the thirty-nine-story Secretariat Building and the General Assembly Building. As usual, the scanning operation had not flagged any packages as potentially dangerous. One item, however, was tagged "Unknown Contents" by the AutoClear operator. This label indicated the x-ray equipment failed to penetrate the package, but no chemical markers of bomb material or radioactive components were detected.

Although unusual, it was not that rare to have occasional items requiring individual inspection. This part of his work was potentially risky, but to Frank, it also meant a certain level of job security. "At least this part of my job isn't going to be automated by some damn machine," Frank thought to himself.

The standard procedure for such items involved inspecting it externally for anything suspicious, then carefully opening the item and further examining the contents. Until thoroughly examined, the package would not leave the mailroom. Since the sender had not addressed it to a specific individual, Frank was able to eliminate the need to contact the recipient's office to obtain permission to open the package. If the package identified a recipient at the UN, the individual had the option of participating in the examination, or of returning it to the sender.

The package simply stated, in neatly hand-written block letters:

> To: United Nations
> New York, NY 10017
> U.S.A.

Covered with standard brown packaging paper and taped at each corner, the package at first appeared to be very ordinary. Then Frank noticed there was no return address and more significantly, no other marks or any indication it had even passed through the U.S. Postal Service.

"This is strange. There's not even postage on the package," Frank thought to himself. The mailroom handled packages and letters from the various delivery services in separate batches, and this entire batch was supposedly received from the regular U.S. Postal Service.

The startling event occurred when Frank tried to move the parcel to the unpacking area. He couldn't lift it.

"What the hell is this?" Frank blurted aloud.

Frank Whippert always figured he was stronger than most men that were his age, so he first wondered if he was experiencing a medical problem. He quickly realized he felt fine, and for a simple check, he grabbed a nearby package and moved it as easily as ever.

"OK," Frank thought to himself. "Let's try that one more time."

Frank tried again to lift the small package. Although it was no larger than a six-inch cube, he couldn't move it.

"That crazy Jack did it again." His coffee buddy Jack Thomas loved to lighten up the usually mundane workplace by joking around, and this time he had really punked him. Now how was he supposed to remove the glue from the table?

He turned aside to deal with the rest of the day's incoming deliveries, and tried to think of a way to even the score with Jack. Although he was not usually the type to escalate shenanigans in the workplace, this definitely called for a response. He'd come up with a still better prank to even the score.

At lunch, Frank entered the break room and saw Jack sitting alone at a table by the Coke vending machine. Jack immediately waved back and simultaneously motioned for Frank to join him. Jack behaved no different from usual as he continued eating his brownbag lunch. Frank immediately questioned Jack, who replied he knew nothing about the package.

"You're lying! You know you're the one who punked me. Who else would have gone to the trouble?"

Although not surprised that Jack would initially deny it, Frank became less sure it was Jack after his repeated denials. It actually was a good joke, so he wondered why Jack wouldn't take credit for it. The situation soon became drastically more confusing and intense.

Chapter 7
June 1, 1:05 PM

"The fucking thing won't move!" Jack Thomas repeated himself as he tried to pick up or even slightly move the package. He had accompanied Frank back to the workroom after lunch, where they both carefully examined the package. When Jack inserted a pry bar under one corner and exerted all his weight, Frank could see under the elevated edge—the package was *not* attached to the surface. Had the table it was sitting on been metal, they might have suspected a strong magnetic attraction. However, the top surface of the table was solid wood—an oak veneer on at least an inch of plywood base.

Wanting to resolve this puzzle quickly, Frank suggested, "OK, let's try to move it to the largest scale and see just what it weighs."

The mailroom was well equipped with four different size scales to accommodate everything from oversized letters to bulky parcels. Between the two of them, they managed to slide the strange package onto a cart and roll the cart to the opposite side of the room. It was now within inches of the largest freestanding scale, typically used to measure large outgoing shipments. With considerable difficulty, they managed to drag the package onto the three-by-four-foot flat metal surface of the scale.

The display clearly read 280 pounds.

They both stared at the scale in disbelief. What could possibly be in the package? The heaviest material Frank was familiar with was lead. On many occasions he had used large lead weights for fishing off the Eastern shoreline. But if someone had filled the six-inch package with lead weights, he figured it still would have been well under a hundred pounds.

Struggling to make sense of the puzzling situation, Jack offered an idea. "You know, gold is one of the heaviest metals. When I toured the US Mint in Washington, D.C. a few years ago, they had solid gold bars on display. I couldn't believe how much each small bar weighed— twenty-eight pounds! I think four, maybe five bars, could fit in this size package. How much would that weigh?"

It would not have been the first time someone had mailed payments or bribes directly to UN officials. But if it was a payment, why wasn't the package addressed to a specific recipient?

Mentally doing the math from Jack's US Mint comments, Frank answered. "Based on your memory, a package of solid gold would still be less than 150 pounds. That doesn't explain it. So what the hell could be in this package?"

Their curiosity at figuring out what the odd package could possibly contain was rapidly being replaced with feelings of apprehension. Frank looked squarely at Jack and nervously stated, "I remember hearing somewhere that uranium is even heavier than gold!" Now both of them were definitely worried—could this be a destructive device, maybe some type of weapon?

After briefly considering calling their manager, the head of Office Communications, or even his superior, the Director of Office Services, they instead quickly contacted Security. Frank pressed the emergency button on the nearby wall-mounted phone, which immediately connected them with the Security Department. He took a deep breath and tried to remain calm, but the cold sweat suddenly appearing on his forehead conveyed his real emotional state.

"We've got a really strange situation here in the Mail Room," Frank anxiously exclaimed to the answering guard. "We can't figure out what's in one of our incoming packages."

Although it seemed much longer, they only had to wait a couple of minutes before one of the onsite security guards arrived and glanced around the room.

"This is what you called us for?" the guard asked incredulously as Frank pointed out the small package. The burly guard suspected he was about to waste time on another false alarm. But his security training emerged as he recognized how worried both Frank and Jack appeared. They both looked genuinely distraught.

Noting the package had not been opened, the guard asked, "Has anyone else touched the package?" He was already thinking ahead if they might need to scan for fingerprints on the outer wrapping.

"Only the two of us, at least since it arrived here," replied Frank. "And check this out—I doubt it really arrived with the normal deliveries. There aren't any mail routing marks on the package."

The mailroom receiving staff stamped all packages with the date/time as deliveries arrived. Furthermore, each package always had a label or other mark designating which carrier delivered it. Only an "Unknown Contents" label was affixed to this package, indicating it had at least been scanned before it left the basement receiving area.

"Yeah, that's strange. Nothing should have entered here without the normal routing. Have to look into that too." The Security guard stared at the 280 pound measurement on the scale, still wondering if maybe he was being set up by both Frank and Jack for some type of joke. He carefully avoided touching the package, but by pressing down on the scale platform, the added pressure moved the scale monitor as one would expect. With more effort, he discovered he could lift the scale platform by a slight amount. Apparently, this small object did in fact weigh considerably more than it should.

"Now what?" wondered the Security guard who was obviously confused. His first inclination was to contact his superior, the Security Section Manager, but following his department's standard procedures, he continued to verify the oddity first.

"No fools on my Security team," the guard thought to himself. "I'm not falling for some stupid prank." Although a few of his co-workers did play around a bit, in the terrorist climate of recent years security jokes were not acceptable in any office environment.

All three of them were now close to the scale wondering what else they could do to figure out this strange package. Suddenly, Frank and Jack gasped simultaneously.

"What?" the Security guard asked. "What's the matter?"

Both Frank and Jack gaped at the digital readout on the scale. Jack's face had turned pale and he leaned against the side of a nearby filing cabinet to steady himself. The guard immediately looked at the readout.

The scale clearly read 560 pounds.

CHAPTER 8
JUNE 1, 4:20 PM

Suspecting the strange package was a destructive device placed by one of the numerous opponents of the UN, Security wanted to move it quickly away from the main complex. A New York Police Department bomb disposal squad promptly responded to the emergency call from the UN Security staff. These first-responders performed standard tests employed with any potentially explosive device. Not detecting any traces of explosive material, they were unsure of the level of imminent risk from the package. Nevertheless, the NYPD decided to move the package out of the UN complex as quickly as possible. Lacking capability to deal with this type of situation, the UN was eager to turn over responsibility for the problem.

The bomb squad was able to unbolt the metal weighing platform from the scale, and use it as a support to move the package. Wearing standard Kevlar protective vests and face shields, a team of four officers struggled to lift the 560-pound package. They managed to place it and the underlying metal panel on a wheeled cart.

With considerable effort, the officers managed to move it slowly down the corridor to the adjacent loading dock and into a waiting fortified bomb disposal truck. Leaving it sitting on the metal platform that they had removed from the scale, the officers secured the package inside the truck. A single driver was assigned to the vehicle and the rest of the NYPD disposal team prepared to ride separately.

The UN's Manhattan location eliminated the possibility of any safe evacuation route. The island's densely populated skyscrapers meant thousands of people would be in close proximity to any route the NYPD selected. Lacking evidence that the strange package was an actual explosive device, the police proceeded to remove it. Had they positively identified it as a particular type of bomb, the police and UN security would have evacuated the building and spent more time determining the best solution. At this point, it appeared to be just an oddity due to its extreme weight.

The NYPD had taken verbal statements from the UN staff that the package had actually increased in weight, but this unsubstantiated claim seemed unbelievable. Regardless of what was causing the mysterious package's extreme weight, it seemed prudent to remove the unknown object from both the UN facility and the Manhattan area.

Since the UN complex was on an island, the Tri-Borough Bridge & Tunnel Authority was included in planning the route. After a brief discussion on the most expedient and relatively safe route to use, the NYPD decided to use a convoy. A police convoy would be the quickest and most efficient way to remove the package, rather than spending many hours trying to clear all traffic and pedestrians from the selected route.

The loading dock of the UN's administration building connected directly onto the southbound lane of Franklin Roosevelt Drive. The NYPD created a moving buffer zone about one hundred yards in front of and behind the bomb disposal truck. As the convoy slowly moved onto the FDR, a constant blare from the police car sirens filled the air.

The driver of the bomb disposal truck carefully maneuvered the vehicle, avoiding any sudden stops or rapid turns. At this location on the FDR, two levels of roadway accommodated the ever-present high volume of Manhattan traffic. Proceeding on the lower level, the driver kept positioning the vehicle to maximize his distance from any of the columns that supported the upper level northbound lanes of the FDR.

Living with danger was not new to the driver who had freely chosen this career path, but the fear of an imminent explosion was never far from his mind. He always wondered if the adrenaline high he experienced during such assignments would eventually diminish, assuming he survived enough years to know. The heightened sensitivity to events and images when close to potential death always intrigued him. Might this be the last time he'd see the gaudy red "LONG ISLAND" sign just across the East River? He also wondered how his wife would cope if he ever died during one of these operations. Although difficult, he managed to suppress the recurring images of his wife as he conscientiously focused on driving the truck.

As the convoy continued southward, the lead escort cars repeatedly leapfrogged each other to block off approaching traffic from the side streets. Other than the pedestrians and drivers along the route who were temporarily blocked, the citizens of Manhattan were oblivious to the disruption. For that matter, traffic disruptions and the blare of sirens in the downtown area was the norm. Only the size of this police escort may have appeared unusual.

The convoy quickly covered the first three miles on the FDR and then crossed lower Manhattan on Houston St. They briefly waited while the police escorts cleared the Holland Tunnel for the four minutes it would take to pass under the Hudson River. As the convoy emerged from the tunnel, less than three miles remained to their destination. It was only a few more minutes before they arrived at a desolate area just south of Union City, a location that the police occasionally used as a bomb detonation site. The bomb squad parked the truck, vacated the immediate area of a few transients and waited for directions from higher up.

With many suspected explosive devices, a standard method of eliminating risk was to destroy the device as quickly as possible. A bomb squad would detonate a charge close to the suspected device, frequently using remote-controlled equipment. The NYPD rejected this approach when the explosive experts determined there were no chemical traces of any explosive material on the package. The bizarre weight of the object caused tremendous confusion—this was not something that fit into any of the standard scenarios practiced by the bomb disposal unit. If it was not a conventional explosive, the fear that it might be a dirty radioactive device or even a nuclear weapon precluded intentionally exploding it and possibly making the situation even worse.

While the object sat at the bomb detonation site, the police continued to examine it in an effort to determine what it was. Still treating it as a possible explosive device, they very carefully removed the packaging paper. It appeared to be common heavyweight paper used to wrap parcels. Chemical testing of the paper might identify who manufactured the paper, but its wide availability in retail stores would limit the value of any such information.

A six-inch cube of some type of metal was the only item inside the wrapping. There were no visible wires, screws, or anything fastening it together. In fact, there were no visible joints anywhere on any surface. There was no way the NYPD could determine if the entire cube was a solid block of metal or if it contained some type of device. It definitely did not resemble anything the bomb squad had ever encountered.

The NYPD took the packaging paper to their lab to process for fingerprints and other evidence. With the maximum priority given to the case, the results were available within a few hours. The investigators quickly matched the only fingerprints on the packaging to the two UN mailroom staffers who initially reported the object. Due to strict security requirements for any personnel supporting the UN, all facility staff fingerprints were already on file. So far, nothing discovered about the packaging was of any immediate value in the investigation.

The U.S. Department of Homeland Security quickly joined the investigation, and provided access to an even more sophisticated explosives detector. A DHS agent brought a portable ion analyzer to the site that was capable of detecting extremely minute chemical vapors and particles. The spectrometry device was capable of identifying over twenty dangerous substances within seconds and it was extremely successful in detecting explosives like Semtex, TNT, Nitrates and RDX.

The DHS agent carefully set up the ion analyzer next to the truck and activated it. Opening a sterile package of two swabs, he cautiously rubbed both of them on all four sides of the strange cube. When the agent inserted the swabs into the scanning compartment of the analyzer, the small display screen quickly showed the results. The sophisticated scanner was unable to detect any explosive material.

For the time being, the NY Police Department maintained primary authority in dealing with the problem. If the initial tests had confirmed the object was in fact a destructive device, Homeland Security would have immediately usurped the NYPD's authority. An explosive device placed at the UN would clearly be viewed as a terrorist act and fall under the jurisdiction of Homeland Security. At the moment however, the investigators were looking for help to just explain the bizarre weight of this small object, remaining cautious that it could in fact still be something extremely dangerous. They also considered it might actually be an elaborate hoax. Consequently, the NYPD turned to contacts within the science department of New York University, asking instructors from the Material Engineering department at NYU to look at the oddity.

CHAPTER 9
TWENTY YEARS EARLIER

Jason was only seven years old when the Morehouse family joined Hope Tabernacle Church in Ventura, California. It was an eclectic congregation, drawing from among the many downtrodden farm workers in the area who had migrated from Central America. Unlike most of the United States, the mild climate of coastal California was appealing to those arriving from a semi-tropical area. The independent Christian church included many of the Pentecostal practices that were comforting and familiar to the immigrants.

Jason's family was one of the few in the church who were second-generation immigrants from Europe, only slightly better off economically than were the farm workers. The fair-skinned Morehouse family easily rose to a leadership role in the growing congregation, as the church gradually became more and more charismatic and cult-like. By the time Jason was a teenager, the local agricultural community viewed the assembly suspiciously and considered it more like a religious cult than a typical Christian church.

The Hope Tabernacle leaders expected all members to demonstrate their primary allegiance to the church in every area of their lives. The church tightly controlled family relationships and virtually all social activities of its members. Multiple families usually lived together in homes, with strictly segregated housing for unmarried members of each sex. The church members dutifully placed all wages as well as any other income into a common pool. Depending on a family's or an individual's needs, funds were distributed to members by the church leaders. Recently recruited members even transferred property titles for cars and homes to Hope Tabernacle.

In exchange for giving up these freedoms and devoting their lives to the church, the congregants gained a peace that had eluded them in their difficult and unsatisfying lives. The reason for their hardships in life was explained as part of God's plan, which was too mysterious and complex for them to fathom as neophytes in the faith. If they could only become more ardent in their prayers and become purer in their thoughts, surely God would meet their true needs. If they could enter even deeper religious trances and speak in tongues more fervently, then they would finally please God and receive understanding.

Growing up in such an environment, Jason was firmly convinced of the importance of absolute authority and the necessity for isolation from the evils and threats of the outside world. Voluntarily living a life segregated from the mainstream of society had another more insidious consequence. Jason and the other church members not only learned to tolerate discrimination from those outside their small community, but they eventually reached a point where they actually craved the discrimination. Ill-treatment by unbelievers only validated their belief that they were suffering in the name of God.

A handsome young man, Jason was a natural leader whom many in the church looked to for direction. Besides being tall for his age, his serious demeanor even as a child helped establish Jason as one to respect. A lean six-footer, he trimmed his own dark brown hair into an uncomplicated buzz cut. He had no interest in impressing friends with his appearance or choice in clothing. For Jason and the entire church membership, even the slightest hint of vanity was a clear indication of weakness. The church leaders banned all forms of jewelry—even wedding bands for married members were considered unnecessary adornment. Only those tempted by the outside world's appeal would be interested in the hollow symbols of affluent society.

The expectations of the church leaders were gradually ingrained into Jason's own self-image, as he discovered it was surprisingly easy to influence and direct those who eagerly sought a leader. His youthful enthusiasm continually led him to raise the standard for "pure" living. A rift gradually grew between his purer standards and those of the majority of the church members. The church elders were increasingly uncomfortable with Jason's continual haranguing for ever-stricter policies.

By the time Jason was twenty-two, he realized he could no longer tolerate the lax morality that had slowly seeped into the congregants of Hope Tabernacle. Worldly pursuits had begun to pollute the church, which he knew were only distractions from following God's plan. Many of the younger congregants were openly socializing with non-Tabernacle members, attending public school dances, attending movies and flaunting their sinful ways. It was as if they wanted to dress, look and act like those in the outside godless world. When the church elders repeatedly refused to punish the sinners, Jason knew it was time to distance himself from this corruption.

There were six other young men in the Tabernacle who shared Jason's view, and had become accustomed to looking to Jason for guidance and spiritual direction. This splinter group left Ventura to start a new life in New York, at the opposite side of the country from the California congregation. Jason believed the three-thousand-mile distance would fracture old relationships and help deter any backsliding by his followers.

Over the ensuing years, the faction bonded even closer as they prayed together and as they struggled to support each other. Facing economic hardships together heightened the members' devotion to their faith and steadily increased their allegiance to Jason. A few discontented co-workers were allowed to join the fellowship, but it was mandatory that all members would maintain a very low profile in their jobs and lifestyle. Their aim was very simple—to avoid pollution from the godless world around them and to practice their pure lifestyle without interference. This self-imposed isolation effectively hid them from the New York community in which they lived.

CHAPTER 10
JUNE 2, 9:00 AM

"Follow the data!" That was the overarching goal of all investigative policies. It worked for investigating crime scenes, debunking hoaxes and interpreting test results. Only a few hours after the bomb squad had removed the strange package from the UN mail annex, the UN's own security staff was in hot pursuit of whoever had delivered it to the mail facility. How did the package circumvent the controls on what entered the mail system? While the NYPD was focusing on the object itself, the UN's own staff focused on how the package might have arrived. If they could identify the source quickly, perhaps it might dampen the expected negative publicity on the UN security failure.

Vincent Marais, the director for the UN internal security force, was reluctant to admit they were clueless. The director had held this position for the past fourteen years, after building a career with security related jobs in several U.S. municipalities and one multinational firm.

He was slightly overweight and mostly gray around the temples, but always performed his role with the utmost intensity.

Since Vincent was personally responsible for the physical site security, he was rightfully worried that this incident would reflect very poorly on his performance evaluation. He was very motivated to identify how the security systems had been breached. Vincent had been working non-stop with his staff since the prior day's discovery of the package, and was now showing signs of fatigue. But their efforts had been unsuccessful—no matter which leads they followed, they could not tie the object to any earlier location or to any delivery route.

"No one saw the package delivered to the mail receiving area. At least, no one will admit to it." Vincent was in the process of updating the FBI investigators assigned to the case. It was painful to admit how little had been detected from the UN's own internal investigation, but he was very forthright with the FBI.

The two FBI investigators were all business. They were both outwardly cordial during the interview, but Vincent couldn't help but sense a thinly veiled condescension. He wondered if this was how they dealt with all their assignments. Maybe their attitude wasn't due to Vincent personally, but more due to the setting. The tense meeting was taking place in Vincent's spartan office, located in a windowless section of the belowground support wing of the UN. He pushed ahead answering their questions quickly, hoping to end the uncomfortable session as soon as possible.

"The loading dock and all connecting hallways and elevator shafts were under constant surveillance by our video security system. Unauthorized personnel don't show up on any of the tapes. Either our security system equipment has been somehow compromised, or the sender had help from someone within the Security department." Either alternative was equally disquieting to Vincent, who had built his reputation and entire career on utmost competency.

Prior to the arrival of the two FBI agents, Vincent had almost completed his own internal review of the related security staff. He had personally interviewed all but one of the security staffers who had been on duty in the proximate area within the past forty-eight hours. Nothing appeared out of the ordinary. The FBI's first recommendation was to place on leave all security guards who had worked over the past weekend and conduct additional interviews with the involved officers.

Vincent frowned, pondering the probable fallout from this security failure. With no one to share his fears, he reflected silently to himself. "Even if it turns out to not be a destructive weapon, even if it's just a hoax to embarrass the UN, our security systems will be publicly depicted as grossly deficient. The press will escalate this fiasco to question the vulnerability of the UN building to any terrorist act. We've got to figure this out before we're all looking for new jobs."

At this point, many assumed that the threatening package was from a radical organization, no doubt one that was opposed to either the UN's actions or lack of action in any of a myriad of areas. The splintering of the radical Islamic movement during the past decade had resulted in a plethora of small, extremist terrorist groups. The only apparent common elements were their loathing of those who opposed their worldview and a willingness to use whatever violent means were available to publicize their cause.

The FBI initially focused their investigation on the Mustafa Azzam Brigade, one of the many militant Islamic groups believed to be associated with al-Qaida. This radical organization had made direct threats toward the UN less than a week earlier. Denouncing the UN as a tool of capitalist infidels, they vowed to destroy it as well as all nations who were enemies of the true faith. Such threats, unfortunately, were too common, and lacking any tangible substantiation, these threats had generated no more interest than had others received every week.

The FBI was trying to determine the current whereabouts of members of the Mustafa Azzam Brigade— several had been recently located in the New York area. Unknown members of the group were always a possibility, but so far, there was no unusual movement or phone activity detected for any of the known members. The FBI assigned four agents to physically track several key brigade members to see if they might discover anything unusual. For the present, the FBI considered the brigade as possibly involved, but the militant Islamists would be only one of many leads to check out.

Vincent knew the FBI would soon be taking over the entire investigation. The full capabilities of the FBI were steadily becoming available, and very soon, he suspected the full attention of Homeland Security would also be focused on this dilemma.

"Great. You can have it. I've done all I can to figure this out," a weary Vincent said as he concluded his briefing to the two FBI agents. He knew it was time to review his retirement options—his days were numbered as soon as this security breach became public. Every PR crisis needed at least one scapegoat. He figured this one would need several.

Chapter 11
June 12, 4:15 PM

1,146,880 pounds

The lab team had spent another two days studying the object, during which time two more weight doubling cycles occurred precisely on schedule. At the current rate of weight gain, only two days remained before it would sink through the lab floor.

The team had utilized every diagnostic tool available to measure, probe and monitor the object. They brought in six types of spectrometers in a futile attempt to analyze the composition of the cube. They also employed a variety of x-ray devices to bombard it with different electromagnetic waves but nothing penetrated the outer surface of the cube. The researchers even tried both low and high frequency radio waves. Their last attempt involved bombarding it with small doses of nuclear radiation but this also failed to provide any clue as to what was inside.

News coverage of the strange object had grown tremendously, parallel to the growth of the cube's weight. The media conglomerates were trying to outdo each other in covering the event as its potential threat dwarfed the significance of all other news items. Since so much of the object was a mystery, the sensationalism of the broadcasts was limited only by each journalist's imagination. There was no end to the speculation and rumors circulating throughout the world. Who could have created such a doomsday device? How many hours before the object destroyed the lab where it was being studied? Would seismic tremors soon devastate the local New York area? Would seismic damage eventually occur throughout the entire world?

Randy Schiller had decided to provide a thorough briefing to the press, rather than the piecemeal research results that had been released to-date. Even though the investigation team's understanding was still very elementary, Randy and the core team members decided that even incomplete information was preferable to the rampant rumors and panic that were spreading across the world.

"At least we have a rudimentary grip on what the problem is, finally!" said Randy to the assembled press. The team conducted the briefing in the largest meeting facility in the lab complex, a windowless room about forty by forty feet. The spartan room had been designed to accommodate a number of purposes, but had never been used for media briefings. Since most of the research at the lab complex had always involved government-classified projects, there had never been a requirement to host large meetings. The room was now equipped with about fifty folding chairs spread out in six rows, all of which were now occupied with press and other media representatives. The entire back third of the room was reserved for the press camera crews, and a small podium at the front of the room was equipped with several microphones.

There was an oppressive sense of gloom in the briefing room, as the press agents tried to balance concerns for their personal safety with a desire to cover the event effectively. The meeting room was located near the edge of the sprawling lab complex, only three hundred yards from the actual object. Some of the journalists had previously been assigned in war zones and consequently were not intimidated by working in dangerous situations. Although the cycles of increasing weight had been predictable so far, that was no guarantee it would not deviate and cause an immediate problem.

Randy continued to address the press agents. "We know we are dealing with something encased in a totally unknown element, which is doubling in weight at a specific rate but not in volume. We believe the mass is increasing from a growth cycle similar to organic cell multiplication. Since this object was discovered eleven days ago at the UN headquarters, the weight has doubled every day, at 1:46 PM.

"The increasing mass has produced an object heavier than anything imaginable on Earth. This undoubtedly sounds bizarre, so I have asked Dr. Stephan Werner of the Max Planck Institute for Astrophysics in Germany to provide some insight. Stephan has been heading the theoretical physics area of our investigation."

As Randy stepped away from the microphone, Stephan rose from where he was sitting in the front row. He was about six-feet tall, wore heavy rimmed glasses and sported a close-cropped beard. Dr. Werner matched the common stereotype for a middle-aged University professor, complete with graying hair, conservative appearing clothes and an overall academic appearance. With only a slight German accent, he articulately addressed the media representatives.

"I will briefly review our understanding of a dramatic yet very common occurrence in the cosmos." Stephan began his presentation like a seasoned professor addressing yet another class of incoming graduate students. A little condescension was evident in his voice, yet the gathered press representatives were not offended—along with the rest of the world, they were desperately hoping for any explanation.

"Neutron stars. Stellar corpses. There are millions of them just in our Milky Way galaxy. How did they form? The extreme gravitational force of a star is balanced by the heat generated from its nuclear reactions. When a star of a certain size—several times larger than our sun—has run through its stock of nuclear fuel, it collapses under the weight of its own gravity and explodes as a supernova. Most of the star's material is blown outwards into space, but a dense rapidly spinning core remains that has slightly more mass than our Sun yet with a diameter less than twelve miles.

"How can such an extreme density exist?" the astrophysicist patiently continued. "You may recall that atoms consist mostly of empty space surrounding a small nucleus. Most people are not aware of the vastness of the space available within every atom. The tiny nucleus that contains virtually the entire atom's mass is only one millionth of a billionth of the full volume of the atom." The professor realized that such scales were difficult to grasp, so he offered an analogy. "If an atom were expanded to the size of an Olympics stadium, the nucleus would be the size of a fly. Yet this fly would be so dense that it would weigh thousands of times more than the stadium." Dr Werner scanned the room to see if his audience was following the presentation, but he mostly saw skeptical expressions.

"Under intense pressure, subatomic particles can huddle extremely close together. Researchers across the world and at my own institute in Germany have used a variety of techniques to measure such occurrences. Common throughout the cosmos, a neutron star is packed primarily with neutrons. A teaspoonful, brought to Earth, would weigh between ten million and a billion tons." The room was silent as the media representatives struggled to grasp these aspects of modern cosmology— concepts so foreign to life on Earth are always difficult to comprehend.

"We also suspect the interior of a neutron star contains exotic particles that we have not yet witnessed. The cube we are now examining in the nearby lab may be composed of some combination of such particles.

"Regardless of what elements or exotic particles compose the object, we are looking at a cataclysmic situation. Based on our calculations, if it continues doubling in weight, the object will soon sink through the Earth's crust and continue descending until it settles near the center of the Earth in one to two weeks. We can expect major earthquakes with increasing damage during this time. The shifting plates of the Earth's crust will reseal the hole formed by the descending object so an eruption of molten core material will not occur—at least at this lab site. However, equilibrium shifts caused by the mass as it continues to settle will cause imbalances to the Earth's wobble as it rotates. This will cause both seismic tremors and volcanic eruptions to occur at the structurally weakest locations across the globe's surface. Tsunamis are inevitable, as well as intense atmospheric changes from the accumulating volcanic debris."

This was most distressing news, but in fact, the dire predictions would actually get worse. Dr. Werner proceeded, in a methodical manner like the experienced professor and scientist that he was. The room was uncharacteristically quiet, a departure from the typical briefing to a crowded room of journalists.

"Although the disturbances to the Earth's crust and the violent climate changes will be disastrous, they will be short-lived, and relatively inconsequential when compared with the eventual effect. If this object continues to increase in weight, there will eventually be a change to the Earth's gravitational center, and a major disruption to the Earth's overall equilibrium. The increased gravitational pull will affect the weight of every item on the planet—everything actually weighs more already, if only by a minute amount. Soon, all orbiting satellites will begin to fall toward Earth. Likewise, smaller tides will occur, caused by a smaller influence exerted by the moon against the increased mass of the Earth.

"If the doubling in mass is unchecked, even at the center of the Earth, the object will become the new center of gravity, and if it continues to increase in density it could draw the entire planet into itself. These predictions undoubtedly sound radical and you may have difficulty accepting them, but these are the same conditions that exist in black holes throughout our cosmos. Could something similar to this object have caused any of the black holes we now observe?"

Dr. Werner continued to address the press agents who were getting more agitated as the presentation continued. "And of course many of you wonder what could possibly be the source of the additional mass that is appearing at set intervals. Mr. Schiller has requested that I convey our current speculation. As we model a number of theories as to how this mass is increasing, we hope to have a more definitive announcement soon. For today's briefing, I will provide only a cursory glimpse of our current theorizing.

"Recent developments in particle physics indicate that all properties of elementary particles are relational and environmental. Although difficult or even impossible to prove, string theory implies that rather than only one unique set of particles and forces being possible, there is an infinite set out of which one came to be for our universe. In different universes, there could be different combinations that would produce unique elements. The object in our lab may be composed of such foreign combinations of particles and forces. Cosmologists have postulated for years that our cosmos may have additional dimensions, most of which are inaccessible to us. This could be the first evidence of a parallel universe which has somehow been interlinked with our own, a universe that has never previously been visible from our world."

Professor Werner was done and quickly retook his seat near the podium. He was not interested in taking questions from the press, since he was certain he had already conveyed everything known about the object. Like most scientists, he was very reluctant to discuss theories at such an early stage, before they had evidence to justify their thoughts. Yet Randy had insisted on disclosing their nascent theorizing, so the astrophysicist complied.

Randolph Schiller recognized that the presentation had been both barely credible and agonizing for the gathered press agents. These media representatives would be the ones communicating this message—or at least their perception of this message—to their respective audiences. The wild rumors that had already circulated had sown the seeds of panic around the world. Randy belatedly realized this briefing would not be allaying any of those fears. The meticulous Professor Werner apparently saw no value in describing whatever minimal signs of hope existed. Randy knew the team had to provide at least a glimmer of hope.

Walking back to the podium, Randy motioned for Rob to join him. "Rob will be handling the Q&A portion of our briefing. But first, I'd like him to mention a factor that several of us believe offers great hope—the immense internal pressure within the Earth."

Standing at the podium to address the crowd, Rob was also sensitive to the immediate need to offer room for optimism. Glancing around the room at the restless journalists, he took a deep breath and began speaking at a measured pace, attempting to bring some calm to the anxious audience.

"We will continue to search for ideas on how we might alter this object's growth. However, if it does continue to descend and it passes through the Earth's crust and mantle, the extremely hot molten core of the planet's interior will surround the object. Due to the accumulating weight of the overlying rock layers and surface features, pressure increases immensely within the Earth's interior. At the center of the Earth, almost four thousand miles from the surface, the pressure is believed to be 3.5 million atmospheres, compared to a value of 1 at sea level. The geophysicists on the team are trying to determine if the intense heat and extreme pressure within the Earth's core could have a containing affect on the object."

One of the press agents interrupted Rob, rather than waiting for the formal kickoff of the Q&A session. The agent was obviously agitated and shouted out, "Why didn't we just destroy the damn thing when it was first discovered, before it had reached this point?"

Rob knew the gathered press agents would grasp this topic more easily and that it might help the overall mood of the session by focusing on a divergent issue. Rob continued, "Was there any way of destroying the object? Likewise, is there any way to destroy it now? Fair questions.

"When initially evaluating the object, the NYPD bomb disposal squad evaluated the option of destroying it with explosives, similar to how many bombs are frequently treated. But that's only done when you have a good handle on what it is that you're exploding. This object displayed no characteristics of a typical bomb, and actually displayed no indication it was even dangerous.

"Everyone initially involved viewed the bizarre weight as more of a scientific puzzle, something of general interest to the scientific community. Once we verified the object was acting contrary to our understanding of physics, it became clear that any attempt to destroy it might in fact exacerbate the situation. When you don't have a clue as to what you're dealing with, any number of outcomes could occur. For example, detonating an explosive next to it might create multiple objects, all likewise increasing in weight. Alternatively, an unknown toxic substance may be inside the cube that could create an immediate threat if it was released to the atmosphere. Likewise, if a nuclear explosion were employed to destroy the cube, the nuclear reaction itself might be compromised or altered by the object, possibly producing an infinitely larger chain reaction than expected.

"Even if we believed it could have been destroyed earlier by a nuclear weapon, that 'solution' was believed to be more dangerous than what we knew of the object at the time. In fact, we are still hoping either we can cause it to cease increasing in weight, or it will stop by itself at some point."

The briefing could actually have been even worse had the team divulged horrific details of a hastily considered option. Rob was careful not to mention the Pentagon's brainstorming the damage a nuclear strike might have on the object and on the immediate New York vicinity, as well as the fallout effect on the entire Eastern seaboard. Sacrificing such a key area might have been a viable option if it was a clear alternative to saving the planet. However, there were entirely too many unknowns for the government to make a decision that would directly kill thousands of Americans. Rob suspected that if the object had been located in a third world area rather than New York, either the United States or another major world power might have further considered such a strike in an attempt to destroy it.

The Pentagon analysts eventually had concluded that attempting to destroy the object with a nuclear strike would have been a disastrous decision. At a minimum, the explosion and resulting nuclear fallout would have killed millions and left a huge area uninhabitable for years. If the object somehow survived the strike, the world would still be faced with the same dilemma. If the strike did destroy the object, there was a significant chance that whoever created it could send another object.

Chapter 12
June 3, 10:00 AM

Within two days of discovering the object at the UN, the FBI was close to seeing the first results from their investigation. The agency had focused its efforts on determining how someone could have delivered the package to the guarded UN complex. The bizarre object remained at the bomb disposal site near Union City while the agents pursued the case. While the FBI was handling the case similarly to a bomb threat, Homeland Security continued to closely monitor the investigation.

"Trace every one of his moves for the past week. My money is on Bob Brolins—he's involved with a terrorist group." Nathan Smith, the FBI investigation head, had immediately suspected inside involvement, most likely with someone on the UN Security staff. It looked like he was right.

Nathan was reviewing the case with the two FBI investigators who had interviewed the UN Security staff and were still struggling to wade through the video images from the numerous surveillance cameras in use at the UN complex. The agents were working out of a temporary office set up within the UN Administration building, conveniently located near the "crime scene" for interviewing and case discussion. Nathan assumed the NYPD or Homeland Security would soon identify some type of weapon concealed within the strange package. He had his own assignment—to determine who had delivered the package and find out how they had brought it into the secured UN facility. He was not about to waste any time in completing his task.

Just past his fortieth birthday, Nathan Smith had reluctantly come to terms with his stalled career. He had joined the FBI upon graduating from college, convinced his efforts would quickly propel him up the management chain. With a plain face, an average build and five feet ten inches tall, Nathan rarely made an outstanding first impression with his various supervisors, but it never took long before they were amazed at how energetically he tackled his assignments—Nathan Smith took his work very seriously.

By quickly resolving this case, Nathan hoped he might finally improve his chances for career advancement. At least his marriage would not be jeopardizing this assignment—his second divorce had finalized a year earlier. There was no doubt in Nathan's mind that his previous two marriages had diverted too much time and energy from his job. Now he could focus solely toward his next career promotion, to be named Special Agent in Charge of any of the FBI field offices in the Northeastern states.

The two FBI agents were blurry-eyed from spending virtually all of the previous night reviewing numerous security video tapes from the UN facility support wing. Due to the large number of intersecting hallways and connections from the basement receiving area to other administrative departments, there were twelve different cameras of interest. Any of these surveillance cameras could potentially have recorded evidence of whoever delivered the package over the weekend. Unfortunately, the entire video system was over ten years old—the grey-scale image quality was barely adequate to identify the individuals.

Any odd activity on the tapes would have immediately focused the investigator's search, but there was no record of anyone transporting an individual package or of anyone tampering with the locked doors or video security system. With considerable difficulty, the agents had matched all the individuals appearing on the tapes to security staffers. There were no unidentified individuals who appeared anywhere within the receiving area or in the mailroom complex.

It turned out that Bob Brolins was the only involved Security staffer who the agents had not already grilled. Knowing that Bob was out on a medical absence, the team tried to interview him where he was hospitalized, but the agents discovered that Bob had been unconscious for the past three days. The acceptable term 'interviewed' was not quite appropriate, since anyone connected to this incident was being thoroughly interrogated. As the case increasingly appeared to be a terrorist event, the agents employed increasingly aggressive tactics to solve the threat.

"Based on this work roster, Bob Brolins wasn't scheduled on any shift during the weekend." Nathan was intently looking over the Security staff work schedule he had received from Vincent Marais. "Vincent stated this list was accurate, but we need to make sure there weren't any last minute changes not reflected on this printout."

Nathan abruptly pointed to the agents' notes compiled from their review of the video tapes. "Brolins was here on Saturday!"

The more senior of the two agents replied, somewhat chagrinned that they had not already compared their list to the work schedule. "Right. We positively matched a photo from Brolins' personnel file to the person entering the annex at 11:45 Saturday morning. He passed by another camera at 11:48 and exited the building through the same entrance at 12:03 PM."

"Was he carrying anything? Was he alone? Did the tape show him with any other staffer?" Vincent was grilling the agents, suspecting they had missed an obvious sign. Although Vincent's years of training usually prevented him from jumping to conclusions, he felt his pulse quickening.

Both agents realized Vincent was upset, but thought they had been working as fast as possible. Rather than dwelling on the implied performance lapse, the senior agent responded. "There's no record on the video tapes of him meeting anyone, and there's nothing obvious being carried. But since the package was only around six inches, it might have been concealed under his jacket. Let's send these three tapes to our lab at Quantico—they can analyze them with their software to see if there's an abnormal bulge anywhere under his clothing."

"OK. Send it off, but we don't have time to wait. Brolins could have just been meeting someone for lunch, picking up a paycheck he forgot on Friday, or any number of harmless things. Let's back up and recap what we know so far."

Nathan was back into his usual methodical form, moving on to review the information obtained from interviewing Sarah Brolins, Bob Brolins' wife. She had been totally cooperative but perplexed at why they would be so interested in her husband's medical condition.

"Sarah Brolins claims she found her husband passed out in the kitchen when she returned home last Saturday evening. As a realtor, she stated that she frequently worked weekends and evenings, but on Saturday, she returned home around 6 PM. After her initial panic at seeing him sprawled on the kitchen floor, she quickly checked that he was still breathing. Sarah immediately called 911 from a nearby phone on the kitchen wall. The paramedics arrived within minutes and the two medical techs verified Bob still had a pulse and his breathing appeared to be normal."

"That's correct," the more senior of the two agents responded. "We located the two paramedics who responded to her call and they confirmed Sarah's comments. They indicated they then placed Bob onto a gurney, strapped his body to the frame and maneuvered the cart out of the kitchen, through the front door and to the waiting ambulance. The paramedics couldn't determine the severity of the medical emergency, so they decided to drive to the closest emergency room. Sarah rode along in the ambulance for the four-mile trip."

The agent handed Nathan a single page memo. "And this is the statement from our interview with the hospital staff. The doctors who treated him stated the cause of his unconsciousness was unknown, but he'd most likely collapsed shortly before his wife found him. The standard medical tests were inconclusive—his vital functions were stable and he didn't exhibit any signs of physical trauma. The hospital physicians couldn't determine any medical reason for his condition, but stated he could regain consciousness at any time."

"Let's go back to the hospital," Nathan said. "I want to see if Bob's status has changed. If his wife is there, we can grill her again to see if we get the same story." Nathan suspected Sarah wasn't quite as forthcoming as she appeared.

Since Bob Brolins' condition was stable yet potentially serious, the hospital had moved him to an intensive care room where they could carefully monitor him. Nathan had already assigned agents to guard Bob's hospital room—he needed to ensure that he or his staff would be the first to interrogate Bob if he did regain consciousness. Nathan had also demanded that full lab tests be performed on the blood samples previously taken, searching for anything unusual.

Nathan and the two agents arrived at the hospital thirty minutes later. Since Sarah Brolins was currently in the hospital room with her husband, Nathan wasted no time in turning his attention to her. Although fatigued from the stress of the past few days, she answered all questions as best she could. Despite her candidness, she was unable to provide any useful information as to Bob's activities during the past week. Sarah seemed very cooperative, readily giving permission for the agents to search their home for anything that might help explain his sudden illness. Since she wanted to stay at the hospital, Sarah gave the agents a key to their front door—by freely cooperating with the agents, she apparently hoped to end their interrogations as soon as possible.

Nathan directed the two agents to check out the Brolins' apartment, while he arranged to meet with several other hospital staffers regarding Bob's prognosis. All of Bob's actions still appeared very ordinary, at least until the search team arrived at Bob's home to look for evidence.

Bob and Sarah's small apartment was located in Lyndhurst, New Jersey. Their home was a ground-floor unit in a large three-story complex of apartments. The surrounding neighborhood was well maintained, and nothing appeared unusual in the unit's exterior.

As soon as the assigned agents entered the home, they recognized that the stock of plain brown packaging paper casually lying on the kitchen table appeared to be the same as the paper used to cover the object. The size of the paper scraps in the kitchen area implied someone had recently wrapped a package that was about the same size as the object. The agents immediately cordoned off the entire apartment and informed Nathan by phone.

Nathan arrived at the apartment within the hour, when the FBI agents had just finished searching the premises. The wrapping paper and other materials did appear to match how the object was packaged, but subsequent chemical tests could confirm that the paper matched that found on the object. The agents also found a pair of latex gloves lying in the kitchen trashcan and surmised someone could have used them to avoid leaving fingerprints on the package. A DNA exam would likely corroborate they were used by Bob. It also appeared that residue from the wrapping paper still adhered to the outside surface of the gloves.

Nathan suspected the carefully lettered addressing would likely match one of the felt pens lying around the kitchen, all of which had been collected for testing in the FBI lab. He methodically laid out to the agents stationed at the house how the facts were falling into place.

"So our man Bob wraps and addresses this object last Saturday morning. He then takes it to the UN mail annex and the video cameras show him entering the facility at 11:45. As a security staff member, Mr. Brolins has authorization to enter the facility without causing any concern. He then carries the package through the receiving area, possibly shielding it from the surveillance cameras by his jacket. He leaves it in the mail annex, returns home and passes out. His wife, Sarah Brolins, finds him at 6 PM and then he spends the next four days in the hospital."

"So what to make of this?" Nathan speculated with the agents doing the search. "There was obviously no interest in hiding incriminating evidence in their apartment—not enough time, perhaps because he passed out before getting around to it? This doesn't really make any sense, since Bob could have destroyed all of this incriminating evidence earlier, before he left to deliver it to the mail annex. No, he wasn't interested in covering his tracks."

One of the agents suggested, "Maybe he expected to eventually be identified. After he delivered the package, he could have returned home with the intent to end his life. Maybe his current medical condition is due to a failed suicide attempt?"

Nathan responded, "There's no sign of physical trauma and none of the blood tests have shown any abnormalities, at least none of the more common poisons or drugs used by someone attempting suicide. We'll get more detailed test data later, but I don't think that'll help."

Nathan continued to talk to the agents, but he was really just thinking aloud. "It looks like we've got our delivery man, but who was he delivering it for?"

All of the agents found it highly unlikely that this security staff person would have the means to construct such an object. Nathan persevered, "We've reviewed Bob's background and it shows nothing that could indicate involvement with a terrorist cell, or even the slightest indication of anything awry. Also, he doesn't appear to have any advanced technical skills of his own."

A painful silence from suspecting they had reached another dead end in their investigation was loudly broken by the ringing of Nathan's cell phone. "Let's go. Bob just came to," he blurted to the senior agent as the two of them scrambled to get back to the hospital as quickly as possible.

CHAPTER 13
JUNE 3, 4:15 PM

"As long as he's in this hospital, your interview time is set by me!" The attending doctor was almost shouting, obviously displeased. Nathan Smith and the physician were arguing in the corridor near Bob Brolins' hospital room. Nathan, in his typical fashion, had attempted to bully the staff treating Bob. He could easily get a court order to have Bob moved to a different medical facility that was more tractable, even a military hospital if needed. But his immediate aim was just to interview Bob as quickly as possible, before he either lapsed again into unconsciousness or worse. Nathan would play along with the medical staff, ostensibly toning down the interview to avoid aggravating Bob's medical condition. The suspect's long-term physical well being was the last thing Nathan was interested in—he had a job to do, and Bob was key to the investigation.

"Fine, fine! If you can just give me five minutes. But I need it now!" Nathan strode into Bob's intensive care room, nodding to the two guards stationed outside the room. They were the ones who had called with the news that Bob was finally conscious. The hospital room was the same as when Nathan was there that morning. An IV was hooked up to Bob's left arm and several monitoring devices displayed the status of his vital systems. The only difference was Bob's position in bed, now slightly inclined allowing him to look around the room. He appeared exhausted, although his color was close to normal.

The physician, somewhat appeased with Nathan's toned-down demeanor, stood close to Nathan and spoke quietly so Bob couldn't hear their conversation. The doctor gave a brief rundown of Bob's status. "Mr. Brolins seems to have full awareness of who he is. We've informed him of where he is and given him a brief status of his medical condition. He's asked for his wife, who we're trying to track down—the floor nurse thinks she may have gone to the hospital cafeteria. I expect her to return shortly. Until Mr. Brolins is stable, you must keep this initial interview to no more than five minutes. If he continues to improve, come back in a few hours if you want to further question him."

Like Nathan, the attending physician was the one usually giving instructions, and he resented the demands of the arrogant FBI chief. The physician realized his authority only existed within the confines of the hospital. If Nathan obtained a court order to transfer Bob out of the hospital, which incidentally was fine with the attending doctor, his physician's responsibility for Bob's health ended.

The doctor edged closer to the bed implying he would be staying during the interview, supposedly to oversee the fragile medical condition of his patient. He typically would have left the room for other tasks, but not with such a high-profile patient—he was curious as to why this case was of such great interest to the FBI. This patient had become considerably more interesting than the typical patients who cycled through the ER—children with influenza, elderly patients with various heart arrhythmias, and gang members with assorted lacerations and gunshot wounds. The government's attention made this case most intriguing and he suspected the local press would soon be hounding the hospital staff for information.

"Bob—we need to talk. I'm Nathan Smith from the FBI. I'm investigating an incident at the United Nations." Standing next to the side of the bed, Nathan positioned himself to face Bob directly. He spoke slowly and clearly, and then paused a moment to try to ascertain if Bob was tracking his comments. With a quizzical look, Bob just stared back at Nathan.

"Do you recall your last day at work?" Nathan was uncharacteristically polite, not wanting to intimidate Bob or to say anything that would stifle his cooperation. Learned from years of FBI experience, he constantly scanned Bob's face for any signs of lying or nervousness.

"Well, not really." Bob's voice was weak as he struggled to respond to Nathan's question. He spoke slowly, as if he were struggling to stay awake.

"Everything seems to be very blurry up to a few minutes ago. I do remember going out to dinner on Friday night, and then going to bed sometime around 11."

"And did anything unusual happen that night, or the next morning?" asked Nathan.

"No, I just woke up here in this bed. But it's not Saturday is it? What day is it?" Bob sounded entirely credible, although obviously confused. He also appeared to be quite coherent, even articulate in his responses.

Nathan continued, "Bob, it's now Wednesday. You've been here in the hospital since Saturday night." Nathan paused and carefully observed Bob's reaction. So far, only blank looks, as Bob slowly comprehended Nathan's remarks.

Nathan proceeded, still carefully studying Bob's reaction. "Try to recall what you did Saturday morning. Did you see or talk to anyone?"

"I don't know. As I said, the last thing I remember is going to bed Friday night. Was I supposed to have done something? Is that why you're talking to me?" Bob was slowly grasping the implication of being questioned by the FBI and that he couldn't recall anything of the last four days. He glanced through the open doorway of his hospital room and saw what looked like armed guards outside his room. The developing picture was becoming more and more unsettling. In fact, he was now wondering if he might be in some major trouble.

"Where's Sarah? Is my wife OK? Is she here?" He was getting visibly agitated now. It appeared the interview was over.

The attending physician stepped forward and in a low voice, reminded Nathan that his five minutes were up. The doctor then addressed Bob "Your wife Sarah is fine. She was here earlier and we're currently trying to locate her."

Nathan quickly left the room and headed to the hospital's Department of Neurology. When the usual clinical tests given during the first two days in the hospital had not diagnosed the cause of Bob's unconsciousness, the neurology department had been contacted. A hospital technician had informed Nathan that the results of the brain scans and neural system tests would be available by Wednesday afternoon.

Nathan curtly introduced himself to the head of the neurology department, who had been expecting him. Word of the FBI's intense interest in the unconscious patient had piqued interest throughout the hospital staff over the past several days. The admitting staff had learned Mr. Brolins worked with the UN when the paramedics had brought him to the Emergency Department the previous Saturday evening. Just two days after his admittance, the first news reports had circulated that the NYPD allegedly had removed some type of weapon from the UN. Rumors quickly began circulating among hospital staff that the unconscious and guarded Mr. Brolins might be involved with some terrorist activity.

"I just had a brief conversation with Bob Brolins, who became conscious only a few hours ago." Nathan did not expect the neurologist to be aware of Bob's current medical status, since he knew the medical specialists only responded to requests from other departments in the hospital.

"That's encouraging, but it's still too soon to know if there's any permanent damage," responded the doctor. He incorrectly assumed Nathan was concerned about Bob's overall health.

"Brolins claims to not remember anything that happened just before he was hospitalized." The coldly efficient FBI agent continued, plainly not interested in wasting any more time. "I need to know if he's lying."

The neurologist was put off by the agent's cold manner, but if the terrorist rumors were true, he recognized the FBI's need to rapidly interrogate this patient. He launched into an explanation of what he had discovered, in non-technical language that he believed Nathan would understand.

"In many cases of amnesia or repressed memory, a patient can eventually recall more and more details. But I don't believe this will be the case with Mr. Brolins—someone may have intentionally erased his memory. Are you familiar with electroconvulsive shock therapy?"

"Somewhat. Isn't that an obsolete method of treating mental patients? Zapping their brains with electricity?"

"Yes, although it actually is still used in rare situations. It's virtually impossible to determine if such a treatment has been administered to someone. There's no chemical residue to show up in toxicology tests. Likewise, carefully applying electrical current may not leave any physical evidence of the treatment." Nathan was beginning to sense that this conversation would also not yield any definitive answers.

The neurologist continued, "What prompted us to suspect something similar to an electrical shock was the slight skin damage on the front of Mr. Brolins' head, hidden just above the hairline. Heat or another type of energy wave undoubtedly caused it. That specific area of the skull protects the frontal lobes, which are responsible for many functions including short-term memory. If these memories were erased before they were converted to long-term memory, they'll never be recovered no matter how long we wait." This was not what Nathan wanted to hear—he was increasingly dismayed as the neurologist continued.

"In addition, the brain scans that we ran two days ago showed no areas of damage which might have occurred if there'd been head trauma, or loss of blood flow to the brain due to a stroke."

Nathan was rapidly running out of leads. Who would have the equipment and the expertise to give Bob an electroconvulsive shock treatment? Could someone have done so in Bob's home, perhaps after he returned home from delivering the package on Saturday? The doctor's findings only heightened the mystery, rather than helping to solve the problem.

Nathan made a note to set up a polygraph test for Sarah Brolins, but he suspected it would not help. He also now suspected that subsequent interviews with Bob would yield no additional information. Whoever had directed Bob's actions had somehow erased his memory of the events as well. It was beginning to appear to Nathan that Bob was just a pawn in this case, and whoever manipulated him did so without leaving a trace. Someone was able to get him to package the object and deliver it in such a way that it would take several days to unravel it to this point.

Nathan speculated to himself, "Maybe whoever manipulated Bob wanted us to spin our wheels for a while until some other development occurred. It's as if a delay of several days were needed before we started to investigate its source. Interestingly, they also apparently used Bob in a way that he incurred no permanent physical or mental damage. That's definitely not the MO for a radical terrorist group, who could view the loss of thousands of civilians as insignificant collateral damage justified by their end goal.

"Whoever created this object didn't leave any clues as to its origin," thought Nathan. His fears were crystallizing as he mulled over the evidence. Trying to trace the source of the object through Bob's involvement had led to a dead end. Nathan would continue going over and over the information and evidence they had collected, but for the first time, he now feared he might never discover who was responsible.

Chapter 14
June 4, 3:30 PM

4,480 pounds

While the object remained at the bomb disposal site in New Jersey, its peculiar nature became the focus of the investigation. What the NYPD and Homeland Security investigators were learning defied all conventional weapon descriptions. They hurriedly contacted a number of scientists to provide advice on exactly what they were dealing with.

The first consultants brought into the investigation were professors from local universities to confirm the bizarre weight of the object. Their initial involvement was primarily to rule out the possibility of it being an elaborate hoax. Two Materials Engineering instructors at NYU were the first scientists brought to the site. Their first experiments eliminated the possibility of any magnetic attraction to the truck's chassis or any other nearby object—the strange cube had absolutely no magnetic quality.

Lacking the tools to identify the unusual metal surface, they focused on confirming the most bizarre aspect of the object—its extreme weight. The NYPD borrowed a forklift equipped with a weight scale to provide accurate measurements of the object's weight. The on-board scale was normally used to prevent overloading the forklift. The scale worked by sensing the hydraulic pressure needed to extend the lift cylinder for raising the forks—the heavier the load being lifted, the greater the pressure of the fluid in the hydraulic lines.

A mobile spreader, usually used for extricating victims from automobile accidents, was used to lift the metal platform underlying the object. Carefully employing the hydraulic rescue tool, the NYPD elevated and blocked the platform about eight inches above the floor of the truck. This clearance was adequate to allow inserting the forklift prongs under the metal platform.

The university instructors, the NYPD officers and the Homeland Security representative were all present to observe the weighing. Adjusting the location of the forks to balance the load, the operator slowly lifted the object. Everyone present was amazed to see the six-inch cube actually measured 4,480 pounds. Checking their equipment, the team recalibrated the scale on the forklift and confirmed it was within its stated accuracy range of 98 percent. They again calculated the minimal weight of the underlying metal plate and carefully repeated the same measurement two more times. Each time, the scale displayed 4,480 pounds. Between measurements, the team replaced the object within the heavily armored walls of the bomb disposal truck to help contain any possible explosion.

From those present at the bomb disposal site, it seemed there was some type of change occurring around 1:45 every afternoon. A few of the officers thought there was visible movement of the truck chassis around that time, possibly due to an increase in weight. The investigators decided to closely monitor and make a video recoding of the object at the next expected expansion time.

CHAPTER 15
JUNE 5, 1:30 PM

4,480 pounds

The following day provided an even greater shock to those performing the tests. With trepidation, the investigators gathered to observe and record any possible change in the object. Intrigued by the unexplained weight of this small cube, representatives from NYU, Homeland Security and the FBI all joined the NYPD officers. At 1:30 PM the officers began video taping the object through one of the opened rear doors in the bomb disposal truck, as they stationed themselves behind a concrete barrier about a hundred feet away from the vehicle.

The group of about a dozen investigators and officers waited nervously, watching a remote monitor from the video camera and occasionally eyeing the truck itself over the top of the concrete barrier. They wondered if another weight gain would actually occur and they worried about what else might happen.

At 1:46 PM, several of the observers saw the truck suddenly bounce slightly, as if something had briefly jarred it. But that was the only visible change that occurred. The investigators apprehensively waited another half hour, and then proceeded with another weight test, as performed several times on the previous day. It only took a few minutes to repeat the practiced steps of removing and weighing the object with the forklift.

The object had in fact doubled in weight to 8,960 pounds.

The investigators were simultaneously stunned, intrigued and frightened. The instructors and the government agents were at a total loss to explain the phenomena.

Although the NYPD had blocked off the bomb disposal area from the news media, several enterprising journalists were able to take long-distance photographs during the weight measuring. News articles spread rapidly over the Internet as well as in printed media. The news media was going wild over these new developments— the NYPD had apparently removed a bomb from the UN complex. Was a devastating terrorist incident just avoided? Was anyone claiming responsibility? The news and wild rumors were rampant once the bizarre facts of the package's weight started to circulate. It also appeared that an anonymous source within the police department had leaked or possibly sold to the press several of the NYPD's own photos of the strange cube.

The truck holding the object was visibly showing the effects of the object. The heavy-duty chassis was obviously under strain simply by viewing the gradually flattening tires. The NYPD contacted additional experts to help explain the strange phenomena. None was able to provide an explanation as to how the object was increasing in weight, especially in light of its size remaining constant. It appeared to be increasing in weight at the same time every day, at 1:46 PM.

Homeland Security was coordinating information about this strange event through related government agencies, including the military. The Department of Defense was now fascinated with the possibilities of using the technology that could have created such an object. The destructive potential of a material that stealthily gained in weight was immense. If the bizarre substance could be controlled and strategically placed, it could have an immense impact on an enemy's infrastructure and war machinery.

For a number of years, munitions manufacturers had been using depleted uranium to increase the armor-piercing capability of bullets and larger projectiles. Uranium was the favored material solely due to its extreme weight. Whatever made up this strange object was apparently vastly heavier than depleted uranium or any other known metal. The military possibilities were intriguing, which ensured the effort received top priority from the government. It would be critical for the DOD to maintain a low profile until the scientists unraveled the mystery.

Both the Homeland Security Secretary and the Secretary of Defense were adamant that the Administration identify the most capable research team available and to assemble it as quickly as possible. President Arbust and the highest levels of his Administration were involved in assuring this happened immediately. The risks of delay were too great, and the president realized they also needed to address the gradually spreading public alarm. After consulting with his closest staff, President Arbust concurred with the recommendation of his science advisor and appointed Randolph Schiller to head the research team. The well-known physicist was considered eminently qualified to unravel this mystery based on his long career of successfully managing difficult projects.

Randolph Schiller's first task was reviewing the list of team candidates identified by the top science advisors scattered throughout the government. The candidates had to be available immediately and be willing to place themselves in a potentially dangerous environment. However, the intrigue of unraveling the mystery was a strong motivator, particularly among the physics community. Being the first to identify a new element was exciting, but having the opportunity to work directly with something that defied the known laws of physics was a chance of a lifetime. It would only be a few more days before the scientists first realized the calamity that was about to threaten the Earth.

Chapter 16
June 6, 2:30 PM

17,920 pounds

The authorities were puzzled as to their next step. For lack of a better plan, the NYPD considered driving the bomb disposal truck to an even more remote location. The police and the consulting scientists speculated it would likely be no more dangerous on the road than at its current site. They began planning a route that would involve the smallest possible damage in case it exploded in transit.

Based on the measurements made in the UN mailroom and at the bomb disposal site, the strange object appeared to be doubling in weight every day. That would mean the 560-pound package measured in the mail facility would now be at 17,920 pounds. Besides approximating the figures from the forklift scale, merely viewing the visible stress on the vehicle further substantiated the estimate. They would have to move the object quickly, or it would soon be too heavy to transport anywhere. Clearing the selected route had actually begun, but they had to abandon this plan when the truck tires collapsed under the increasing weight of the object on the fifth day.

The consensus of the scientists who tried to explain the object was to transfer it to an advanced lab site where a broader collection of investigators could more thoroughly examine it—perhaps physicists and chemical engineers could unravel the mystery. The quicker they could relocate it to a well-equipped lab, the better. Homeland Security, NYPD and the scientific community all were eager to resolve this mystery for their own purposes.

The Department of Defense agents working with Homeland Security first considered all military installations in the general area, but none of the government sites was adequately equipped for the type of testing required. Since time was critical, finding an established lab facility with advanced test equipment already installed was essential. The agents next contacted several private business firms, but they quickly eliminated all of these labs due to inadequate security at the sites.

Pressed to hurriedly move the object, the scientists finally found a lab complex with high tech testing equipment—Harriman Systems Laboratory. The large site was relatively close—less than fifty miles away near Harriman, New York. The research and development facility not only had extensive testing equipment onsite, but also had highly secure facilities. Several agencies within the Department of Defense had previously established R&D contracts with Harriman Systems Laboratory. These classified contracts had required a variety of security enhancements not present in commercial settings.

Randolph Schiller, with several team members who had already started working on the project, toured the facility and was excited to move quickly ahead with the project. Having gradually extended his authority over most aspects of the investigation, Randy made the final lab selection. The Defense Department negotiated an emergency contract with the lab's owners, an open-ended contract that would cover the full cost of the entire lab complex and cause all other work at the site to cease immediately.

The police brought a heavy-duty hauler to the New Jersey site that evening, and winched the bomb disposal truck onto the hauler's flatbed for transporting to Harriman Systems Laboratory. The convoy began to traverse the route, again using a police car escort to create a moving buffer zone around the rig. The carefully chosen route included a small detour to pass through a truck scale on the interstate. Despite the consistent weight measurements made so far, Randy decided another independently performed measurement couldn't hurt. The investigators were still having difficulty accepting the bizarre reality of the extreme weight. Subtracting the known weight of the flatbed rig and the bomb disposal truck, they quickly verified the object did in fact weigh between 17,000 and 18,000 pounds.

The U.S. military was now intensely interested in the mystery, seeing the chance to obtain an entirely new type of weapon. The Department of Defense had always funded basic research in a wide variety of areas, not for the advancement of science alone, but frequently just to ensure that America did not lag behind an enemy's discoveries. Although not publicly acknowledged by

Homeland Security, the military was actually one of the first organizations they contacted when they were scrambling for anyone to turn to. Only the utterly bizarre increase in the object's weight forced the military to concede that they also did not have a clue as to how to handle the emergency.

Randy was in his element, now in control of the entire effort to understand and hopefully control this strange object. He was formally placed in charge of all aspects of dealing with the object, as all the affected agencies were so informed by Homeland Security. The DOD would remain in the background, at least until the mystery was solved.

If the military could only replicate this strange weight expansion, there would be tremendous value in the destructive potential of such an object. They needed to monitor closely every action of the investigation team and ensure that when the underlying mechanism was understood, all team communications would immediately be restricted. The DOD would have to embed at least one member on the research team, one who recognized the military value of such a device and who could be relied upon to inform the Pentagon immediately of any discoveries by the team.

Most of the members of the team would soon surmise that this monitoring role was the real agenda of Taylor McCracken, a physicist from Los Alamos. He held degrees similar to the other team members, but had never distinguished himself in any creative way. His sole public role was membership on a committee advising the Pentagon on nuclear weaponry—both current and potential future methods of deployment. Since the team's task was so urgent, the other team members were not overly concerned about any possible covert role, as long as Taylor did not thwart or delay the team's progress.

When the police had hauled the bomb disposal truck to the Harriman lab site, they had to continue solving logistical problems due to its extreme weight. They parked the transporting vehicle adjacent to a building identified as C Lab, extended the rig's loading ramp and opened both rear doors of the truck. Noting that here was no visible change to the cube since they left the New Jersey site, the officers removed the straps that had secured the object during the move. Using a forklift, they removed both the object and the underlying steel panel to the outside of the vehicle. The object and panel were then placed on a platform used for transferring building construction equipment.

Due to an on-going expansion of one of the buildings in the lab complex, a variety of heavy construction equipment was already present on the lab grounds. One of the pieces of equipment was a construction crane used to hoist rooftop air-conditioning equipment to a building adjacent to the lab. By attaching the winching cables to the transferring platform, the crane was able to hoist the object and position it above a removed skylight in the lab building.

Moving the object by crane was risky, particularly if it doubled in weight in the midst of moving and upset the entire balance of the huge crane. However, since the cycles had all occurred at exactly the same interval of time, the team felt it was an acceptable risk to transfer the object between expected cycles. The construction crane operator carefully and very slowly lowered the object to the floor of the lab.

And there the object sat, about to be examined over the next week with virtually every possible non-destructive test known to modern science.

CHAPTER 17
JUNE 12, 8:15 PM

1,146,880 pounds

"We have to act. We have to act soon, before it's too late." Jason Morehouse spoke passionately to the "true believers," the nine adults who had gathered in his home for their habitual prayer session. The members sat on the floor in Jason's small living room, in three rows of three penitents each. The all male group quietly faced their revered leader who also sat on the worn carpeted floor.

Although Jason was only twenty-seven, his followers viewed him with the same respect normally reserved for an elderly rabbi or mullah. Jason's words and actions always inspired his followers—no matter what he was doing, his piercing dark eyes and rigid movements always projected an austere image. Living in an evil world was not supposed to be easy or simple. When surrounded by heathens, maintaining a pure existence was a difficult and ongoing challenge, but understanding and following

God's true dictates was the only life worth living. There was absolutely no doubt in any of the members that Jason would lead them in knowing God's will for each of them.

It had been five years since the core members of the faction had moved to New York. They had never contacted Hope Tabernacle in California, where the roots of their cult life had formed. There was no need—this small band was now their family, their entire support system.

Jason's home, which served as their regular meeting site, was in a struggling working-class neighborhood. There were empty lots scattered around the neighborhood, including one just across the street scarred with the remains of a redevelopment project that was suspended after the foundation had been laid years earlier. Residents in this neighborhood worked long hours and generally kept to themselves, which meant that Jason's followers arriving for their frequent meetings drew little attention.

Jason's followers had always eagerly anticipated the specific end-times prophesied in the book of Revelation. They firmly believed in the horrific conditions on Earth during the last days: widespread wars, violent struggles everywhere between believers and non-believers, famine and plagues. They wanted to be ready to protect themselves and wage whatever battles might be required against the expected forces of the Antichrist.

The members also viewed the current world as a constant threat to their group and fully expected they would someday need to defend their faith—true soldiers of Christ had to be prepared for any onslaught from evil forces. Over the past several years, they had quietly assembled a small collection of guns, all too easily obtained in the spotty enforcement environment that existed in nearby New Jersey. Their intermittent hunting trips to upstate New York and Connecticut had been a suitable cover for their training maneuvers. Deep in the back woods, they succeeded in hiding their marksmanship practice and stealth drills from public view.

The devoted followers were aware of the frequent news reports that forecast increasing destruction from an unexplained object, and like everyone else, were frightened by the predictions of a possible end to the world. Like most people, they desperately focused on trying to understand the situation. In this group, however, there was no panic at the thought of helplessness. These devotees had been completely mesmerized by Jason, especially by his descriptions of how he directly received messages from God. Jason would lead them in these final hours and he would receive instructions as to what they needed to do.

Everyone in the small group admired Jason for his pure, ascetic lifestyle. Although he supported himself as a postal worker, he filled his private life with "pure" pursuits—living ascetically, praying, avoiding temptation to both mind and body. His unusual early life in the Hope Tabernacle community had prepared him well for his present role.

Jason led his anxious members in a ritual prayer to calm their fears and bolster their solidarity. "Lord hear our prayers. Lord hear our prayers. Lord hear our prayers...."

The chanting was steady, repetitive and very effective at blocking out extraneous thoughts that might distract the members. It was calming, providing a soothing mental state that they had grown comfortable with over the past several years. Even the occasional sirens of an ambulance or police car went unnoticed by the supplicants.

"Praise His name! I have received instructions!" The group was silent, but the excitement in the room was palpable as they waited for the revelation from Jason.

"The sacred container itself is our altar, a Holy Ark, the conduit for our direct communion with God. It must be protected and treated with proper respect. Are all of us worthy enough to be chosen to protect this Holy Ark?"

The gathered followers were riveted by the revelation. *They* had been selected by God. The members waited expectantly as Jason continued, "We must rescue it from the sacrilegious treatment it's receiving in the laboratory. It's being ceaselessly subjected to heathen touch, to radiation tests, to chemical analysis. When we show the world how to properly respect the sacred vessel, it will stop increasing in weight and the destruction of Earth will be halted.

"God does not want to destroy the Earth, only to demonstrate his displeasure with humanity for ignoring his will. The entire world will know this is a final warning from God. The sinners of the world must finally abandon their evil ways.

"We must be willing to make the supreme sacrifice, to martyr ourselves if necessary in this holy act. This is God's command to us. All of us are totally subject to God's will and mercy."

Rescuing the Holy Ark would undoubtedly be dangerous, and they might even have to kill heathens and faux Christians to accomplish their mission. Nevertheless, there was no doubt or moral reservation about what had to be done. When one is channeling God, the laws and conventions of mere humans are of no consequence.

The group continued chanting their comforting mantra as Jason formulated plans to rescue the sacred ark. "Lord hear our prayers. Lord hear our prayers. Lord hear our prayers...."

CHAPTER 18
JUNE 13, 8:00 AM

1,146,880 pounds

As Randy and the team reflected on the challenges of the past week, they now realized that physically moving the object to the lab was a relatively simple part of this project. At the time, the numerous obstacles in moving it first to the bomb disposal area and later to the lab complex seemed daunting, but possible. After studying the object with the most sophisticated technology available, understanding this bizarre object now seemed beyond their technical and intellectual resources.

Lacking any headway in explaining how the object could be increasing in weight but not size, the investigative team shifted focus to its origin. If they could identify the sender and the sender's background, they might be able to gain insight as to how it was assembled and how it could function.

Most of the team had gathered that morning in the lab's conference room for a general brainstorming session. The coffee was flowing as usual in an attempt to keep their mental faculties at a peak. By freely tossing around ideas, they hoped to identify new angles to research—and they desperately needed new angles.

Everyone was acutely aware of the worsening crisis. A few members had dropped off the team, overwhelmed by both the intense pressure to come up with a solution and the apparent hopelessness of their task. Randy had not replaced them, electing not to waste time bringing new team members up to speed. Besides, he figured that with fewer team members there would be fewer to share the glory when they eventually solved the crisis. Randy's optimism persisted despite the lack of progress to-date.

Ever since 9/11, the first reaction to catastrophes was to assume they were the result of terrorist activity. Whenever a number of individuals died or dramatic destruction occurred, terrorism was always a possibility. It was almost a given that every major airplane crash would be initially attributed to terrorism, rather than the result of mechanical failure or pilot error. Assassinations, workplace shootings and kidnappings of political leaders were also typically suspected to be the work of terrorists. But in almost all cases a deranged employee, a drug-crazed individual or just old-fashioned greed turned out to be the real cause. Even natural calamities had become suspect—were the 2005 breaks in the New Orleans levees helped by someone attempting to maximize the economic damage? Was that tragic train derailment only due to a naturally eroded rail bed?

Wreaking havoc on an enemy's economy as well as their collective state of well-being and safety was undoubtedly in line with many terrorists' goals. One of the most critical dilemmas facing the world was how to understand and deal with individuals willing to martyr themselves and kill innocents by the thousands. How could anyone commit such horrific acts in order to force their worldview on others?

With the recent advent of weapons of mass destruction, the world had moved into a radically more dangerous era of terrorist capability. For the first time in history, small and unpredictable groups of people, operating independently of any state, were capable of doing unimaginable harm.

"My dollar is on al-Qaida! This would be a perfect venue for getting maximum publicity for their cause." Taylor McCracken was laying his cards on the table in his usual direct manner. Although he was not highly regarded by other members on the team, they all appreciated his candidness and willingness to put his views on record. For Taylor, a terrorist organization must have created the object—if not al-Qaida, then some other radical faction with similar aims.

"What better target to attack than the United Nations, symbol of the world's attempts at global cooperation? If a terrorist could gain access and spectacularly damage the well-protected UN headquarters, think of the global news coverage. Extreme anti-terrorism safeguards have been in place in New York since 2001. With the UN headquarters in such a heavily guarded city, any successful terrorist act in New York would dramatically demonstrate that no place on Earth is outside their reach." Taylor's confrontational attitude never failed to irritate his associates. Whatever the issue, Taylor always seemed to have a preformed opinion.

Randy was the first to fire away, with his usual lack of concern that he could be stifling the free flow of ideas. "No," he abruptly interjected. "If this were a conventional weapon, you might be right. But this really doesn't make sense for a number of reasons. How could a terrorist organization construct a device that's beyond the comprehension of the most advanced scientists in the world? Any underground cell has to operate under lots of constraints to keep its work secret. I don't see how something as complex and innovative as this object could have been produced by a terrorist group that has to spend so much of its energy hiding their activities from the world."

Randy continued, "Perhaps we should be looking at established research organizations that are known to be pushing the frontiers of basic physics. It's possible that a phenomenally intelligent individual is responsible for this object, and the development has been carefully concealed from the world. Perhaps a modern-day genius of the likes of Leonardo DaVinci or Newton is operating off the world's radar. With adequate time and financial support, an advanced research group might have secretly discovered or created a new element, or found an ingenious way to bypass the known laws of physics."

"And you think a genius who was capable of creating such a device would actually unleash it on the world as a doomsday weapon?" objected Taylor. He was operating under the common conception that someone with an extraordinary intelligence would still share the same moral values as most of humanity—a somewhat debatable point.

"Maybe." Randy was not about to be corrected, especially by Taylor. "But it doesn't matter whether the creators actually concurred with the use of the object. Many weapons have been created by scientists who later regretted their involvement in unleashing them on the world. The method of use may have been totally out of their control. Just consider how our own nuclear weapons were initially developed by the world's most esteemed scientists but then subsequently controlled by military and political powers."

Rob saw an opportunity to bring the discussion back to territory that was more plausible. His credibility on the team allowed him to be as direct as necessary with Randy. "Let's back up a second. The 'mad genius' scenario fits into a Goldfinger or Dr. No story, but it's not plausible with today's advanced technology. The frontiers of basic scientific fields such as physics are extremely complex in the twenty-first century. Advancing these frontiers requires the collective efforts of many individuals, funding by immense grants, and support by large infrastructures—so immense that it generally means large governments. The days of the lone 'mad scientist' are long gone."

Persevering to attribute the crisis to an enemy of the United States, Taylor countered. "Then why not a government-funded effort, perhaps by a rogue government with lots of funds and the right sympathies to try to effect a global change? Several oil-rich nations could provide immense funding for such an effort."

"Sure, we all know several countries that are sympathetic to terrorist causes," Rob conceded to some extent. "There are also quite a few very wealthy benefactors who could bankroll advanced research projects. However, one of the biggest successes in global anti-terrorism efforts has been how the banking system has curtailed much of the funding for known terrorist groups. So it would seem the billions of dollars of required funding for such an effort would have to be totally contained within a rogue country."

"Regardless of where it might have been created," Rob continued, "whether here in the States, in another developed country or in some rogue nation, the larger question is how such a huge effort could have possibly been kept secret. I believe it's very unlikely that such a large-scale project could have been kept submerged for the decades needed to develop it. I'm afraid we're coming up short."

It was not the answer Randy wanted. There was another briefing with President Arbust that afternoon and there was absolutely nothing encouraging to report to the president or to provide for the media. The team and the world would soon realize the research efforts could not have been further off base.

CHAPTER 19
JUNE 13, 9:45 AM

1,146,880 pounds

"Woe to anyone who disregards the laws of God! Woe to anyone who refuses to believe in the truth and prophecies of the Bible!" Tirelessly, Pastor Matthew Robinson hammered the message home—again and again.

Most of the research team members had left the conference room after the morning work session, but a few were watching a live broadcast on a TV monitor. Feeds from several of the main networks were always active on the TV monitors that lined the back of the room. Observing news reports helped the team know just how much information presented in the press briefings was actually passed on to the public. They also provided at least one indicator of the level of panic spreading across the world.

Over the years, Pastor Robinson's televised broadcasts attracted more and more of the dissatisfied populace, offering solace to many seeking a clear solution to their problems. Like many charismatic evangelists before him, he had ridden the televised airwaves to enthrall an audience now numbered in the millions. His projected image of sincerity and certainty in all of life's questions provided an anchor for many struggling with the problems and complexities of life and the unknowns of the afterlife. Understanding there was a simple reason for all one's problems, and even better, that there was a simple solution for addressing them, was enticing.

Matthew Robinson's messages had always appealed to those anxious about a crisis in their personal life, but now it offered a solution to the crisis facing the world at large. As with all other dilemmas, the arrival of this object provided Pastor Robinson with an opportunity for inspired interpretation: it was a direct message from God himself.

The main networks were now actually vying with one another to be the first to air his broadcasts. After years of struggling to fund his programs either on syndicated channels or during low-cost late nighttime slots, Pastor Robinson was elated. Audiences were desperate for any news on the escalating disaster, and they were even more desperate for any proposed solution. He was offering one, and he quickly seized the opportunity to explain the reason for this strange object.

To Pastor Robinson, this was not a fortuitous event for him to capitalize upon. This was all part of God's plan—he was merely one of those selected to explain God's will to the world. Although the good pastor would never have publicly referred to himself as a prophet, he knew in his heart that he was one of God's chosen communicators.

"God's word is clear! He who rejects it will spend eternity in Hell; he who accepts it and believes will spend eternity in Heaven. God sent this object to test us—will we continue to rely on our worldly tools to save us from this crisis, or will we repent our sins and plead to God for mercy? None of the trials and plagues that God has previously sent has awakened us to seek Him. HIV, tsunamis, earthquakes—all have been explained away by the false gods of modern science. So, God has sent us a final warning in this object.

"Many believe that God works in mysterious ways. There is no mystery to His acts. The world's calamities are all divine retribution for our failure to accept the Truth. Hurricane Katrina didn't just happen to occur in New Orleans—the hedonism, paganism and homosexuality rampant in New Orleans were a direct affront to God's laws. When Americans turned their backs on God and embraced feminism, allowed abortions and took the Bible out of the schoolrooms, God allowed the terrorists to attack us on 9/11."

The pastor's voice boomed with certainty and conviction. "God will not be mocked! Wasn't it obvious to everyone that God struck down Prime Minister Ariel Sharon with a stroke when he carved up the Holy Land and gave away territory in the Gaza strip? The devastating 2010 earthquake in Haiti was clearly a punishment for their country's founders forming a pact with the devil. There's no escaping God's wrath."

Since the networks were realizing greater numbers of viewers than at any time in their history, the television media gave Pastor Robinson maximum coverage, occasionally with rebuttal dialog from less radical evangelists. Yet

the liberal religious factions with more complex and less
certain interpretations were rarely given the same amount
of airtime. Not only were those viewpoints less dramatic,
but they were not easy to ponder. Contemplating events
with patience and a clear mind was becoming more and
more difficult as the level of fear increased along with the
object's weight.

Never ceasing to be astonished by the fundamentalist's
simplistic and unquestioning answer to all dilemmas,
Sharon Catwold voiced her concern to Rob as they took
a brief break before the upcoming daily status meeting.
She found it easy to be candid with Rob, who was always
open to hearing her ideas. Although their opinions often
differed, they had steadily developed a close relationship
where they could both openly share their thoughts. Each
had discovered they shared a common base of core values
that resulted in similar attitudes toward the world in
general.

Both Sharon and Rob had chosen career paths that
could potentially make significant improvements in the
world. Immediately following college, Sharon spent the
next two years working with the Peace Corp in Burkina
Faso. Seeing firsthand the extreme difficulties faced by
the citizens of a struggling nation, Sharon developed
an enduring desire to assist those in impoverished
countries.

After Sharon's Peace Corp tour ended, she had a clear
vision of how she wanted to spend her life—developing
low-cost medications for ailments that plagued the poorest
inhabitants of the world. Sharon consequently devoted
the next several years to earning a doctorate in Biology
and then completed several post-doctoral programs. She

was currently involved in studying potential vaccines for malaria when the selection committee urgently recruited her to help study the object.

"So why are we working so hard to understand this object, when all we need to do is pray?" asked Sharon. "Just repent for our sins and ask God to halt this object. But pray to which God—Allah, Yahweh, any of the thousands of Hindu deities, or even Thor? There have been over thirty thousand gods worshipped since man first began thinking about them—and we continue to create more gods and religions.

"When I was working in Burkina Faso, I was always fascinated with the indigenous religions. Although half of the country is now Islamic, about a fifth still practices traditional animistic beliefs, especially in the rural areas."

Rob was not sure how this related to the team's problem, but he wanted to know more about Sharon's line of thinking. Although not always immediately obvious, her observations were always relevant. For unknown reasons, he also found himself curious about her attitude toward religion.

"Sharon, aren't you really talking about ancient religions, where new gods were readily invented?"

"No, actually we continue to create more gods and more religions. Did you know that the Falun Gong movement claims to have 100 million adherents—mostly in China—and it was founded only a few decades ago? It was started by Li Hongzhi, a former soldier and grain clerk from northeastern China."

Rob replied, "I didn't think they considered themselves a religion."

"Most followers think of it as a spiritual movement, but their combination of concepts from both Buddhism and Taoism sure fit the definition of religion. They're best known for their slow-motion exercises that they believe channel unseen natural forces through the body. Although their practices promote health and living a virtuous life, the Chinese government labels them as an evil cult. The number of adherents clearly pushes them beyond the cult category into a mainstream religious organization."

"Wait a minute. You think the only difference between a group of believers being a cult or being a religion is the number of members?"

"Just who's considered a 'cult' depends on who's doing the labeling. Despite having millions of members, many Christians consider organizations like the Church of Scientology or the Latter Day Saints as cults. The degree of deviation from one's own religion has a big influence on how one views other faiths, particularly since the label 'cult' is always used negatively. It seems a degree of 'mind control' may be the most distinguishing criteria of a cult, where different viewpoints are absolutely forbidden and any questioning of authority isn't tolerated."

"OK. I give up. So what does Falun Gong or cults have to do with this?" Rob was trying to figure out where Sharon, who was usually very focused, was taking this conversation.

"My point is only that new beliefs, deities and religions have been created continuously for tens of thousands of years, ever since the first religious symbols were placed in graves. It never made sense to me how the members of most religions think of themselves as having the sole, or at least the best, path to salvation and an eternal reward—

they can't all be right. If there's only one God or one true religion, then all the rest of the world's inhabitants are wrong."

Rob hesitated to pursue this conversation, but wanted to provide another approach for Sharon to consider. "Then again, I wonder if they all could be right—not in terms of specific beliefs being true or false, but that they all satisfy a similar need for their followers. One could argue that all religions might be honoring or worshiping the same God, and only their practices or theologies are different. Islam, Baha'i and other religions view many of the world's past religious founders all as prophets of the true God, each being sent with a message unique to a specific time or culture."

Sharon must have heard Rob's comment, but she kept venting her frustration, a frustration ignited by the famous televangelist's arrogant claim to fully understand the object's purpose. She was surprised how easy it was to communicate her thoughts to Rob, wondering if he was simply a good listener or if they related on more levels than just the team's research.

Sharon continued, suddenly realizing she truly enjoyed these discussions with Rob. "And exactly what sins does Pastor Robinson want us to repent for? Practically all religions agree on a few egregious acts as sins. But it seems to me that every religion has defined a set of behaviors it considers right or wrong, righteous or evil, sacred or profane. Hundreds of millions of devout followers believe that it's a sin for anyone to drink alcohol, to expose one's face in public, or even to criticize their faith. Just exactly which sins is Pastor Robinson talking about?"

"Don't try to think too much about it—that's not the intent of his messages. His audience didn't grow into the millions by any critical examination of his pronouncements. Rather than just seeing the highlights on the nightly news, maybe you should attend one of his services?" Rob quickly averted his face to prevent Sharon seeing his smile.

CHAPTER 20
JUNE 13, 3:00 PM

2,293,760 pounds

"This is just another Western plot. The imperialists want to force the entire world to perform some yet-to-be decreed action, probably something to ensure their oil supply or to further support the state of Israel." Only a few team members were in the conference room when the afternoon broadcast from Al Jazeera filled one of the TV monitors. The news channel from the Qatar-based television network reached a huge audience as the world debated the events that were unfolding in New York.

The current show was an interview with a popular cleric in Iraq who had recently become one of the most influential religious leaders in the Mideast. Mullah Akbar Farouf was an unknown clerical student before Saddam Hussein was removed from power in 2003, but as the sectarian violence in Iraq continued, the mullah's radical sermons had been attracting a growing audience.

As with other religious groups, the followers of Islam likewise varied in their reactions to the mysterious object. The most radical Islamic fundamentalists simply did not believe the newscasts they were receiving. Yet even those who viewed the entire event as a sham had to admit most of the world was mesmerized by the news of the purported dilemma. Whether the news was actually true or fabricated, they recognized that the global powers would soon be acting on such news.

Of those radical Islamists who did accept the legitimacy of the news reports, many believed the object was a new weapon that the United States itself had secretly created. They assumed that only a superpower like the United States with its wealth and scientific capabilities could secretly create such a destructive object.

The Al Jazeera program continued with the interview of the popular Shiite cleric from Iraq. "What do you expect from these infidels? These reports are coming from the same country that arrogantly claimed the right to attack other countries preemptively. America has spent hundreds of billions of dollars and thousands of lives in an invasion of Iraq based on fabricated reasons. Such a country is clearly capable of spreading false information to justify their other quests. The question is this: What do the devils in Washington want to control this time?"

Most of the Western world readily dismissed the inflammatory broadcasts, yet denizens of the Mideast and other Islamic areas considered the cleric's pronouncements to be the same matter-of-fact coverage as weather or traffic reports. Tens of thousands of such people believed that the Americans would soon force the entire world into a yet-to-be announced but undoubtedly self-serving action.

Islam had been the world's fastest growing faith for decades. Over the previous thirty years, the number of Muslims worldwide had doubled to 1.5 billion followers. At the current rate of expansion, one fourth of the world's people were projected to be Muslim by the year 2025. If the object was eventually tied to a radical Islamic faction, or a worldwide effort was needed to deal with the object, the team recognized they needed to have a better grasp on how the Islamic segment of the world was interpreting this dilemma.

Recognizing the incredulity of people around the world toward the object, and the tremendously reduced credibility of the U.S. government, the investigation team had invited representatives of doubting nations to directly observe the lab's testing. The team also specifically solicited respected scientists and world religious leaders, as well as influential UN delegates already present in New York.

To gain a better understanding of the more widespread moderate Islamic reaction, the team contacted Mullah Mahmoud Rezai. He happened to be staying in New York at the time, participating in an ecumenical council of a number of Islamic factions that resided in North and South America. The mullah was one of the religious leaders previously invited to personally observe the investigation, hopefully to help mitigate the widespread skepticism. He had visited the lab site a few days earlier and directly observed the testing of the object.

The team had asked Mullah Rezai to join them for a briefing on how the Islamic world was interpreting what was happening. Eager to enlighten the team, the mullah was talking to a small group consisting of Rob, Sharon,

Randy and Taylor. The respected mullah was surprisingly confident of the source of the object.

"This appears to be a delivery from Allah—just as Muhammad, praise be upon him, received the Qur'an fourteen hundred years ago. We must unite in prayer and ask for guidance for what we need to do, for guidance as to how we should respond to this object. If Allah's will is for our civilization to end, so be it. To Allah we belong, and to Allah we will return. If we ask Allah for mercy, and we're blessed by the Almighty to survive, it will be made known to us."

As the meeting progressed, it was apparent that much of what was happening was compatible with Islamic theology. Mullah Rezai continued, "All Muslims believe that God has sent messengers throughout the history of mankind—twenty-five prophets are mentioned in the Qur'an. Five of these prophets delivered specific messages from God, delivered at different times to humanity: the scrolls to Abraham, the Commandments to Moses, the Psalms to David, the Gospel to Jesus and finally the Qur'an was revealed to Muhammad. Allah sent the same message repeatedly commanding us to worship the One God alone and to follow His guidance. Yet over time, man has altered most of the messages. Modern day translations of all the other messages have been corrupted and only the Qur'an still reflects the authentic word of Allah."

Sharon protested, "But if Muhammad was the final messenger, then why would another one be sent? Isn't that a conflict with what is in the Qur'an?"

Sharon was familiar with a few of the core beliefs of Muslims. During her two Peace Corp years in Burkina Faso, she had many opportunities to discuss aspects of life with the local citizens. The Burkinabe were more than happy to help educate this unusual foreigner in their midst. Sharon had learned that a key Islamic belief was that Muhammad was the final prophet, and that there was no need for further prophets since the scripture of the Qur'an would guide humankind. Consequently, Muslims have always viewed religions like the worldwide Baha'i and the Qadiani in India as heretical. The Baha'i believe God sent earlier messengers to humanity like Krishna and Buddha, as well as prophets after Muhammad like their own spiritual guide Bahaullah who died in 1892. Throughout the centuries following Muhammad, any splinter groups that recognized subsequent messengers as prophets were treated severely.

The mullah responded without any hesitation, "There is no conflict. Muhammad is still the final prophet. This message has clearly come to us without any human messenger. We only need to pray that we may truly understand the message we have been given by this object."

CHAPTER 21
JUNE 14, 1:36 PM

2,293,760 pounds

"A bowling ball in jelly! That is what it will look like in about ten minutes," Rob informed the gathered press agents. As with all recent briefings, journalists completely packed the pressroom at the lab complex. Rob was the only one at the podium, giving a brief update to the gathered journalists and potentially to millions watching the televised briefing. As he checked his watch, he continued, "The next cycle will occur in precisely nine minutes, thirty-five seconds. All of the previous cycle times have been very exact. We have made a number of preparations for this next cycle, which we anticipate to be the most spectacular to-date."

Rob continued, "As some of you have observed, the supporting structure under the object has been under increasing stress. The first surface under the object is the stainless steel plate that the NYPD removed from the scale when they first discovered the object in the UN mailroom. Since the plate is steel, it has only shown minimal deformation so far. The floor of the lab however, being six inches of reinforced concrete, actually deformed noticeably with yesterday's expansion cycle. Cracks in the concrete floor now radiate outwards in all directions from the object."

"So how much does it weigh now?" asked the closest journalist, trying to quantify the disconcerting information they were trying to process.

"We calculate the weight to currently be 2,293,760 pounds, which we anticipate will double in another eight minutes. This will place it at a weight sufficient to collapse through the floor and into the layers of soil and rock under the building.

"We have taken steps to isolate the object from the surrounding building structure. Yesterday, all layers beneath the object were detached from the building—the underlying three-by-four-foot steel panel, the concrete floor and the underlying foundation structure. These layers were separated from the object by using a heavy-duty reciprocating saw to cut a thirty-six-inch diameter circle around it. We believe this will allow further compression under the object without causing the collapse of the entire building.

"The immediate area has been evacuated except for two volunteer observers, and as you can see on the overhead monitors, we have installed additional cameras to view the next weight doubling cycle. If it helps to visualize the dynamics we are about to observe, think of a huge vat of jelly, perhaps the size of a grain silo. If you were to place a bowling ball on the top surface, its weight would cause it to sink slowly through the jelly. The density of the underlying layers would set the speed of descent. Depending on the strength and density of the surrounding material, the developing shaft above the descending ball—or above this object—will either retain its shape or collapse."

Rob wanted to provide an accurate assessment of what would soon occur, to minimize the anxiety from unexpected developments. However, he was very aware that forecasting what would happen after the object began sinking through the ground was extremely difficult. In fact, it was almost impossible.

Maps from the U.S. Geological Survey provided the most detailed information on the underlying strata, but this data was limited to only the top few miles. The ground surface consisted of clay and sand, deposited during the retreat of massive glacial ice sheets that covered half of North America in relatively recent time. Sedimentary formations provided the next layers, laid down during the Paleozoic era. The varying density of all of these underlying strata would dictate the rate and angle of descent.

The presence of at least three known lava flows under this specific area of New York further complicated making predictions of the object's descent. These flows resulted in large deposits of denser basalt interspersed between limestone and shale layers. Depending on the amount of this hard substance, the basalt could abruptly halt the object's descent. On the other hand, any subsequent expansions in weight could restart its descent.

Establishing any influence from existing fault lines was even more problematic. Although a number of faults from earth movements had been located in outlying areas, the risk of undetected faults was very high. The closest known fault line was over fifteen miles away, an inactive fault caused by earth movement millions of years earlier.

Fortunately, the team had an extremely effective tool to determine the object's weight, even after it would soon descend through the Earth's floor. The researchers relied on both ground-based and satellite-based gravimeters to determine the mass of the object. These devices measured changes in the gravitational field and were typically used for determining anomalies in underlying ground strata in geological studies. Once the local gravitational constant was determined for the site of the lab, the instruments accurately measured the increase in the object's mass at each cycle.

Determining the object's location would be less straightforward. If it descended through the lab's floor, sophisticated calculations would have to be employed to determine the object's changing location. The team hoped the sensitive gravimeters would also aid in determining the exact depth of the descending object.

Checking his watch again, Rob blurted to the group, "At this moment we're only three minutes from the next expansion, so I'll be leaving you now—I'm one of the two designated observers. Randy Schiller will take your questions."

Rob immediately stepped back from the podium and headed out of the pressroom. Although it was only a few seconds until Randy stood before the front of the group, the journalists were already clamoring for answers. They had learned they could expect more candid and more detailed answers from Rob, and were hoping to direct at least a few quick questions to him before he left the room.

Randolph Schiller, however, was not about to give Rob any additional exposure to the media. As head of this project, Randy was sure he could field the questions more than adequately. He grasped the sides of the podium and turned ever so slightly to the right, showing what he considered his best side to the television cameras. He scanned the room deciding which privileged journalist to acknowledge first as Rob hastily stepped out of the pressroom.

Rob was relieved to be away from the television cameras and the frenzied attention from the journalists. Never comfortable in the limelight, he had perfected a public persona that at least appeared to be at ease. It only took a minute for Rob to cross the short path to C Lab and enter the room to join Sharon.

"Cutting it awfully close, aren't you? Leaving me to my fate alone?" Sharon halfheartedly chided him, but she was genuinely glad not to be alone in the lab. They both knew the risk outside the three-foot isolated circle of flooring was small, but they agreed with the team's security manager that there was no point in risking more staff than necessary. Despite all previous cycles being consistent, there was no guarantee that the next weight doubling would be the same. They positioned themselves at the rear of the lab next to a windowless concrete wall, where they could still see both the object and most of the monitoring screens.

"Scared?" Rob quietly asked.

"Oh yeah, but we both know better than anyone, that unless we solve this, everyone's days are numbered."

30 seconds to go.

"If we survive this, we deserve a long break," Rob suggested, as he found himself watching Sharon more intently than usual.

"You got it, Rob—but the key word now is 'if'. Assuming it sinks through the floor as we expect, we'll need to calculate how many more cycles the planet can tolerate."

Sharon was thankful that Rob was in the lab experiencing this dangerous situation with her, but a strange thought briefly caromed around her mind as she studied the monitors. She was surprised to realize she could think of absolutely no one with whom she'd rather share this intense moment.

The room was silent, except for the steady hum of the air conditioning system. The overhead monitor displayed the dwindling number of seconds. Just as the monitor displayed zero, there was an immediate change in the object.

A loud crunching sound emanated from the center of the room where the object sat. Sharon grabbed Rob's arm as they both stared at the center of the room. This had suddenly become much more frightening than either of them had expected.

Whoosh.

The crunching of the surface concrete blended with the sound of air being sucked into the vacuum of the hole. The loud crunching sound emanated from the steadily deepening hole where the object has previously sat.

The floor isolation strategy worked. The building only experienced minor movement, as the underlying soil layers were compressed and displaced by the object.

When the dust settled from the pulverized concrete, the overhead camera showed a visible hole about three feet across. With the limited camera resolution, limited lighting and vaporized dust in the hole, the depth was unknown. In fact, the hole was continuing to deepen.

As the engineers had predicted, the hole was the same size as the three-foot diameter section that had been cut from the steel panel. As the object descended further into the Earth's crust, they reasoned the hole would be diminishing in size as the underlying concrete was pulverized and the circular section of metal bent around the object.

Sharon imagined that if the object had been sitting on the bare surface of the earth without the underlying steel and concrete base, the hole probably would have been limited to the size of the cube itself, only six inches. It might have resembled a typical fence posthole and it certainly would have sunk out of sight days earlier.

"All right!" Rob was the first to speak.

"At least our isolation technique saved the lab building from ruin." The sucking sound of the surrounding air moving into the deepening hole continued to diminish, and now was barely audible.

Rob continued, "Now we'll see if our other monitoring tools will work." Since the object was no longer in sight, a variety of different sensors had been set up to monitor its continuing weight increase and its varying location. "We still have the same key questions: Will it continually descend or will it stop at some point? Can we determine if it's still increasing in weight just on seismic monitoring? Is there anything else we can use to measure its activity?"

The team engineers had previously attached a transmitting beacon to the top of the cube. They expected the beacon to work at least for a few days, but these types of transmitters had never been tested beyond two thousand feet under the Earth's surface.

The higher temperatures encountered as the object descended would add a major unknown dimension to their estimates. The deepest mine in the world was the TauTona gold mine near Johannesburg, South Africa. It extended over two miles beneath the surface, where geothermal heat cooked the rock to 130°F. In order to make the area workable, the miners pumped chilled water onto the tunnel walls. In 1970, Soviet scientists began drilling a hole to explore the Earth's interior. Nineteen years later, the scientists gave up the effort after reaching a depth of 7.6 miles. The temperature at that depth was over 350°F.

After the object initially sank out of sight through the Earth's surface, the fact that it was no longer visible provided a delusive respite of sorts—a few factions took credit for their prayers being answered by removing the object. These presumptuous groups would need to halt taking credit if the object's weight expansion cycles continued as it descended through the planet's interior.

The media was relentless in its typical hindsight analysis—why wasn't the object somehow destroyed when it was first discovered? Could a nuclear weapon have stopped it? The reasons for ruling out that option were still as valid as when reported earlier in the investigation. Now however, even if they discovered a means of destroying the cube, that option was no longer possible. The object was no longer directly accessible after sinking below the Earth's surface.

At this point, the outlook could not have been more dismal. What could they possibly do now? An astonishing discovery was about to answer that question.

CHAPTER 22
JUNE 14, 3:30 PM

4,587,520 pounds

"This is fantastic!" exclaimed Rob, talking to himself just as Taylor entered his office doorway. Taylor had stopped by Rob's office to learn any scrap of new information in advance of the next status meeting. Although Taylor had been keeping his Pentagon contact well informed of events as they developed, he was somewhat chagrined that the public news channels were comprehensively reporting most of the investigation. His participation as a covert member of the team had so far not been of any value to his superiors or to his own ego. Still, he hoped today would be different.

Rob was rapidly pacing back and forth behind his metal office desk and he had a very noticeable smile on his face. Rob's first thought as Taylor entered his office was to avoid wasting valuable minutes discussing this latest development with him. Yet the discovery was so surprising he needed to share the excitement of the moment with someone, even Taylor.

The markings on the cube's exterior had been obvious from the first detailed inspection eight days earlier. It appeared to be simply random marks, similar to what might occur in a metal milling operation. The FBI had diligently investigated numerous metal fabrication facilities, especially any that had an alleged connection with a terrorist organization. So far, the agents had not discovered a connection to any fabrication shop.

"Last week Sharon and I magnified the markings and passed the digitized image through a language translation program. The FBI had obtained permission for us to access the DOD's advanced software used to interpret foreign communications. This system, called LNGTRN, contains over fourteen hundred languages, mostly those in current use but also a significant number of dead languages."

Rob was not concerned about violating any security regulations by discussing LNGTRN with Taylor. To provide access to any classified tools that were needed for the team's research, the DOD had granted emergency security clearances to Rob, Sharon and other team members. A few of the members, including Taylor, already possessed high-level security clearances from working on previous government projects.

As with all government-classified information, the details could only be discussed with others under two conditions. First, both parties needed to have the appropriate level of clearance. Consequently, the DOD granted a high level of security clearance to all the research team members. Secondly, an individual could only disclose the information on a need-to-know basis.

Taylor was already aware of the LNGTRN system, but wanted to avoid emphasizing that his background actually included experience with DOD classified systems. He responded only in general terms, "Why couldn't the marks be part of a language not in that system, since there are far more languages in the world—I seem to recall something like seven thousand."

"But all the others are only rarely used," Rob countered. "In fact, half of all current languages will actually disappear within the century since they're used by so few people. All significant languages have been included in the LNGTRN database.

"After rotating the images of the marks to all possible angles, the system still couldn't relate the odd marks to any known language characters. All six sides of the cube were distinctly different, further indicating they were meaningless random marks. Hitting a dead-end, we moved onto researching other aspects." Rob paused to catch his breath. He knew this next revelation would shock Taylor, as it did himself just minutes earlier.

"After the object descended through the floor earlier today, I was trying to come up with anything we might have missed. I went back to the images of the cube's markings, and it suddenly occurred to me that perhaps the marks were only a fragment of a composite image. Could I combine them somehow into a meaningful pattern?" Taylor just stared back at Rob, intrigued at what could have caused Rob's uncharacteristic liveliness.

"So I overlaid the images from all six sides of the cube, creating a composite image of all six layers. The odd marks on each of the six sides were in two parallel lines, so to retain the marks in horizontal lines each side could only be viewed upright or inverted. Since the side images were already positioned in the same axis, I started the comparison by keeping all four sides oriented in the same direction. I only had to rotate the top and bottom views of the cube as they overlaid the side images. This resulted in eight different combinations. Even without the computer doing any of the analysis, it was immediately apparent that one combination resulted in a clear string of flowing characters."

Rob brought up the image on his monitor. Due to the afternoon sun reflecting into the office, Taylor moved close to Rob to get a better view. The combined marks were now clearly visible as an inscription. A relatively brief string, it was only two lines of about seventy characters.

هل بالآخرين ما كنت ستفعل أنفسكم منعزلة.
الانتظار لمدة ستة صفر صفر أربعة ستة

Taylor could not take his eyes off the screen. The silence in the office was shattered as Taylor's voice exploded in a sputter, "That's Arabic!" His mind raced to comprehend what he was viewing. "Islamic terrorists sent this!"

It did appear to both of them to be Arabic writing. Although as far as Rob or Taylor could tell, the flowing characters could also have been any number of dead languages used millennia ago. Arabic letters are more complex than those in most other languages since they can change depending on whether they appear at the beginning, middle or end of a word, or by themselves. But this string of characters could now be passed through the same language database that had previously processed the partial characters.

"If it's a known language, maybe now we can identify who sent this and why," Rob stated. He was trying to remain composed, but this really looked like a major breakthrough.

Taylor felt his covert positioning on the team was about to pay off—he had to get this information to the DOD immediately. The Arabic shaped characters clearly identified the sender as a radical Islamic group. He now had no doubt that a demand or taunt to the United States would soon be deciphered.

Taylor was certain that the cautious research team would delay the release of this information until they had fully analyzed it. By then it would be too late to make the necessary retaliation strike at the heart of the Islamic world. Taylor imagined possible scenarios for a show of force that would compel the radicals to halt this device. Perhaps it would require an actual strike at a few of Islam's holiest sites.

4,587,520 pounds

It only took a few minutes for Rob to format and transfer the composite image to Sharon's computer. Her office PC was the only one in the facility that the DOD had authorized to link with their classified language system. If the LNGTRN program contained the language in question and it accurately matched with the symbols submitted, the system would generate an exact translation. Rob anticipated a successful match, since the newly composed characters certainly appeared to be from an Arabic language. Although there were numerous variations, similar symbols had been in use for almost two thousand years.

Rob informed Taylor, "I just called Randy—he wants to join us here when the message is translated. With any luck, Sharon should be back with the results in another

ten minutes or so." Randy's office was in a separate
administration building only a few hundred yards away.

Taylor left the room for a few minutes, ostensibly to
use the restroom down the hall. It would be enough time
for him to pass on a quick status report to his Pentagon
contact through his encrypted cell phone. Standing by an
exterior window down an adjacent hallway, he hurriedly
entered a phone code, a number that his assigned contact
always answered regardless of the time of day. Waiting
for the phone link to complete, Taylor silently cursed the
barely adequate cell phone reception from this location.
He knew the encrypting circuitry in his phone would
prevent anyone from listening to the transmitted message,
but he still had to speak softly into the phone to prevent
any possible monitoring within the lab. His contact picked
up the call immediately, and Taylor quickly passed on the
alarming news of an Arabic message on the object. He
confidently stated that the creator of this amazing weapon
was about to be known, and would definitely be a radical
Islamic organization. Not wanting to risk missing any
results from the translation, Taylor hurried back to Rob's
office.

Representing the Pentagon's interests, Taylor had to
be constantly cautious not to expose that he had received
background information about his fellow team members.
He knew that Rob had studied linguistics during his
college years at Stanford. He also knew that Rob grew up
in Silicon Valley with his immigrant father from Scotland
and a mother from Sweden. Living in a multi-language
home primed his ability to become fluent in several
languages and fostered an early interest in linguistics. Rob
was also proficient in numerous programming languages,

mostly used in his physics research, but there was no record of any exposure to Arabic languages.

Attempting to act normally, Taylor formed what he thought was a simple and innocent appearing question while they waited for the LNGTRN results. "So if we get a translation, do you think we'll finally know what the sender of this object wants?"

Hoping to bring Taylor up to speed on what would be a more realistic expectation, Rob replied, "Unfortunately, it may be much more difficult—particularly if we're dealing with an obscure or even ancient language. Lexicographers have always struggled with defining words used in different places or eras. Words don't have a fixed definition that means the same to different cultures, different eras or even consecutive generations. They only have referential meaning that in the case of a lost or ancient language, applies to a world now lost in history. We can only guess as to what specific words pointed to in that era, but we can guess more closely the more we understand about the total culture of that period.

"Universal concepts like 'Mother' are the easiest to translate, since they aren't culture-specific. But if an early Roman plutocrat is quoted 'Let the buyer beware', could he have merely been reminding his slave who purchased goods that he constantly risked beatings, or was he instructing someone to be alert to a seller's possible motivation to defraud the buyer?"

Rob was not sure Taylor was following, but he continued. "If the LNGTRN gives us a message, hopefully it will refer to words or concepts that occur in many languages and in many different eras. If so, then I believe we can more safely assume it has similar meaning to multiple cultures." Rob also hoped the message was composed exclusively with common terms so that no further linguistic research would be needed. Given the object's daily cycle of weight expansion, they were desperate to understand it quickly.

Randy entered the room, not the least bit out of breath from his fast-paced walk to Rob's office. Dispensing with any pleasantries, as was his custom, he immediately blurted to Rob and Taylor: "It looks like we finally have a breakthrough. Assembling those hash marks into a character string was brilliant, Rob—although I'm not sure why the team didn't discover that earlier." Randy always had difficulty complimenting subordinates—he found positive remarks were doable only if they were followed by some mitigating comment.

Randy was about to continue demonstrating his leadership acumen when someone could be heard moving quickly down the hall outside the office. Sharon hurriedly entered the room with a printout and an excited look.

"You won't believe this! The message matches with 99 percent accuracy to classical Arabic in the database. Like modern Arabic, the words read from right to left. Here's the English version."

"Do unto others as you would do unto yourselves. Waiting 200646"

All four of them just stared at the printout.

This was incredible. They had no idea what to expect, but something more along the line of a ransom demand would have been much less surprising. Yet here it was—the widely recognized Golden Rule, the synthesis of religious edicts in practically all mainstream religions.

Taylor couldn't restrain his frustration, "So we still don't know who sent this! And what the hell does this message mean to us?" He collapsed into a chair near the office door, devastated that a solution to the object was still not at hand.

Rob responded, in a subdued voice and with carefully chosen words. "It does appear to be a religious exhortation. Some religious group may actually be responsible for this object."

It had always seemed highly unlikely to the team members that a religious organization could have been involved in funding or developing the object, but the possibility could not be ruled out. Could zealots actually be using the object to force their worldview on others?

Sharon zeroed in on the two new questions now facing the team. "We've got to learn more about the religious source of this statement. We also have to know why the Arabic language was used."

Beads of sweat were forming on Taylor's forehead, which he attempted to wipe off before his associates noticed. This was not what Taylor had foreseen. He was certain the inscription would have contained a demand, and that the terms of the demand would have indicated who had sent the object. He feared his Pentagon contact had already initiated some threatening show of force, based on his earlier phone call about the Arabic message. The panicked Taylor knew he had to contact them immediately and he hoped that the frustrated military brass had not already authorized a preemptive strike. He quickly left Rob's office to place another call.

Halfway around the world, the guided missile cruiser USS Tacoma was on patrol in the Persian Gulf as part of the 6th fleet. Acting on an urgent message from naval command, the crew had readied two cruise missiles for an imminent launch. Captain John Tidwell, the commanding officer, was only waiting to receive the strike coordinates when the authorization to launch was abruptly countermanded. The captain swore to the nearest officers on the brig, "Crap! Those idiots in Washington can't get anything right. I hope whoever jerked us around ends up paying for this damn false alarm."

Chapter 24
June 14, 6:00 PM

4,587,520 pounds

Jason Morehouse had gathered his close group of followers the same evening that the news media had broadcast the latest development—the object had sunk through the lab floor and disappeared from sight. He was initially shocked at the announcement, in that it conflicted with his clear mission to rescue it. How could they fulfill their calling if the Holy Ark had in fact sunk out of sight?

Praying and meditating, Jason's followers continued sitting in silence in the dimly lit living room. As in previous summer evenings in New York, the warm muggy air and the closed window shades made the room seem smaller. The members were used to being uncomfortable, forgoing frivolities like air conditioning. In fact, they welcomed any opportunity to further discomfort themselves in God's service. The members had no doubt that Jason would soon explain how their sacred mission was affected by the ark disappearing.

After praying, the answer became obvious to Jason. Not unlike many true believers, his practical response toward data that conflicted with his beliefs was either to ignore it or reject it outright. Jason pronounced the solution to the gathered members.

"They lie. They always lie. The sacred ark has not sunk into the earth—it was a ruse to throw us off. They only want us to believe that so we'll think rescuing it is hopeless. But their falsehoods won't deter us from our sacred mission. The godless scientists fear someone might come and try to halt the sacrilegious acts being performed on the Holy Ark."

Jason confidently reaffirmed the continuing need for urgency. "Do not believe the evil men of this world. The sacred container has not sunk into the earth—it is waiting for us. God is waiting for us. Every day the sacred ark waits is another day for which we must explain our delay. We'll rescue it before tomorrow morning, before they can defile the ark again with their lies."

The followers were in awe of Jason's certainty and felt consoled as they surrendered their individual thoughts to his clear and uncomplicated vision. There was no need to contemplate options or entertain conflicting views; it was much more soothing just to follow their charismatic leader.

Almost every week there seemed to be news of some radical Islamic group's holy war on their enemies. The Muslims were wrong not to worship Jesus as their Lord and Savior, but Jason felt they at least got one thing right—how one spends the afterlife is what really matters.

This life on Earth is inconsequential compared to how we will spend eternity. Jason and his followers were ashamed at the lack of vigor in the so-called Christian community. The world was full of faux Christians, unwilling to forego this world's temptations and unwilling to follow God's will.

Jason's loyal band of followers was ready to do God's bidding. They had regularly prayed that one day their skills would be utilized in serving their God, and now they finally understood the purpose for which they had all been chosen and for which they had trained over many years. Over the past several evenings, the group had reviewed and memorized the plan-of-attack formulated by Jason. Tonight they moved their hunting arsenal out of the home's basement into the living room where each gun was carefully checked and loaded. The group was ready.

"Lord guide us in Thy service. Lord guide us in Thy service. Lord guide us in Thy service...." The repetitive praying calmed their nerves and focused their thinking. It was now just a matter of hours until each devotee would fulfill his life's purpose.

Chapter 25
June 14, 6:45 PM

4,587,520 pounds

Professor Josef Ramon was eager to help. He had been closely following the daily news reports and like everyone else was trying to make sense of the strange object. When Randy contacted him, he immediately agreed to come to the lab complex to provide whatever assistance he could offer. How could he not be intrigued after Randy relayed the message found on the strange cube? As head of the Religious Studies Department at NYU, he was well versed in the world's religions, and was a recognized expert in Islamic studies.

As the government-provided limo pulled into the lab complex, the professor continued to speculate on what other information the research team might have. Surely, there were other facts that were not shared with the media. Perhaps they had identified a specific group of religious zealots and they wanted to better understand their motivation. On two occasions within the past several years, he had provided briefings to Homeland Security staff regarding such questions.

Professor Ramon was in his mid-fifties, but looked much younger—too young in fact to be a department head in a prestigious university. His dark brown hair, almost black, was thick and long—as if he was at least a few months past his last haircut. His full beard was also of a deep brown color, which framed his lively eyes. With a light olive skin complexion, he could easily have been a member of a Mediterranean or Middle-Eastern ethnic group.

It was now 6:45 PM, only one and a half hours after Randy first contacted the professor. As he entered the conference room, the first thing the gathered researchers noticed was his calm appearance. Everyone on the team had been operating in crisis mode for the past week, so the difference between the demeanor of the group and the visiting professor was obvious. Rob wondered if that might have anything to do with his exposure to so many different religions, particularly the Eastern meditative variety.

The team members present were Rob, Sharon, Taylor and Randy—the same ones who had shared the discovery of the message earlier that afternoon. After very brief introductions, Sharon spread out two documents on the conference table. The first was a printout of the Arabic characters Rob had assembled from the cube photographs and the second was the translation report from the LNGTRN program. The initial task was to verify the translation was correct.

Professor Ramon scrutinized the string of Arabic characters, and confirmed the translation as entirely accurate. He paused for a few moments, as the room remained silent in anticipation of his next comments. Ever since Randy had relayed the message to him on the phone, the professor had thought of little else.

"There are literally thousands of exhortations in the Bible, the Qur'an, the Hindu Mahabharata and other major religious texts. But if you were to pick one rule that best represents their teachings, this would probably be the one. Virtually all mainstream religions constrain one's selfish actions by promoting respect and assistance to others.

"Why have all religions found it necessary to speak out against selfish actions? We wouldn't have evolved to our current level over these past millions of years without a strong drive for self-survival. Whenever resources have been limited, the ensuing struggles determined which life forms survived and which disappeared. By satisfying this self-survival drive, all life forms have been able to benefit themselves and, over the eons, some have evolved into higher life forms. The self-survival mechanism is deeply imbedded in our genetic code. It enables our brains to rapidly distinguish our family and tribe from 'others'. Unfortunately, this self-centered behavior also promotes intolerance for 'others', which is potentially catastrophic in today's world of modern weapons and destructive technology."

Professor Ramon continued. "This message to assist others has been around for thousands of years. Many religious leaders and philosophers have reminded us of it, and here it appears yet again, but this time it's not just a simple exhortation.

"This time the ancient message has arrived in a most dramatic fashion, in a tangible format that the entire world can readily see. This time the message doesn't require faith in abstract beliefs. This time there's no opportunity for gradual dissemination by a growing band of followers. An object has accompanied the message that transforms it into a demand that we cannot ignore. If I understand the media reports, this device has the capacity to destroy our world. And this destruction isn't predicted for some point in the distant future—that point is within a matter of weeks."

"How can this be a demand?" exclaimed Randy. "The message may sound like it's some sort of command, but it's extremely vague as to any specific response."

Avoiding the obvious question of who had sent the message, Randy focused on the message itself. "What if it's not here to force us to a particular action? What if it's merely a notice from someone that we're being destroyed because we've previously ignored this message?"

Rob hesitated a moment to clarify his thoughts. "No. If that were the intent, why take so long to do it? The device has a paced growth cycle that allows us time to investigate it, time to discover this encrypted message, and time to respond. It appears we either need to figure out how to stop this doomsday device—something we so far are incapable of—or, we need to somehow demonstrate to someone or something that we can comply with the directive to 'do unto others as we do unto ourselves'."

Taylor was now literally pacing back and forth through the open office door and was obviously the most agitated one in the room. He was very concerned about the phone calls he had made to the Pentagon, realizing he had prematurely provided information that was now apparently wrong. Taylor wished he had waited until Sharon had returned with the translated message—his credibility with the Pentagon had been needlessly damaged.

"So the fact that the message is in Arabic doesn't imply that there's an Islamic connection?" asked Taylor, still hoping to justify his prior assumption.

Professor Ramon responded emphatically, "No. In the Christian world, the most famous source of this mandate is that attributed to Jesus himself, noted in several gospels. The Bible implores us to 'Love our neighbors as ourselves' repeatedly throughout the books of the New Testament. But there are dozens of ancient references to this same concept, including one written two thousand years earlier in the Old Testament book of Leviticus. The Talmud also states that 'Whosoever saves one life saves the world entire.' Muhammad specifically said 'Not one of you is a believer until he desires for his brother that which he desires for himself.' The Hindu Mahabharata, written around 150 BC, teaches 'This is the sum of all true righteousness: Deal with others as thou would thyself be dealt with.' Similar messages to love others as ourselves occur in the writings of Confucius, Buddhism and Greek philosophy.

"So no religion owns it. It's essentially a classical mandate, incorporated into the moral code of every major religion. Of course, humanity hasn't always followed this precept. In fact, it's rarely been applied to people outside one's own tribe or nation."

Taylor was having difficulty seeing beyond his original frame of reference. "So the message is more universal than one culture. Still, why would it be written in Arabic? This has to be from a radical Islamic group!" he fumed. "This is *not* good. Even if it weren't from one of them, other Islamic radicals will interpret this use of Arabic as corroboration of their holy war against the Western world."

"Slow down, Taylor." Rob was used to dealing with Taylor's narrow interpretation of the world. But Rob also knew that millions of people would be asking the same question when the news media eventually circulated the translated message.

"Not necessarily," Professor Ramon interrupted. "Arabic is the sixth major language of the world. More importantly, the Qur'an is the most widely used religious text that's survived in its original language. Since Muslims view it as the final revelation from God to the world, they always recite it in the original Arabic. If they used any of the numerous translations into other languages, that would involve interpretation and be subject to human errors. Although most Muslims don't speak Arabic, they do attempt to learn classical Arabic in order to recite their prayers and to understand the Qur'an. As with all languages, numerous local dialects have formed over the centuries, but the classical Arabic used in the Qur'an has been preserved for over fourteen centuries."

Taylor persisted "I'd be more at ease if the message had been in anything other than a Middle Eastern language—it's alarming."

Professor Ramon responded, not only in an attempt to expand Taylor's simplistic view of the world but to construct a cohesive argument as to why the sender may have chosen Arabic. "I don't believe this object is directed solely at the Western world." Looking directly at Taylor, he asked, "Perhaps you'd have been less disturbed if the message had been written in modern English, or maybe in the original language of the Bible?"

"That would have made more sense to me," exclaimed Taylor. He couldn't understand why his associates didn't see the obvious connection to a radical Islamic group.

"Actually, the languages used for the Bible have continually changed over the years," Professor Ramon patiently continued. "The Old Testament was first translated into Greek in the third century B.C., into what's known as the Septuagint alluding to the seventy scholars assigned to translate it. This then became the source for later translations into Latin, Coptic and Armenian. The Latin version—known as the Vulgate—was created in the fifth century by translating manuscripts from Hebrew, Aramaic and Greek. During the Protestant Reformation, a number of religious groups created additional translations, including Martin Luther's German version, a Polish version and later the King James Bible in English. Incidentally, the King James Bible used a Hebrew text as the source for the Old Testament, and the source for the New Testament was a different set of manuscripts than those used for more modern versions like the New American Standard Bible.

"So if the Bible were the source of the message, a key question arises. Which translation should be used? Perhaps this is why the sender chose Arabic to convey the message. The language is original, eliminating at least one variable of language translation. Of course, the word usage has changed between ancient and modern Arabic, but since the same message appears throughout man's history, the ancient meaning of the message is likely the same as today."

Randy and the rest of the team were openly receptive to Professor Ramon's logic. Sharon, as usual, was processing the information quicker than the others were, as if she just processed thoughts at a higher baud rate. She had been thinking about another possible connection and did not hesitate to share it.

"I seem to recall seeing this exact same quote at the UN building. There's a Norman Rockwell painting in the visitor lobby that includes this same message overlaid on the painting. I can't help but wonder if there's significance in that the package was found at the UN where this identical message is already displayed."

It was 8 PM when the small group began to break up, each leaving to pursue their different agendas. Professor Ramon agreed to continue participating on the team, and seemed pleased that he might be able to help them unravel this mystery. Randy returned to his own office to prepare a briefing of the surprising news for the president. He was uncertain how the president or the world at large would receive this news, but he would dutifully report it as well as describe how they were attempting to understand it.

Taylor hastened to relay the latest information to his Pentagon contact, relieved that the surprising nature of the message might overshadow his earlier premature comments. Taylor was now less alarmed by the Arabic nature of the message, but the Defense Department would make their own assessment. He was confident the DOD would have other analytical tools.

Sharon headed for her own office, mulling over the ramifications of the translated message. To her thinking, this was definitely a directive, but who could have possibly sent it? Moreover, why didn't they identify themselves?

Upon carefully reviewing the day's events, Sharon realized she hadn't received a response from her inquiry to the Palo Alto Astrophysics Institute. She was still hoping to find relevance to the precise time of the growth cycles—maybe there was a message on her office answering machine.

CHAPTER 26
JUNE 14, 10:30 PM

4,587,520 pounds

Exhausted from the day's efforts at the lab, Rob was finally able to relax in his small hotel suite for a few minutes. Although he had not spent much time here since flying into New York to join the investigation team, this was a place of respite from the ever-present stress of the project.

It was here in the hotel suite that Rob allowed himself the brief luxury of recalling his life before this project. His former life now seemed so far removed. Being single, Rob's thoughts would usually drift to his family members: his only brother farming in Oregon, his twin sister practicing medicine in Spokane, and his deceased parents. His siblings knew Rob was totally immersed in the project and that he wasn't at liberty to discuss the team's latest efforts. Rob made a mental note to contact them and see how they were doing—perhaps he'd call them tomorrow.

Rob's mental wanderings would next turn to his small circle of friends, all of whom dated back to his college life at Stanford. These ruminations frequently culminated with the same thought: Rob would be reminded yet again that he didn't have a single romantic relationship among his friends. He found it amusing that his train of thought would then segue to images of Sharon. Such thoughts were an unwanted distraction while working on the project, but here he found the thoughts pleasing, even arousing.

Grabbing a cold Guinness and a chilled glass from the room's mini-bar, he collapsed onto the small couch and began surfing through the cable TV channels. Anything that would take his thoughts off the crisis for a few minutes would help.

Skipping past a half dozen or so reality shows, he paused on a late night news station that was interviewing a well-known professor. Dr. Branson was famous for his radical sociological theories, and recently had been receiving a lot of media attention. His theory of how society will change in future generations from the pervasive effect of electronics and unlimited access to information was both fascinating and disturbing. This was not the desired distraction from the crisis, but the ongoing commentary was captivating.

"Imagine for a moment an alien civilization, one that's expanding its understanding and use of technology at a rate similar to our world. In just the few hundred years since the Industrial Revolution, consider the fantastic advances we've made in all areas of science. Extrapolate that same level of advancement by ten times as long to two thousand years, or to twenty thousand years, or even to two million years—the capability of such a civilization is unimaginable to us. Yet this is only a nit in the fourteen billion year age of our cosmos."

The futurist continued, "Although we can only guess at what such an advanced civilization would be like, I think one aspect might be boredom with their 'aloneness'. Wouldn't it be interesting for them to observe how life could develop in various environments? With numerous habitable planets scattered throughout the cosmos, they could create any number of experiments and leave them to evolve not unlike the cultures in our own Petri dishes. Naturally occurring calamities would periodically alter the 'experiments' but not obliterate them. Disruptions from droughts, ice ages, massive earthquakes, plagues, volcanic activity—all of these would radically affect a portion of the planet's inhabitants, but not erase what may have taken millions of years to evolve.

"On our own planet Earth, we hominids have been developing for more than five million years. Yet if a few enterprising humans developed something that could decimate their entire species—that would be 'game over' and the end of the experimenters' amusement. Perhaps such a scenario would provoke an advanced civilization to interfere with the natural order of events."

This was almost too much to handle this late at night. Rob couldn't help but speculate to himself, "This is preposterous. Throughout history, man has always struggled with his destructive side. So if an advanced society were monitoring us, why would they intervene now? Surely, we live in a much less dangerous world than previously. Then again, WWII alone cost the lives of over fifty million people."

In fact, Rob recalled, many historians view 1962 as the most dangerous point in human history, where we were perilously close to annihilating a billion people in the escalating Cuban missile crisis. "If we were being observed by an alien civilization, why wouldn't they have intervened at that point?

"Or did they?" Rob struggled to resolve conflicting thoughts. "It's never been clear exactly how the crisis was defused between Khrushchev and Kennedy. A global nuclear war undoubtedly would have devastated the entire developed world. Civilization would have reverted to a pre-industrialized state or worse if the radiation effects spread to all areas of the globe. Could there have been an intervention at that point?"

Rob turned off the TV, just after the interview finished. Attempting to stretch out on the too-short couch, he couldn't stop thinking through these radical ideas. "For the past half century, mankind has had the capability to wipe out entire countries and even decimate whole sections of the globe with nuclear weapons. Despite such widespread destruction, life would continue somewhere and humanity would continue to develop, albeit more slowly. What new cataclysmic threat could this Branson be talking about?"

This line of thinking was not helping Rob to fall asleep, but his thoughts were gaining clarity. "This theory of an advanced civilization intervening in our world would only make sense if there were a new doomsday technology secretly present, or perhaps about to be developed."

This was a most depressing situation. Besides the dark forecast for the world, another entirely separate and disconcerting aspect came to Rob as his mind continued to wander. "If this object was sent to somehow halt a fatal development, it would also mean that these global developments, and potentially all of our activities, are somehow being monitored by a type of advanced intelligence." This was too sobering a thought to be absorbed immediately, especially when he was so exhausted. "Maybe tomorrow would be a better time to think about this."

About to give up trying to fall asleep, Rob closed his eyes and again tried to still his active mind. "It's way too far-fetched a theory to be taken seriously anyway."

4,587,520 pounds

A single shot caught the guard squarely in the center of his chest. He slumped to the floor of the security kiosk, his life ending within a matter of seconds.

The gunman knew there would only be one guard at the entrance station. Two of Jason's followers had scouted the perimeter of the lab complex the previous evening. Driving calmly to the entrance gate, they had pretended to be lost and had innocently asked for directions. The ruse established that there was only one guard on duty at the station, at least at 2 AM.

Tonight, Jason had been the only occupant in the car that arrived at the entrance gate—he wanted to get as close as possible to the guard's kiosk without raising any suspicion. Just as the security guard politely asked for identification to enter the complex, Jason fired a 9 mm Beretta and then quickly jumped out of his car and entered the unlocked door of the kiosk. Shoving the guard's bleeding body out of the way, Jason stepped inside and quickly scanned the few controls by the door. He calmly pressed the button to open the gate that blocked the driveway.

Two more cars filled with Jason's followers quickly pulled up to the open gate. The attackers had been waiting just out of sight of the guard station, listening for the sound of the gunshot to signal them to move to the entrance gate. Jason jumped into the first of the two waiting vehicles, abandoning his original car next to the kiosk.

"Faster! Faster!" Jason shouted at the driver who already had the accelerator pressed hard against the car floor. Both vehicles were crowded with the entire band of ten zealots, each carrying their own weapons. The two cars headed straight to C Lab, driving as quickly as possible on the winding roads within the complex. In their efforts to provide full coverage, several news broadcasts had included clear images of the building that contained the object. Jason had easily accessed both its location and their invasion route from Google's satellite maps.

"This is our life's destiny. We are the ones chosen to rescue the Holy Ark." Jason's words directed the thoughts of his followers away from their fears and toward their simple and holy mission.

Jason shouted over the roar of the car's engine, "We'll protect the sacred Ark from their profane tests."

The group was confident they did not have to secure an exit from the lab complex. Once their mission achieved success, the attackers had no doubt the world would recognize them as heroes and that they would be protected from any harm. Only then would the sacred container cease its incessant growth. The world's future was at stake and they were the chosen ones.

The lab's security had been significantly increased when the object first arrived, but the perimeter security for the lab complex proved to be inadequate. Other than the team investigating the object, few individuals were expected to endanger themselves by willingly coming to the lab complex. Only assigned representatives from governments, scientific assemblies and selected media were anticipated. Many residents in the communities surrounding the research complex had even evacuated their homes, considering the danger similar to a bomb about to explode.

As with all first-of-a-kind events, the team investigating the object was ignorant of many possible problems. They never anticipated that there might be individuals passionately desiring to get close to something that was potentially hazardous. However, these invaders were not typical people—zealots throughout history had always challenged what the majority considered reasonable.

The central guard station was equipped with a bank of surveillance monitors which covered all entrances and other key areas of the complex. The facility's central security staff was immediately alerted to the forced entry, and had viewed the brutal murder of their associate on the security monitor.

The night manager in Security immediately broadcast an emergency message to all security staff stationed throughout the site. "Armed intruders have broken into the complex! One of our guards has been shot. The intruders are in two vehicles and appear to be heading to the center of the lab complex." The manager then quickly placed a 911 call for support, relaying the same information to the local police dispatcher.

Because Jason had been scrutinizing every detail released through the media, he knew the lab complex had increased the size of the security staff. Additional guards had been added to ensure the safety of the various foreign dignitaries who visited the complex to confirm the validity of the object's threat. Since these foreign visitors only visited the lab during the day, Jason knew these additional guards would not be onsite during the middle of the night.

Unknown to the invaders, Homeland Security had stationed a small contingent of their own agents at the complex. They had not publicized their presence since their initial assignment was to ensure that none of the team members would act unilaterally. In effect, they were there to ensure that no actions would occur without the consent of the U.S. Government. They also monitored communications from the complex, to prevent any researcher from secretly disclosing any discoveries. As the number of foreign researchers increased, Homeland Security surreptitiously added even more onsite agents.

The invaders would be at the lab within a few minutes, winding their way through the complex of lanes toward C Lab. There was barely enough time for the onsite staff to set up a defense. The nightshift manager of Security knew he had to warn those few still working in the lab.

"Attention! This is a lockdown condition!" blurted the Security manager on the internal PA system. "Armed intruders are in the complex; they appear to be heading toward the lab facilities. Stay within your offices until further notice."

The security staff was in the process of securing all entrances to the lab buildings when everyone in the complex heard a volley of gunshots. Several shotgun blasts hit the electronically secured entrance door in the front of the facility.

"They're attacking C Lab!" One of the guards radioed to the central security site, as he began to return fire, shooting through the damaged doorway at the invaders attempting to enter the building. Only designed to operate with magnetically encoded badges, it was useless as a deterrent to a forced entrance. But the broken glass did slow down the invaders, and the doors were now jammed from the shotgun blasts destroying the door locks and door hinges.

Sharon was one of the few researchers still working in the lab. Sitting at her office desk, she froze, reluctant to believe what she was hearing. She cried out, "This can't be happening!"

Sharon wondered if her sleep-deprived state could be fueling her imagination, or if she might have fallen asleep at her desk and this was only a dream.

More gunshots.

This was no dream. Sharon checked the office clock—2:21 AM. She stood next to the desk, her mind racing to figure out what to do. Run? But which way? The sound of the gunshots seemed to be coming from several different directions. Should she close and lock her office door, which was at the distant side of the room from her desk? She didn't want to expose herself by moving closer to the doorway so she just sat down on the floor, using the metal office desk as a shield between herself and the hallway. Along with the other scattered researchers who had also been working late into the night, Sharon continued to hear more shots, including rapid-fire automatic volleys.

The presence of heavily armed agents had surprised the invaders who tried to reorganize their attack in the chaos. The zealots had expected an easy entrance to the lab building but were now engaged in a full-scale gun battle with the Homeland Security agents. The agents were gradually pinning down the attackers, who were in more exposed positions outside C Lab's entrance.

"The Ark, the Ark!" Jason continued shouting, encouraging his dwindling number of followers to keep attacking.

Two of the invaders abandoned the doorway attempt, and broke through a glass window in one of the corner offices of the lab building. The two had hoisted themselves through the broken window and were moving among the lab's offices, frantically searching for the Ark.

As the few scattered researchers huddled in their respective offices, some wondered if they should try to flee the building. One of the researchers called across the hallway to Sharon, "Let's get out now! The gunshots are getting closer!"

Sharon yelled out her still open doorway to her associate and any others within earshot, "No! Stay where you are! Get under a desk or anything solid—the gunmen can be anywhere. Anyone moving around could get shot by our own security staff!"

Hunkering down under her own metal desk, Sharon's next thought was regret, "Why didn't I head home earlier like most of the team?" She had been working nonstop ever since they had translated the message, unable to think of anything else.

"What idiocy," thought Sharon to herself as she listened to the shots and shouting around the complex. "Why would anyone want to attack the lab? How could anyone be so violently opposed to our efforts to understand this object?" But she knew the answer—it was the same reason throughout the history of humanity. "For whatever cause, some group has decided to resort to violence to satisfy their personal interests. Whoever is attacking us wants to exert their will on others, regardless of the consequences. Could this be the reason this object has been sent to us?"

The shots continued but were staggered and much less frequent than before. A few sounded like they were only a couple of offices away. Sharon could hear vehicle sirens in the distance, undoubtedly police or other agents arriving to assist. After what seemed forever, the gunshots finally stopped. All Sharon could now hear from her office was muffled shouting and a few additional sirens in the distance—it seemed the assault was over.

The Security staff notified Randy immediately and gave him a complete status report when he arrived onsite a few minutes later. Based on the surveillance cameras throughout the site, they determined that ten attackers had been involved. All ten were quickly accounted for, so the entire lab complex remained locked down for only a few hours.

It would take another two days for Homeland Security to determine exactly what Jason and his followers planned to do at the lab. Yet the presence of well-worn pocket Bibles on several of the attackers provided an early indication they were most likely members of a radical Christian group. Also, as the Homeland Security agents took one of the injured attackers into custody, he had vehemently shouted, "You must stop defaming the Ark! God will not allow you to treat it with such sacrilege!"

Randy telephoned Rob and several other key team members a few hours later. When he reached Rob, he informed him, "Seven invaders were killed in the assault. None of our researchers was injured, but three security staff members were also killed and one Homeland Security agent was injured. The agents had captured three of the invaders, who would be interrogated if they survived their injuries."

Rob only asked two questions of Randy: "Was Sharon still onsite?"

"Yes, but she's OK. Pretty shaken up, but not injured. The Homeland Agents are interviewing her now—I imagine she'll be leaving soon to get whatever sleep she can manage."

"Great!" Rob was surprised at how relieved he felt.

"And what about the lab? Did they damage our monitoring equipment?"

"No. They never got into the main lab room, just the entrance area and a few nearby offices. The attackers were heard shouting, "Rescue the Ark!" I'm afraid we're guilty of ignoring an old adage: never underestimate the danger of groups of stupid people."

Randy had other calls to make so he cut the conversation short, "We'll have more information in the morning. Get some rest."

Rob thought to himself, "An attack of this size wasn't coordinated by stupid people. Their intelligence level was never a real factor. More aptly, the adage should be: never underestimate the danger of groups of zealots, of true-believers."

The highly educated, technology-savvy researchers had not anticipated anyone would venerate the mysterious object. Having spent their lives rationally studying phenomena, they were poorly equipped to recognize how some people might interpret this event.

Rob immediately called Sharon at her office, hoping to catch her before she left. As she answered the phone, Rob was filled with relief to hear her voice, which was still slightly shaky from her harrowing experience.

"Rob, can you believe anyone would act so violently to stop our work? Randy said the attackers were shouting something like 'Rescue the sacred Ark!' What were they possibly thinking?"

"We'll know more after the police investigate them," Rob responded. "But there may not be any reason we could relate to. They apparently believe the object has some major religious meaning. People hold strong beliefs, with or without valid reasons. Despite all the advances in learning, over a billion people still have only the most basic understanding of how the world functions. Lacking a better explanation for this object, I can easily see how these people might revere it."

"I suppose you're right," Sharon replied, her voice starting to sound steadier. "Remember the major earthquake in Pakistan a few years ago when almost one hundred thousand people died? Pakistan's media was full of pronouncements by their mullahs that the quake was punishment for their sinful behavior. Not one major scientist in the entire country challenged that belief."

Rob continued, "Right. And look at our own country. Many Americans want to believe the world is only six thousand years old despite overwhelming evidence establishing billions of years of history. And, over 80 percent of the entire world's population believes prayers change the natural order of the world. Every day, millions of prayers are made to change every imaginable facet of life, from ensuring victory in football games to victory in wars."

Sharon agreed, her voice now sounding more normal. "That's true. Most wars have been fought with both sides praying for their own victory and for their enemy's defeat. But don't you see a parallel to what we're doing?"

There was a slight pause in the conversation before Rob responded, "What do you mean?"

"How are we doing any different?" Sharon replied. "How are we treating this object any differently than ancient cultures would treat it? All ancient civilizations believed in a plethora of gods, many requiring sacrifices. This object has mysteriously appeared, threatens us, and now we're trying to figure out how to appease whoever sent it. This sounds pretty similar to the early Greeks, the ancient Egyptians or any of the numerous groups described in the Bible—they all acted in ways they thought would appease their gods."

"Yeah, I see your point but what else can we do?" Rob struggled to come up with an insightful comment, or at least a few words of encouragement. He was coming up empty. "We just have to keep studying this thing and try our best to figure out a way to stop its weight expansion."

Rob was trying to help Sharon make sense of the ordeal, but he realized they were both exhausted.

"We need to get some rest. I'm just so relieved you're OK after the attack." Rob felt awkward at not being able to close the conversation with anything more personal, maybe even intimate. He made a mental note to think about that lack, but the best he could muster at the moment was simply, "See ya in the morning."

Sharon finally headed home for a few hours of rest, talking to herself as she headed out of the office, "If we could only get a better grasp on who sent us this message or even why it was sent."

Chapter 28
June 15, 10:00 AM

4,587,520 pounds

Within hours following the previous night's attack at the lab, a full maintenance crew was busy cleaning up the debris and replacing the damaged doors and windows. Most of the team offices and equipment were already operational since practically all of the damage was limited to the entrance area of the C lab building. A mixture of additional NYPD and Homeland Security agents were scattered throughout the complex, guarding all of the entrance gates as well as all key buildings.

As the researchers arrived for their morning work session, all were soon informed about the previous night's carnage. Seeing the damaged facility was a shock, but learning of the fatalities from the violent assault was too much for a few of the researchers. Two members immediately left the complex, grabbing the few personal items stored in their offices. Several other researchers were trying to decide if they should also abandon the group.

The stress had already been intense for everyone on the team, exacerbated by the continued failure to stop the object's weight expansion. For the scientists, the threat of death from the object was still tolerable—always a high probability, but importantly, it was not yet imminent. The physical assault that had just killed or injured close to a dozen people vastly changed the situation—the lives of all the researchers were now in immediate jeopardy. Each team member would need to decide if their personal reasons for staying on the team still outweighed the risk from any future assaults on the lab complex.

There was never the slightest doubt in Sharon's mind about staying on the project—she had to understand why this object had been sent. There had been no damage to Sharon's office, so she lost no time getting back to her research. The first thing she did after entering her office was to check for any messages—voice and e-mail.

"200,700 to 200,600 years ago. There's a 95 percent probability that's the century you're looking for. At that point in Earth's history, we can calculate the solar day to have been exactly 23 hours, 59 minutes and 55.385 seconds. Let us know if we can be of any further help." The single recording on Sharon's phone messaging system was clear and concise. The call had been received early that morning from the Astrophysics Institute in Palo Alto, California.

Sharon replayed the phone message and thought to herself, "So the amount of time between the object's growth cycles exactly matches the length of Earth's solar day around the year 198,650 BC, give or take fifty years."

"OK. So the Earth's slowing revolution time apparently can be accurately matched to a specific point in history. Could anything significant have possibly occurred on Earth in that distant era? And if anything did occur, what bearing could it have on today's crisis?" she wondered.

The research was taking a surprising turn—from investigating an initial bomb threat, to unraveling a physics mystery, and now to researching a historical question. None of the research to-date had helped to understand this object, let alone to halt its destructive path. Now history was entering the picture as a potential factor. Was this just another false path that would waste valuable research time? Sharon was obliged to communicate this new information to the entire team as soon as possible but was afraid that it would be squelched out-of-hand by Randy, the 'hard science' oriented team leader.

Since Rob had initially suggested the Astrophysics Institute, Sharon knew he'd be interested in its response. She briefly considered transferring the phone message to Rob's phone, but really wanted to see him. She felt a growing connection to Rob and wanted to meet with him to discuss this new information. Since Rob's office was only twenty yards away, Sharon didn't bother calling to see if he was in and just headed in that direction.

"Great, you're here," she said upon reaching his doorway.

"And good morning to you, too" Rob responded, chiding her lack of civility, but at the same time also noticing how great she looked. With all the stress and violence from last night's attack at the lab, he figured she couldn't have gotten more than a few hours sleep.

Rob had already given considerable thought to his reaction when he was first informed of the attack. Was Sharon still working at the lab? Was she injured? He'd given even more thought to why he'd even have such a reaction, particularly in the midst of the dilemma facing them. Rob now realized he'd never been so attracted to anyone. This didn't seem to him like a passing infatuation, but more like a deep level of relating. This was a new experience for Rob—he found it disconcerting but amusing that his pulse noticeably increased when she entered his office.

"Sorry. Good morning to you, too." Sharon smiled back briefly, but she was too excited to slow down and talk. She wanted to tell him all about last night's attack, but that could wait.

"You have to come over to my office. I finally got a response from the Astrophysics Institute."

They quickly walked the short distance to Sharon's office. "Rob—listen to this voicemail! After you hear it, I need your help with a decision. Should I present this new angle now and risk Randy ruling it useless and directing me not to pursue it? Or should I continue researching and violate procedures by not including it in our daily status updates?"

As Sharon pressed the play button, she knew Rob would be open to examining any possible connections but wanted his view on whether an ancient historical angle could really be relevant. For that matter, she also wanted his opinion on whether the strain of the project might be muddying her reasoning.

Rob managed to shift his focus from Sharon back to the project. His eyes widened as he listened to the recorded phone message. "Oh my God! This is incredible! That was a pivotal time in human evolutionary history." Rob was visibly excited—he recognized this might be the first break in understanding the 'why' of this doomsday device.

"For the past fifty years, comparative psychologists have struggled to explain why humans are the only species to perform complex intellectual tasks. Why do we appear to be so much smarter than all other species? Why wouldn't random mutations provide other species with advanced intellectual capacity?"

In this area of biological development, Sharon was considerably more knowledgeable than Rob. She immediately responded, "Fossil records show our brain size started to increase about two million years ago. A radical change happened at that early point to our ancestor's genome that separated hominids forever from all other species that had evolved. The hominid brain eventually expanded to be three times the size of the forerunners of chimpanzees, our closest evolutionary cousins. Several studies have found that one part of the genome, the HAR1 region, is essentially the same for all mammals except humans. In humans, it differs in eighteen different places."

Rob was moving around the office as Sharon talked, certain they were close to identifying a significant piece of the puzzle. "Right," he responded. "But that was two million years ago. Some anthropologists have also predicted a more recent sea change event occurred in the hominid brain. This change finally allowed humans to utilize the unique cerebral cortex that had been gradually expanding for the past two million years. This key change occurred about 200,000 years ago."

The usually even-tempered Rob continued, surprising Sharon by becoming more animated as he spoke. "A number of anthropologists have speculated there was a key neural change that gave rise to consciousness—actually being aware of ourselves. This new capacity was passed on genetically, and gradually allowed social emotions and moral concepts to develop. A few theologians have even described this early event as the advent of the soul, equating it with the creation of man in the Garden of Eden. In fact, the first relics indicating concerns about an after-life—food, flowers and art objects—have only been found in human grave sites after this era."

"Whoa," Sharon sat down in her desk chair, intrigued at the possibilities of this revelation. "This could still be merely a coincidence. Is there any way to corroborate this? Or for that matter, if we grant that this period was critical for human development, how can that event be related to the object?"

Rob, now speaking softly and again in his more measured manner, looked straight at Sharon. "The last part of the inscription: 'waiting 200646'. It's not an insignificant postscript but represents a number of solar years. Whoever sent this object is telling us they've spent '200,646 years waiting'."

Chapter 29
June 15, 1:30 PM

4,587,520 pounds

"We'll know in about fifteen minutes." Randy wasn't speaking to anyone specifically, only attempting to project a calm appearance. There was no need for his subordinates to be aware of his real emotional state—he was just as anxious and scared as the rest of the team members.

Most of the researchers were moving around the lab, closely watching the monitoring equipment. In only a few more minutes, the next expansion cycle was expected and one of the team's most critical theories was about to be tested. Since the object had sunk into the Earth's crust during the previous day's cycle, this would be the first test of how the object would act within the Earth's interior.

"Ready?" Sharon asked the equipment techs as she scanned the signals displayed on the lab's overhead monitors. Eight separate screens lined the front of the room, each display mounted about six feet from the floor.

The monitor on the far right showed a cross-section view of Earth, indicating the thickness of various internal layers. A bright pulsing dot highlighted the location of the object, or rather, the best estimate of its location. Three numbers were displayed on the bottom of the screen: the latitude and longitude of the surface point directly above the object and the estimated depth of the object. The researchers believed it was now at a depth of 2.4 miles, in an almost plumb position beneath the lab complex.

Aside from the numerous ground-based sensors monitoring the object, several orbiting satellites were also measuring critical changes. One of the overhead screens displayed live feeds from the satellite sensors, which would immediately show the instantaneous increase in the Earth's gravitational pull with each expansion cycle. The same satellites were also capable of detecting even minute changes to the Earth's spin and wobble.

As one of the technicians completed a last-minute test of the satellite communication link, he remarked to Sharon, "If the object continues to increase in weight, the increased gravitational pull of the Earth will soon doom these and all other orbiting satellites to crash. So far, the relative increase in the Earth's total mass has only been large enough to alter their orbital height a minuscule amount."

Rob, standing near Sharon, overheard the tech's comment and couldn't refrain from responding. Usually the most optimistic member of the team, Rob's comments were disturbing to those within hearing.

"Losing the satellites is the least of our worries. If this damn object continues to gain weight, the entire planet will be irrevocably altered. A new and changing center of gravity for the planet will cause a realignment of the Earth's interior layers as well as all surface features. All life will certainly be destroyed as the planet goes through a rebirth process to achieve a stable structure. This process lasted over a billion years when the Earth and the solar system were forming."

The prayers and hopes of the entire world were that the device would somehow halt its periodic growth cycle, and perhaps stay suspended and dormant at a point deep within the interior of the Earth. The investigation had so far provided no clues as to how they could stop the object's incessant growth in weight. In fact, the team knew of nothing that could affect it in any way. The world was desperately clinging to the hope that the extreme pressure and heat within the Earth's interior would somehow stop the object's relentless growth.

The nervous talk around the room subsided, leaving only the faint hum from the computer equipment to fill the void. Everyone present was keenly aware that so far they had completely failed to understand this device. They also knew that unless the situation changed, none of them would live to see the end of summer.

The largest monitor was currently displaying the Earth's relative mass, graphed as a bar chart over the past month. The graph indicated the object had exactly doubled in weight at each of the past cycles. The same graph also displayed the exact recurring time intervals. The overhead digital display adjacent to this monitor was set to show the remaining time to the next cycle. The three-inch digits clearly showed the number of seconds remaining.

9 … 8 … 7 …

Rob's memory flashed back to more pleasant countdowns at New Year's parties. He wondered if they would ever see another New Year's celebration.

6 ... 5 ... 4 ...

Would the cycles continue? Although the viewers in the room would be the first to see evidence of the cycle, millions of people would soon experience tremors as the shock waves spread to the surface.

3 ... 2 ... 1 ...

The graph jumped suddenly and the entire room gasped and sighed in desperation.

"Damn!" exclaimed Rob, as he and Sharon locked eyes, both of them acutely conscious of the diminishing window of time to solve this dilemma. There would be no respite today.

The researchers knew that very soon the ground throughout the lab complex would begin to tremble. Through an ever-expanding radius, the seismic waves would steadily progress outward from the object's location deep within the Earth's crust. They also knew the weakest buildings in nearby cities would be the first to collapse, as would countless others as the range of seismic activity steadily increased. If these expansion cycles continued, every part of the planet would eventually be directly impacted. Everyone on the planet was one cycle closer to annihilation.

CHAPTER 30
JUNE 16, 4:00 PM

18,350,080 pounds

"All of the individuals who attacked this lab have been identified. As we first suspected, all of them are members of a radical religious group." Agent Sanderson of Homeland Security was briefing the entire lab team during a late afternoon team session. The middle-aged agent looked like he would be more at ease in a battlefield setting. Dressed in camouflage field gear with his side arm very conspicuous, Officer Roger Sanderson presented an imposing image. He'd been coordinating the investigation nonstop since the attack and lack of sleep didn't seem to affect his appearance or his level of energy. His buzz haircut matched his demeanor—no time for any non-essentials or pleasantries.

Agent Sanderson clearly was not one who wasted time or words. "One of the injured attackers still hasn't regained consciousness. The other two survivors have freely talked to our investigators." The agents were more used to working with criminals who did everything possible to impede investigations, but these perpetrators purposefully wanted to explain their actions. They wanted the media to know how their attack on the lab was justified by their holy cause.

"All of the attackers were from a previously unidentified group of religious zealots. The organization's self-proclaimed leader, Jason Morehouse, is one of the three survivors. He claims they're Christians and that they're not affiliated with any organized religious body. He also states that he'd received explicit instructions to 'rescue the Ark', which is what they call the object. According to Jason, 'God sent the object to threaten the evildoers on Earth. All of mankind must acknowledge their sins and respect the Ark.' Because the sacred Ark was being subjected to 'profane' experiments rather than being revered, Mr. Morehouse told us he was 'instructed to intervene'."

The team was astounded at this explanation. Several team members were firing questions at agent Sanderson as everyone was trying to make sense of the startling explanation.

Randy Schiller brought focus to the dialog simply by talking more loudly than the others. "What were they hoping to do? Didn't they know the object had already descended below the Earth's surface, out of their reach?" Randy's typical domineering manner irritated the other attendees at the briefing, but it did rein in the chaotic session.

"According to both individuals we've interviewed, all of the attackers thought the object was still in the lab. They believed that the media reports of the object descending through the lab floor were part of an elaborate hoax designed to discourage any attempts to 'rescue the Ark'. Actually, since they never reached the center of the building, they still believe the object is located in the lab. Mr. Morehouse is convinced that once the truth of their mission is known, the Ark will finally be revered and the daily tremors will cease."

Sharon, one of the few team members who had been present during the attack, voiced a pragmatic concern of many. "Are there more members of their group who may try again?"

"Our agents are still investigating all of the attackers—lifestyles, relatives, employment, neighbors. So far, we've discovered no interactions of interest with anyone outside of the band of ten attackers. Essentially, these ten appear to be a tight knit group who have avoided unnecessary contact with anyone outside their cult. To anyone they would have encountered, each would have appeared to be an asocial loner. Regarding any continuing threat, we believe the entire group has been neutralized."

"OK. Then what about others like them? Couldn't other zealots come up with a similar rationale to attack us?" Sharon questioned.

"Yes. In fact, we can expect more such attacks. The object has worldwide coverage, so there are myriad interpretations of what the arrival of this bizarre object means. Likewise, there are myriad ideas on how to satisfy whoever sent it. For prudent threat assessment, we now expect a small percentage of these interpretations to result in hostile incidents, directed either toward the object itself or to those studying it. As the devastation from the tremors is expected to increase each day, the desperation and willingness of various groups to resort to violence will similarly increase."

Rob pointed out another concern. "Then I recommend you continue to keep their leader, this Jason Morehouse, isolated from the media. And don't pass on to the press any quotes from your interviews with him. From the news reports I saw this morning, some fringe groups are already referring to the slain attackers as martyrs. If any more people believe the attackers were truly obeying a dictate from God, we could have lots of crazies who similarly want to be martyrs showing up here."

Randy jumped back into the discussion. "So how do you plan to protect us? We can't waste any more time being distracted by lunatics—we have to focus solely on stopping this damn thing."

Agent Sanderson had expected this question and was prepared. "We've already implemented numerous safeguards. I'm not at liberty to discuss all of our security measures but I can assure you that the increased number of agents you've undoubtedly seen around the lab complex is only one aspect of our heightened security measures. We're controlling all ground traffic in the surrounding area as well as the air space in the vicinity. You won't need to worry about any intruders." For future visitors to the site, the complex would appear more like a secured military base.

Taylor lobbed the next question. "It's only been a day and a half since the attack. How can you be so certain these idiots weren't acting for a foreign government or aren't part of some larger organization? Being able to control this object would provide immeasurable power to any radical group or government. We know al-Qaida has funded clandestine cells, and like this group, they're usually unknown until they perform their mission."

"It's a remote possibility, but not likely. During the interrogation, Jason Morehouse did express admiration for what he called 'Islamic jihadists'. Although he seemingly despises the Islamic faith, Jason was impressed and undoubtedly inspired by the Islamic concept of holy war. A willingness to sacrifice one's life for one's beliefs was something he felt was lacking in most of the world's Christians.

"I can state that all of the group's known members have traceable backgrounds that so far have not indicated any interaction with foreign governments or causes. Even if a connection is eventually detected in our investigation, I can assure you we're positioned to protect this site against any threat—from either homegrown or foreign terrorists."

The team was not convinced that they were now safe from future attacks, but every member recognized the urgent need to push ahead with their research. The short-term threat from zealots attacking the lab was indeed frightening—a few more researchers had lately abandoned the project and returned to be with their families. All those who remained on the team realized that the danger from another assault was actually minor compared to the threat of devastation that could eventually result from the object itself. They had to find a way to stop its daily expansion.

Chapter 31
June 17, 1:47 PM

36,700,160 pounds

"Not again! This feels just like yesterday!" Teresa Fortino was more perplexed than scared by the unusual ground movement. Growing up in California, she had experienced many small earthquakes in her younger life and had learned that they only rarely caused significant damage. Now at the age of forty-five, she had made her home in Albany, New York for the past twenty years. Her home was on level ground and solidly constructed, so Teresa was not overly alarmed by the minor tremors she felt.

Struggling with the challenges of creating a good life for her family, virtually all of Teresa's and her husband's time was dominated by an over-filled daily schedule. Typical of many families, very little time was left to pay attention to anything that lacked an imminent need. Paying bills, driving kids to after-school programs, hosting play-dates and maintaining their sixty-year-old home consumed all of their attention. Keeping up with national and world events was way down their list of things-to-do, so watching news reports and reading newspapers had become less regular since their second child was born.

Until the previous day, Teresa had never personally experienced even a slight earthquake here in New York. She knew the surrounding area was not prone to earthquakes, at least in the past several centuries. But this was the second one in two days.

As a mother of young children, Teresa's first thoughts were about the safety of her three kids who were attending a summer camp program at their nearby community church. All the children at the camp usually spent the early afternoon playing some outdoor sport, which explained why none of them had even realized there was an earthquake the previous day. "They might not even notice this quake if they're running around on a soccer field," she told herself.

But the ground was still moving. "Definitely more movement than yesterday," Teresa thought. It seemed like a slow rolling motion that followed the initial jolt. When she first felt the house jerk, she immediately moved to the front doorway of her home. A standard response learned during her California days was to seek the most structurally sound area of a building. As she glanced down the street from her front doorway, the scene reminded Teresa of watching small ocean swells.

Although it seemed much longer, the slow undulating movement lasted less than thirty seconds. In Teresa's neighborhood, yesterday's tremor had only damaged a few brick chimneys and one very old Colonial-style residence. This earthquake was stronger, but Teresa thought the amount of damage would probably be similar to yesterday's tremor. Her kids would be OK, but she'd call the church office to check anyway.

"But didn't yesterday's quake also occur just at lunch?" she thought to herself. She quickly realized it occurred at the exact same time of the day. Like yesterday, the daily episode of "As the Earth Turns" had just concluded and Teresa had started to throw together a salad for lunch. Her husband occasionally teased her about being addicted to the daily soap, but he knew it provided a brief respite from her home-based sales business.

"Earthquakes are rare enough around here—but why in the world would two occur at exactly the same time of day? This is crazy." She carefully reentered the living room and began scanning the TV channels for a local news program. Teresa figured there would soon be news coverage of the quake and maybe an explanation for the strange spacing of yesterday's and today's tremors.

Teresa's family would no longer be ignorant of the topic that had begun to dominate the daily news reports. As predicted in the media, the seismic activity was affecting more people every day. The daily tremors and the eventual fate of Teresa's family were becoming connected to the bizarre object that was baffling the scientific community.

Chapter 32
June 17, 2:30 PM

36,700,160 pounds

"You can't really believe all events across the planet are being monitored," Sharon argued. She was using their brief lunchtime to challenge one of Rob's earlier comments that she considered too far-fetched. "How could someone or something possibly observe everyone in the world?"

Rob and Sharon were now eating all of their meals together, which was essentially the only downtime they had from the stressful project work. They usually dined in the onsite cafeteria since it was much more convenient than leaving the lab complex. The food was actually fairly good, but if they had more time, both of them would have opted to leave the complex. Although it was extremely difficult to separate mentally from their work, at least being offsite would have provided a brief physical separation from the exasperating research.

There were only a few minutes remaining before the next afternoon work session with the entire team. Forcing himself to skip the last half of his bagel sandwich, Rob was eager to answer Sharon's question.

"Why does this sound crazy? Over 80 percent of the entire world's citizens already believe we're being monitored, and furthermore that all our actions are being recorded." Rob glanced at his watch to make sure they still had a few free minutes left and then continued.

"The billions of people who pray to God are communicating with someone they believe is already aware of everything they do. Most of these same individuals also firmly believe their fate in the after-life will be based on a judgment of actions that were permanently recorded throughout their entire life."

"But even if someone believes God is monitoring us, isn't it an enormous jump for them to believe God would intervene and deliver this message to us?" asked Sharon.

Rob downed the last of his iced tea and continued describing his reasoning. "It's not a jump at all. Virtually everyone who prays for an event to occur is essentially asking for a supernatural intervention. Interference with the order of events in the world is requested every day by billions of people." His speech was gaining momentum as the solution was becoming more apparent to him.

"The world needs to take action now. First, we need to convince the entire team that whoever sent this is looking for a revolutionary change in our behavior. Whoever sent this is looking for actions that demonstrate we understand the message and that we'll comply with it."

"All right. I really can't see any other options," Sharon interjected, with a resigned tone in her voice. "Our planet is already on its way to annihilation in a matter of weeks. I suspect that whoever or whatever has the sophisticated ability to send and activate this object, also has the means of deactivating it. At this point, we have absolutely nothing to lose by trying to respond to the object's message."

They left the cafeteria and walked quickly down the corridor to the conference room, where the researchers were gathering for the daily briefing. Ever since the team was first assembled, Randy had insisted on holding daily sessions to update each other on their respective research efforts. They immediately noticed Professor Josef Ramon, the head of Religious Studies at NYU, was present. After the professor's previous consultation on the object's Arabic message, Randy had asked the professor to be an active member on the research team. The members had been hoping a better understanding of the object's religious significance might help determine who might have sent it.

Several team members were discussing the message and the interpretations proffered by different religious groups with Professor Ramon. Rob waited until the current conversation started to wane and seized the room's attention with his opening remark.

"We've spent a lot of effort these past few weeks analyzing the object and attempting to identify the sender. I realize it's difficult to accept, but at this point it doesn't really matter who or what sent this object." Rob continued, aware that everyone who had assembled in the conference room was listening intently. He knew what he was about to say would be very unsettling to many of his fellow team members as it would be to most of the world's citizens.

"All of our efforts to learn how the object functions so we could dismantle it have been futile. Despite our technical abilities, we're completely powerless to halt this device. Our only remaining option is to comply with the message on the object: 'Do unto others as you would do unto yourselves'. I propose that our historical failure in not treating others as ourselves has brought us to a point where we now face our imminent destruction. I believe that either God or an advanced benevolent life form has decided for whatever reason to give us an assist, to help us get beyond this fragile phase in our development so that we can evolve to a more peaceful species."

The room was uncharacteristically quiet for the next twenty seconds or so, as the impact of Rob's concept was absorbed. Most of the team members had always considered spiritual concepts as being distinct from the physical world. As humans increased their understanding of the world, thoughts of what constituted God and spiritual issues had continually been modified to be congruent with what was learned.

Rob pressed ahead, concerned about the derision which usually resulted from what he was proposing—the possibility of extraterrestrial life. The scientific world preferred to deal with tangible concepts, or at least with ideas that they could test experimentally. By its nature, science requires uncompromising skepticism by those validating new theories, particularly those theories that move radically away from established laws of the natural world. But at the same time, increasing understanding of the world requires being open to new ideas.

In normal circumstances, Rob would have avoided proposing the possibility of alien involvement, but this was not a normal situation. Ever since the team initially verified the increase in the object's mass, long-established physical laws had become suspect—probably invalid. Radical viewpoints were now essential, especially in view of the limited time left to deal with this doomsday device.

Rob noticed that Randy was visibly frowning—their distinguished leader might want to shut down this line of reasoning as too fantastic. Rob quickly continued to address his fellow team members before they could voice the first of many criticisms. "The recent discovery of planets throughout the cosmos has forced many to speculate that finding extraterrestrial life is merely a matter of time. We now discover new planets every week—we're limited only by the ever-increasing capacity of our tools to view them. The conditions necessary for life to exist definitely limit the number of potential life-sustaining sites, but the incomprehensibly vast size of the cosmos provides many possibilities. There are between one hundred and four hundred billion stars in our own Milky Way galaxy, and there are at least a hundred billion other galaxies.

"It's arguable that probability-wise life must exist elsewhere, particularly when you consider potentially different bases and structures for life. Eventually our tools may enable us to actually locate and observe a distant planet that's suitable for sustaining life. In much of the world, our ancestors viewed humans as the focal point of all creation, but we now know that the Earth is an extremely small part of an enormously vast cosmos. As with past advances in knowledge, our religious and cultural beliefs will accommodate these new discoveries. Why couldn't other worlds also be created by God?"

Taylor voiced the first of many questions that were raising the anxiety in the room. "You seem to be referring to both aliens and God at the same time. Are you saying that it doesn't matter whether the object was sent from God or sent from aliens? Or are you implying that they could be one and the same, that what we've always thought of as God could actually be an alien life form?"

Rob doubted this line of discussion would help them solve their immediate problem of how to respond to the object, but decided to pursue it anyway. The topic had already surfaced and it was now too late to avoid it.

"If there were an advanced civilization that was monitoring us and occasionally intervened in our development, what would that look like? If we were given messages periodically to point us in some desired direction, how might that be accomplished?"

Professor Ramon, the most knowledgeable one in the room where religious interpretations were concerned, offered his opinion. "Perhaps I can help illustrate what I believe is the essence of Rob's argument. Humans are hard-wired for religion. From the earliest days in our development as sentient beings, we've made sense of our world by attributing mystical aspects to whatever we didn't understand. Whether it was lightning, floods, droughts or the presence of wild game, all were attributed to the actions of a spiritual presence. Our ancestors gave most of these spirits humanlike behaviors and appearances. Appeasing these spirits led to continued benevolence, displeasing them led to misfortune. Virtually every society throughout history has identified one or more gods to account for the unpredictable events that we now view as the natural order.

"As human civilization matured, it gradually recognized that there was consistency in nature. Whether sacrifices were made or not, the sun still rose and set every day. The reasons for storms, diseases, eclipses, birthmarks and plagues were all eventually attributed to natural causes. As more and more natural laws were discovered, spirits were believed to be responsible for a diminishing number of events."

The team seemed receptive to Professor Ramon's comments as he continued the animated discussion. His clear presentation reflected years of teaching experience. "The religions that have survived over thousands of years are among the oldest human institutions. Most have provided great comfort to their followers by providing direction in our daily lives and by establishing an opportunity to rectify this world's injustices in a future life. From a humanistic viewpoint, their greatest benefit has been in creating a sense of community and encouraging charity and support of others. Although many of the global problems we face today are related to or even the direct result of religious fervor, religion isn't the root cause. Age-old human traits of greed, pride, intolerance, vengeance and hate exist regardless of the presence of religion."

Taylor McCracken had been uncharacteristically quiet during the briefing. It was apparent he was very uncomfortable with the topic of religion and the direction the conversation was heading. Along with the rest of the team members, he had expected the afternoon briefing to cover technical aspects of the different ongoing studies of the object. A discussion of religious implications was a new twist for them.

Shifting nervously in his chair, Taylor interrupted Professor Ramon. "I'm having difficulty with Rob's claim of equating an advanced civilization with what we've thought of as God. Sure, the physical world is more understandable now. But what about issues other than explaining physical events in the world? What about miracles or answers to prayers?"

Professor Ramon didn't hesitate to answer. His articulate manner indicated this topic might have been part of one of his class lectures. "All the miracles described in the predominant religious texts occurred long ago, and are far beyond the scrutiny of modern tools. For virtually all events that are considered modern miracles like healings or answers to prayers, there are usually other plausible explanations. As to those that can't be explained, the absence of an explanation doesn't provide proof of divine intervention. I believe such unexplained events merely indicate we're too ignorant to comprehend the reason. Much of the randomness that we perceive in the world actually is a reflection of our lack of knowledge.

"Most progressive religious groups no longer try to prove the presence of modern-day miracles—it's just too difficult. Many theologians also reject the validity of ancient miracles as well, and view most, if not all of them, as totally unnecessary to the core purpose of religion. One of my favorite quotes from St. Augustine, a Christian theologian in the fifth century, sums up this whole issue: 'Miracles are not contrary to nature, but only contrary to what we know about nature.'"

Professor Ramon unconsciously tugged at his dark beard as he continued. "As to the human tendency to interpret unexplained events as miracles, consider the result whenever vastly different societies have interacted with each other—just within our own recent human history. Whenever there was a significant gap in the level of development, particularly in the understanding of how the natural world operates, how did the members of the less developed society view those in the much more advanced society? They were treated as gods, with spiritual power that gave them the ability to perform magic or even miracles.

"When the Spanish and Portuguese explorers first contacted the societies of the New World, they were immediately viewed as gods with superior power and magic. When New Guinea natives first witnessed the modern world, they thought likewise. Many other indigenous cultures have similarly viewed their first contact with more modern explorers."

By the affirming head nods, it was apparent the team had no problem in accepting Professor Ramon's specific examples. The researchers recognized that any technological society possesses capabilities that were likely viewed as magical only a few generations earlier. To the eighteenth century citizen, traveling by aircraft to the opposite side of the planet in a matter of hours would surely seem magical. Traveling to the moon or communicating instantaneously with millions through the worldwide Internet would likewise seem magical.

"Wouldn't billions of today's uneducated citizens be similarly impressed if they encountered some feat that was beyond their comprehension, yet might be within the capability of an advanced technology? Perhaps objects disappearing or relocating instantly would be viewed as magical. Instant healing by selectively destroying or replacing diseased cells would surely appear miraculous. Mentally communicating with others or accessing infinite energy sources would appear to be supernatural. These events would be most disturbing to many in the undeveloped countries of the world and mystical reasons would be created to explain what couldn't be understood." The professor's remarks made sense to the gathered researchers, but they needed to figure out how this would influence the team's next efforts.

Rob figured that at this point he might as well drive his radical idea all the way. It was imperative to convince the team if they were to buy into the action plan that he and Sharon would soon be proposing. "Exactly what would be the distinguishing differences in how we describe God and how we might describe an advanced alien civilization? I propose that there are no qualitative differences, only differences of degree."

Randy couldn't sit still any longer. He recognized he either needed to halt this discussion before the press got wind of it, or, if in fact there was no better alternative, jump in and support Rob in this new direction. "So Rob, from what you're stating, you believe we need to respond to the object's message as a direct command, and also that it doesn't matter whether this message came from either a god-like advanced civilization or from God."

Rob was more than ready for this discussion. "Yes, we've run out of options. I'm not claiming an advanced civilization could attain a god-like status, only that their advanced state would make them appear to us as god-like. Natural laws would still constrain their actions. The knowledge available to a more advanced civilization might allow them to manipulate what we consider as inviolate physical laws. Furthermore, if it turns out alternate universes do exist, as predicted by many theorists, different natural laws within any given universe would allow them a corresponding different set of actions."

Randy was warming to this radically new approach. It was evident by the reflective look on his face and the fact that he was not bullying the team toward a preconceived plan of his own. He had to admit, this multi-disciplined team was actually coming up with scenarios he never would have imagined. Maybe there was more to this collaborative work style than he had realized.

"Can you imagine," Randy asked, "the tremendous negative reaction if we can't convincingly present this theory to the world? There's no way we can adequately address the philosophical implications of Rob's proposal. So where do we go from here?"

Sharon, in her typically efficient manner, steered the researchers back to a task that they could successfully achieve. "So if we're being monitored for a response to the object's message, then what do we need to do to demonstrate that we can 'treat each other as ourselves'? Also, how can we demonstrate that very quickly? I believe whoever sent this device will stop its growth if we can show we can alter our self-destructive ways."

The room was silent again, but this time not from shock at the discussion content. By the silence and absence of alternate theories, the team was tacitly agreeing to follow this new approach.

Sharon hammered away at the next step while the team was receptive: "I believe a new paradigm is required, where self-survival at the cost of others is no longer acceptable. So what must we focus on? What has been a threat to humanity for the entire period identified by the message on the object—the past 200,000 years?"

"That would leave out recent problems like terrorism and nuclear weapons," Randy offered. "It must be very generic, something our ancestors experienced 200,000 years ago and that we still experience today."

"To my thinking," Sharon countered, "it's intolerance—refusing to respect other's interests, rights and beliefs. Intolerance has been present in all wars and genocidal actions, as well as environmental destruction and misallocation of limited resources. So if we're being asked, or rather commanded, to change our ways and to essentially 'clean up our act', then how would this new world appear?"

The exhausted team members realized they couldn't continue without getting at least a little rest. It was just before 11 PM when the group disbanded, each member tasked to be ready with ideas for the following day's work session. Although their jeopardy from the object increased with each passing day, the team finally had a clear direction for their efforts.

CHAPTER 33
JUNE 18, 3:00 PM

73,400,320 pounds

"What could be so threatening to our world that someone or something would have to intervene to save us?" asked Randy. The team had been struggling to come up with ideas on how to respond to the object's mandate to "do unto others as yourselves." Yet the related question kept arising—what could possibly be so dire for humanity that an intervention would be necessary?

"I can think of several potential cataclysms," responded Rob. He had been pondering this for the past several days since he saw the televised interview with the futurist Dr. Branson.

"Aside from the continuing threat from nuclear war, recent technology advances provide a number of possible means for creating worldwide catastrophes. With the widely available biotech tools, could a tech-savvy band of radicals have figured out how to create a new virulent strain of microbes? The devastation from a new viral strain could definitely be catastrophic. The Spanish flu epidemic of 1918 alone caused the death of over fifty million people worldwide. The virus that caused it was a form of bird flu that had mutated into a form that could spread easily between humans. Infectious diseases introduced by the Spaniards decimated the Native American tribes. As much as 95 percent of the native population disappeared in the sixteenth and seventeenth centuries."

Randy was ready to discount microbes as a threat, having spent his life promoting science and technology as the answer to all problems. "Not a problem! Most of the Indian deaths in the New World were due to smallpox, which has probably caused the deaths of hundreds of millions over the past centuries. But scientists found out how to immunize people and ran mass immunization and treatment programs to eradicate it completely. The smallpox virus is now extinct—a great example of technology solving a problem."

"Really?" Rob blurted. "Since it was eliminated, there was no need to continue costly vaccination programs. So now, no one in the world under age thirty-five has ever been vaccinated against smallpox. It may be extinct in nature, but what about samples of the smallpox virus that are in government labs around the world? If a bioterrorist gained access to one of those labs, how quick do you think the world could reintroduce a global vaccination program? Smallpox passes easily through the air between people less than six feet apart. Usually, 30 percent of those infected die, but some outbreaks have had deaths near 100 percent. Besides, even if the existing samples in labs were secure, couldn't some enterprising lab genetically alter another virus to become as lethal as the smallpox virus?"

Randy shot back, "The scientific community has debated the risks from biological engineering for years. Those few scientists who have been unreasonably concerned with the potential risk of creating new microbes are just alarmists. Modern technology can develop a means to counter any new virulent microbe."

"Could it?" Rob countered. "Modern-day terrorists have few qualms against using extremely lethal means. What if one of these extremist groups had control of a virus that could spread through the air without killing its host until the entire globe was contaminated? If it spread too rapidly, it might be impossible to develop protection against the virus before it obliterated the entire human population. As far as our ability to contain new influenza variants, look what happened with the H1N1 virus, the so-called "swine flu". Despite widespread efforts to contain it, the World Health Organization still had to declare its spread a global pandemic in 2009. Fortunately, it turned out to not be as lethal as feared."

Sharon cut into the conversation, offering another possible threat from her own field of biology. "It's been years since researchers first merged genetic material from one organism into the chromosomes of another to create improved life forms such as corn or livestock. This type of genetic engineering is becoming commonplace even though consumers don't universally accept it. I suspect some of you aren't familiar with one of the newest biological specialties—Synthetic Biology. SynBio is actually programming cell behavior to produce entirely new life forms that would be self-replicating. The economic potential is driving several research centers to develop this capability as quickly as possible. Could we be on the verge of a catastrophic SynBio breakthrough?"

Rob brought up an additional area as a potential runaway threat. "We could also consider the rapidly advancing nanotechnology field where numerous mainstream businesses are pursuing radically new creations. A few scientists have cautioned against such research, believing that it might unwittingly release a self-replicating nanobot that could consume one or more of the Earth's resources. Most of the scientific world has always dismissed this hypothetical threat, but maybe such a danger is possible."

Taylor offered another possibility, one that he couldn't keep from worrying about after a recent conversation. "I had a discussion last week with one of the German physicists on our team. He told me how excited he was to be involved in the Large Hadron Collider that was recently constructed near Geneva, Switzerland. CERN, the European Organization for Nuclear Research, has created the world's most powerful particle accelerator. It's hoped that this huge device will increase knowledge of the most basic structures of nature, yet I found his description of one of the planned experiments to be very alarming. He enthusiastically described to me how they were hoping to establish the right environment to create a "mini" black hole. He and the rest of the CERN scientists were certain that this creation would evaporate instantaneously and cause no threat to their collider or the world. But do they really know what's going to happen when they activate this experiment? What kind of risk assessment are these physicists using? Could the world's esteemed particle physicists be unwittingly about to open Pandora's box?"

Rob wondered if Taylor's real concern was that the Europeans were the ones running this experiment, without any control by Americans. Regardless of Taylor's bias, there were unsettling questions about the safety of such leading-edge experiments.

Most of the team knew Taylor's background involved a long career in the nuclear arms field. His training would have included the history surrounding the first nuclear bomb experiments by the United States. Rob recalled that similar concerns were expressed by scientists when the first nuclear bombs were about to be tested in the 1940's. Some nuclear scientists feared there might be a runaway chain reaction that could engulf the entire world. As it turned out, an uncontrolled chain reaction did not occur and the world obviously survived, but could the CERN experiments initiate a runaway black hole that would draw in everything around it?

"Why limit the threat to a new exotic creation or weapon?" asked Sharon. "What if a problem with the environment was about to reach a tipping-point that would be fatal to humans? For years, scientists have predicted problems from global warming. Our rampant use of fossil fuels has put nearly a trillion tons of carbon dioxide into the atmosphere over the past couple of centuries."

This was a concern Rob had also held for some time, as he expanded on Sharon's suggestion. "A warmer planet will surely produce a lot of changes, especially for future generations. But rather than merely creating major problems to deal with, could global warming be approaching an irreversible point? Could the ever-higher temperatures we're now experiencing become self-perpetuating and result in a lethal hothouse atmosphere? The first decade of the twenty-first century was the hottest since recordkeeping began, and it included nine of the ten warmest years ever recorded. If the global temperature became high enough, it could become fatal for human life everywhere on the planet."

Several members seemed to have a strong opinion on the issue of global warming. Randy jumped into the discussion and surprised a few of his team members with a more open attitude than he usually expressed. "Sure, there's lots of evidence for major changes occurring, but are they cataclysmic? Everyone knows that half of the Arctic's ice has already been lost, and with less sunlight-reflecting ice, more and more solar heat is absorbed. We've also known for decades that warmer conditions are increasing both the strength and frequency of hurricanes. Could these indicators mean we may be close to a point where global warming is unstoppable?"

Rob mentioned a couple of ominous news articles that had generated accusations that the authors were alarmists. "The British scientist James Lovelock in 2006 claimed we'd already passed the point of runaway warming, and that billions would die from it this century. Another climate expert, John Schellenhuber, in 2004 identified twelve global-warming tipping points, any one of which could cause sudden, catastrophic changes to the world."

Rob was aware of numerous other developments that provided additional warning signals. "These predictions don't seem so far-fetched and can't be readily dismissed. Another recent discovery is that tremendous amounts of methane have been stored for millennia in frozen arctic tundra—400 billion tons. Melting permafrost could release that methane into the atmosphere, increasing global warming and consequently triggering the release of yet more methane from ocean bottoms. In Siberia, melting permafrost has already created so much methane in lakes that many don't freeze even in the coldest winter months."

Drawing on her biological sciences background, Sharon offered additional support to the impact of methane on climate. "That could really be serious. A number of scientists believe a large release of methane into the atmosphere occurred 250 million years ago. This caused the oceans to warm and shut down the ocean conveyor belt, trapping oxygen and nutrients so deep that most of the world's oceans became a dead zone. The resulting absence of sea life to scrub the atmosphere of carbon dioxide caused global warming to accelerate even further. This condition led to the extinction of 90 percent of all marine species and 70 percent of all terrestrial vertebrates, as well as the elimination of forests. Many areas didn't recover for more than 100 million years."

The team members could not help but be dismayed at the many horrific possibilities. Randy tried to sum up the discussion and end the distressing meeting. "All right. What killed off most species 250 million years ago was a natural event, but today we're facing a number of man-made threats to our world. We've been aware of some of these problems for decades—like the use of fossil fuels accelerating global warming. But our recent advances in technology have resulted in a number of new and exotic threats that are potentially lethal for humankind."

Randy wrapped up the discussion in his typical manner. "That's it! We can't waste any more time trying to identify a potential catalyst for this object being sent to us. There are too many dire possibilities. Even if we were able to identify the most likely one, we still need to figure out how we can respond to the message on the cube. That's our only priority at this point."

73,400,320 pounds

Several of the team members were in the lab, comparing notes and trying to plan their next steps. The overhead monitors were displaying the object's current mass, its estimated location and the time to the next expected expansion cycle. After the last expansion, the object had descended to its current depth of just over twenty miles, still within the Earth's crust.

Sharon remarked to the techs who were also observing the monitors, "It's almost as if this thing were designed to get the attention of everyone on the planet. The strongest earth tremors can be predicted to occur precisely after each daily cycle, even though we can't predict the exact strength of the tremors or their location as they ripple through the Earth's interior up to the Earth's surface. If the object keeps descending and its mass keeps increasing, everyone on the planet will eventually experience these tremors. Everyone will have a clearer understanding of the planet's fragile situation and they'll experience an increasing panic over their own impending death."

Sharon continued her conversation with the techs, but she was not that interested in a dialogue. She was primarily thinking aloud—refining her own thoughts on several puzzling aspects of the object.

"The exact timing of this object's cycles has also allowed minimizing massive loss of life, at least so far. The earthquake tremors have been steadily increasing in magnitude each day, so that people have learned to avoid high-risk areas—they've abandoned poorly constructed buildings and moved away from areas prone to landslides."

One of the techs replied "Right. Most of the casualties to-date have been in impoverished and overpopulated coastal areas where the inhabitants had nowhere to flee. Since tsunamis now occur every day, tens of thousands of inhabitants in low-lying coastal cities have already fled to higher ground."

As additional team members arrived in the lab to view the next anticipated cycle of weight increase, Sharon continued speculating. "Since the majority of the world's people inhabit the northern latitudes, that means that most people are currently experiencing mild spring temperatures. This seems fortunate with the millions of people now living out of their homes. I wonder if the seasonal timing of this device's arrival was also set to minimize loss of life."

"Perhaps," offered another tech in the room. "But the seismic damage is escalating every day. The number of casualties will only get worse and probably very soon."

The doubters who originally dismissed the findings as another hoax or even a conspiracy by the Western powers were now witnessing the actual effects. The earlier belief that Allah was punishing infidels by depositing the device in the heart of western capitalism, New York, was abandoned since widely scattered locations were now being equally affected.

Rob entered the lab, immediately spotted Sharon across the room and walked over to her. He looked as exhausted as the other team members did, but somehow his optimistic personality still managed to search for positive angles. Even in this potential doomsday situation, optimism could still survive.

"There's only one bright side to this problem as I see it," he ventured to Sharon and the other nearby colleagues. "Every problem we've ever faced to this point has had skeptics who persistently doubted the problem, despite a preponderance of evidence to the contrary. Just take the relationship of cigarettes to lung cancer or the burning of fossil fuels to global warming. But now there's virtually no skepticism about the reality of the danger from this object. Previous dilemmas could always be dismissed as someone else's worry or something that could be solved by later generations. This catastrophe will affect everyone and dealing with it can't be postponed to some point in the future."

The conversation in the lab became subdued, as the researchers waited to observe yet another expansion cycle. There was still hope that as the object descended further into the interior of the Earth, the increased pressure and heat would have a stifling effect on the object. They would soon be disappointed.

146,800,640 pounds

"A major earthquake occurred at 1:46 PM this afternoon causing widespread damage. In east coast cities, at least two hundred people are known dead and hundreds more are missing. Fortunately, tens of thousands of residents in both the Northeastern and Southeastern United States had already fled to evacuation centers in anticipation of today's quake."

The experienced newscaster spoke in an even voice, belying the anxiety he personally harbored. Jonathan Santone was a rising star in the Channel 4 newsroom. He easily matched the formulaic TV reporter image: strong facial features, reasonably handsome, articulate, a commanding voice and an overall serious demeanor. Only one feature distinguished him from the majority of his newscaster colleagues—his skin tone. It was impossible to determine if his dark complexion was due to a southern

European or Middle Eastern lineage or only due to a carefully maintained suntan.

The special news report interrupted the regular television schedule and was being broadcast on multiple stations. Jonathan Santone had established a reputation for equanimity while reporting horrendous tragedies. He had repeatedly placed himself in harm's way over the past decade, reporting from war zones, from coastal areas struggling against Category 5 storms and from politically unstable sites of government coups. But after reporting the escalating disasters of the past week, signs of stress were beginning to show in his demeanor. His movements appeared too quick, even jerky, rather than the measured, deliberate gestures that he had always displayed when in front of live television cameras. His eyes also blinked more often than usual, as they darted rapidly between the dual teleprompters.

"Only scattered reports of damage are available at this time, but the scope of destruction is extensive. What little information we have is undoubtedly only a small sampling of the devastation that has become more severe with each passing day.

"Near Jackson, Mississippi, at least twenty-four people died when the Hope Cathedral shelter building collapsed. The destruction of this supposedly secure building has unfortunately discouraged others from seeking safety in official shelter sites. Another fourteen elderly citizens were crushed by falling debris as they fled from a high-rise retirement community in Jacksonville, Florida. Thousands of homes across a widening area have collapsed—a number of residents are still trapped in the ruins.

"The area of seismic activity has increased daily, and is now affecting many distant areas of the world. Today's temblors reportedly tore four-foot-wide fissures in the ground in central Mexico, toppled bridges and elevated roadways and destroyed dozens of buildings. Tens of thousands of homes across Mexico and Central America are without water or power. As supplies slowly arrive at the most damaged areas, temporary emergency shelters are being assembled."

Jonathan paused slightly, forcing himself to continue at an evenly measured pace. He recognized the danger of further panicking his viewers. He knew they would be trying to make sense of the uneven and seemingly random locations of earthquake damage. Besides the obvious differences in construction strength between buildings, the underlying terrain was usually the determining factor in which structures would collapse. Ground that appears solid could behave like a liquid from the shaking produced by an earthquake—loose, sandy soil or poorly compacted artificial fill would be the most affected. This type of earth shaking frequently ruptured buried gas and water mains leading to the additional dangers of fires and flooding.

"Reports are just now coming in from sites even more distant from the initial epicenter as the seismic waves propagate farther across the planet. The Japanese islands have been on emergency status for the past several days as they anticipate the effect of each day's tremors. Japan has always been one of the most earthquake-prone countries with four tectonic plates underlying the nation. Japan's long experience with earthquakes has better prepared them for these events than other countries. Consequently, their loss of life to-date has been minimal."

Jonathan prudently decided to skip mentioning several facts that had been collected by the newsroom researchers. The last major quake to hit Tokyo killed 142,000 people in 1923. The Meteorological Agency of Japan had been predicting for decades that the capital has a 90 percent chance of suffering a major quake in the next half century.

"An uncorroborated report has been received that the city of Bursa, Turkey, just south of Istanbul was hit particularly hard by today's temblors. Widespread collapse of buildings may have resulted in thousands of deaths and tens of thousands of injuries."

The newscaster paused again to gather himself. He struggled to maintain his professional demeanor, yet he couldn't block the distracting images that flashed like a horror slideshow in his mind. As with most people his age and younger, Jonathan Santone had always expected to live a long life. Death was a hazy and ill-defined concept, something to deal with at a distant time. Death was also something not faced directly. But producing the daily newscasts of constantly increasing destruction and death around the world underscored everyone's probable fate. Jonathan Santone was acutely aware that his life could also end in a matter of days.

U.S. geologists were particularly alarmed with the record number of tremors being detected at Yellowstone National Park in Wyoming. The seismometers that continuously monitored the geologically active area had never previously recorded so many tremors. The entire park sits squarely atop one of the biggest volcanoes on Earth, one that last erupted about 640,000 years ago. The volcano is still very active—half of all geysers on the planet are located in Yellowstone. Geologists had determined that the Yellowstone volcano had erupted on a cycle approximately 600,000 years long. Since the next eruption was overdue, it was feared that tremors from the object's expansion would likely hasten the next explosion.

Were the Yellowstone volcano to erupt, the destruction would be immense. When it last erupted, the explosion buried areas up to a hundred miles away with molten lava and threw so much ash and dust into the atmosphere that the entire Earth endured a darkened, continuous volcanic winter for several years. Aside from the immediate deaths from another eruption, just this one volcano could eventually cause tens of millions of people to starve due to the loss of crops around the world.

Jonathan Santone had prudently avoided reporting the Yellowstone concerns—it would unnecessarily amplify panic. "Besides," he reasoned to himself, "the newsroom researchers had informed him there were 169 geologically active volcanoes in the United States alone, and far more in both Indonesia and Japan. Eruptions could be triggered just as easily at any of these sites, maybe even at all of them." Jonathan forced himself to sit upright in his broadcaster's chair and focused on continuing with a calm delivery.

"We have been informed that the lethal object which is the cause of these quakes is now positioned close to the lower edge of the Earth's crust. The crust is about twenty-five miles thick at the site where the object descended beneath the surface of the Earth.

"There are so many aftershocks, occurring in so many far-flung areas that the U.S. Geological Survey organization cannot keep up with isolating and reporting them. A high-ranking official speaking anonymously stated, "The widespread tremors and their countless aftershocks have swamped our data collection system. If the quakes continue to grow in strength and frequency as they have this past week, we'll not be able to keep forecasting probable sites of tsunamis or aftershocks.'"

Jonathan somberly added, in an apparently unscripted commentary, "If the shocks continue to get stronger every day, our capacity to report the increasing damage will soon be very limited. In fact, any televised coverage may soon be impossible."

146,800,640 pounds

"It was like a vision—an incredible experience. It happened while I was sleeping last night." Rob was uncharacteristically rattled. He had called Sharon and asked her to meet him for breakfast at the Cup and Saucer restaurant, only a few miles from the lab complex. He needed to reveal his experience as soon as possible, and she was the only one he completely trusted.

Sharon immediately knew the meeting was important—Rob had never before arranged an offsite meeting for the two of them. When she had arrived at 7:15, there were only a few other customers in the small restaurant. She had easily found Rob, who was sitting at a small two-person table close to the entrance door. Based on the number of empty coffee creamer containers, he had apparently already downed at least two cups of coffee and was plainly excited.

"It makes so much sense! Everything seems so much clearer about what we need to do. The object *is* from an advanced civilization."

"How can you be so sure? How do you know you weren't just dreaming, maybe building on that futurist's TV talk that you told me about a few days ago?" Sharon prodded.

"I suppose his comments could have started my thinking in this direction. But it was quite different from a dream. Dreams always have bizarre parts to them, with logical inconsistencies and things morphing into other things. Everything was so consistent throughout the vision, and the experience was so vivid. It began with a graph that I can still see with amazing clarity."

Rob pulled out the hand drawn chart that he had recreated earlier that morning and placed it on the table between them. It showed a steep downward sloping curve, which Rob had labeled across the top "Civilization Life Spans."

"Whoever provided this chart to me had apparently been observing the evolution of life throughout the cosmos. This chart depicted life spans of civilizations before they self-destructed. The vast distances in the cosmos and the tremendous gaps in time have assured that the numerous civilizations that evolved had rarely interacted with each other. Only one—themselves—had survived long enough for their technology and knowledge to place them in the unique position to recognize this."

Rob pointed to the bottom axis that he had labeled "Earth's Solar Years," ranging from zero at the left to 500,000 years at the extreme right. He had labeled the vertical axis "Sentient Civilizations"—which ranged from zero to 700,000. The essence of the graph was immediately obvious.

"Just look at this. Within 140,000 years of achieving sentience, two-thirds of all civilizations self-destructed. They defined the term 'sentience' as the state of self-awareness and tracked all life forms that had evolved to this point. Within 200,000 years, 99 percent had self-destructed. Only one had survived beyond 300,000 years. *They* were the only survivors. The graph stopped at 500,000 years, but I got the impression it only stopped because there was no relevance in identifying how old their civilization is—whether it's 500,000, millions or even billions of years old. Their advanced knowledge of the universe has enabled them to travel throughout the cosmos, extend their lifespan to thousands of years and monitor anything of interest."

Although usually skeptical, Sharon found herself intrigued by Rob's explanation. The novel concept directly addressed several long-standing questions. "That's amazing! If this were true, it would explain why the cosmos isn't teeming with advanced civilizations. But why would they be giving us this information?"

"We pique their interest because we've evolved in a manner similar to them. They've interfered in our development because they want to see another advanced life form besides themselves."

Sharon interrupted, incredulous at Rob's revelation. "Just how did you find this out? You said you could see the graph, but how did you get this explanation? Were you talking with someone in this dream?"

"First, I'm telling you it was no dream! As for the detailed explanations, I don't know. It's as if the thoughts were just there. There was no one I was conversing with and no image other than the graph was involved. It just seems so clear to me that an advanced alien species was communicating with me at a level appropriate to my ability to understand.

"But it turns out that the message on the object isn't the first such communication. They've attempted to aid us a number of times in the past. Messages have been sent to us at several points in our history, by controlling the thoughts and memories of selected individuals. Humanity ignored most of these messengers who passed into oblivion—they were viewed as antisocial cynics or more recently as psychotics. Several messengers, however, have ended up being revered by their followers as the founders of various religions: Buddhism, Christianity and Islam being the most successful.

Sharon now knew why he didn't want to divulge this "vision" at the lab. They both knew that more than a few team members would be delighted to cast doubt on both Rob and her as the current leaders of the investigation and redirect the team's efforts. She waved off the waitress who approached their booth to see if they were ready to order breakfast.

Rob continued with the amazing revelation he had experienced. "This advanced civilization has tried various methods to see if the same key message would stick—the message being, in order to survive self-destruction, you need to subjugate the natural drive to preserve and benefit oneself, and replace it with a perspective that values all humans as equals. They gave several messages to pre-historic man, but the first messenger we could relate to by name would have been Imhotep, a Sumerian leader in one of the early Egyptian dynasties. After that early civilization totally ignored the message of tolerance, they elected to avoid intervention for the next two thousand years to see how our civilization matured on its own."

"They eventually tried again using a low-key approach with Siddhartha Gautama. His teachings of compassion and non-judgmental acceptance of others were successful and gradually spread throughout Asia. Yet over the centuries following the Buddha's death, the philosophy subsequently morphed into a religion filled with ritual and mysticism.

"Five centuries passed before a more direct message was provided through Jesus, and this attempt eventually proved to be more successful. The essence of Jesus' message was conveyed when he specifically stated that all the teachings of Jewish law were based on just two commandments: to "love God" and to "love your neighbor as yourself." Unfortunately, his followers systematically obscured this simple expression of reciprocal altruism with a rigidly structured religion. Six more centuries passed before the same message was again tried through an in-your-face attitude with Muhammad, but this also was subsequently reinterpreted by some of his followers into intolerance for most everything, not just selfish behaviors."

Rob's revelation fascinated Sharon—it actually was starting to make sense. She suggested, "Maybe it's almost impossible to advance beyond our stage where both destructive technology and intolerance for others simultaneously exist." Sharon recalled her disgust at an event reported just a few weeks earlier. One of the extremely rigid Islamic countries was threatening to execute one of their own Muslim citizens for abandoning the faith—it would be difficult to imagine a stronger example of intolerance.

There definitely were many similarities in the world's religions. It seemed to Sharon that all religions sought a relationship with God, generally promoted positive values and encouraged constructive actions. Yet why had they so frequently morphed into aggressively intolerant institutions? Sharon wondered if perhaps the real problem wasn't religion itself, but an underlying flaw in the human character. Extremists occur in all areas, not just religious circles. Could there be a genetically driven need to control others? Or, at least a need to force others to share one's own world-view?

Continuing, Rob described a number of lesser-known messengers that had also attempted to give a similar warning to Earth's humans. "Dupre the Elder only lasted a few weeks before he was burned at the stake as a heretic in the sixteenth century. A mugger killed Joseph Schwartz, a New York City homeless man, before he could spread the message in the twentieth century. Humans unfortunately have not been interested in listening to advice. I also got the impression that we humans have managed to develop numerous threats to our own existence, whereas most life forms elsewhere in the cosmos succumbed to merely one."

Sharon could immediately see where this was heading, and voiced the key connection to their current crisis. "So after all those failed attempts to assist us, they realize we're getting very close to our own point of self-destruction. We're about to be another tick mark on the graph you saw, so they decided to make one last attempt to intervene."

"Right," Rob excitedly blurted. "They decided to send one last warning. But this time, no messenger would be used who could be ignored or whose message would be corrupted. They chose to give us something we're forced to relate to. What do people best react to?"

Rob leaned across the table and animatedly answered his own question. "A physical threat! A threat with fatal consequences! Give them a doomsday device that'll tax their ingenuity; let them utilize their esteemed technology and conclude for themselves that they must alter their ways to avoid certain destruction. This weapon will in fact destroy the Earth, but progressing as we are, in the grand scheme of the cosmos it will only curtail Earth's civilization by a few years."

Both Rob and Sharon knew they couldn't share this vision with the team, as it would only raise more questions—there was absolutely no way they could verify it. Perhaps they might be able to discuss it openly at some later point. But at least for the moment, they both had a heightened sense that at last they were on the right course. After the past frustrating weeks, they finally knew why the object's message had been sent.

Now there was yet another seemingly impossible task. They had to come up with a way to convince the world's diverse groups to halt their self-destructive actions.

Chapter 37
June 20, 11:30 AM

146,800,640 pounds

"The sacred land must be cleansed!" Someone had left the front-page article of that morning's New York Times on Rob's desk. Despite the disturbing commentary, he continued to read the inflammatory proclamation that was rapidly spreading throughout the Middle East. "All non-Muslims within two thousand kilometers of Mecca must immediately be removed! The daily earthquakes clearly are a punishment for allowing the holy land to be defiled by the presence of infidels."

The radical Islamic party Fatah al-Islam was raising the stakes with their own fervent interpretation of the object. The fiery group's message was gaining adherents throughout the Middle East almost as fast as Pastor Robinson's pronouncements to the Western world. Most of the area encompassed within this radius was already predominantly Muslim, with the very prominent exception of Israel. There were also large Christian populations in Lebanon and Ethiopia that were similarly threatened by this intimidating announcement.

The research team had recognized for some time that much of the world was now viewing this dilemma from a religious framework. The team would have to balance whatever steps they might eventually recommend to halt this object with widespread and conflicting religious interpretations. Extremists in many faiths were bombarding the airwaves and the newspapers with specific demands. Every day, more and more radical religious proclamations were surfacing in a desperate attempt to convince followers to appease the sender of the object. The message from the different fundamentalist groups was clear—the lethal seismic waves would only be halted by obeying the commands of God.

In many religious organizations, the more fundamentalist their beliefs, the less tolerant they were of the beliefs of others. Typical examples were those who followed the teachings of Pastor Robinson or those who blindly accepted the hostile declarations of the mullahs speaking for Fatah al-Islam. Insisting their beliefs were beyond criticism due to their sacred authority was reminiscent of most of civilization prior to the Renaissance. Even acts of violence could be justified if needed to convert others to one's religious viewpoint. It was perilous that many denizens of the twenty-first century still held such radical beliefs.

All major religions and long-lasting cultures have incorporated common moral principles such as honesty and responsibility. These principles have been tested by their consequences and found to be essential to stabilizing a society. Yet other ancient cultural and religious teachings that denigrated those outside one's group or promoted divisive behaviors have also endured through the centuries. Billions of people still followed ancient traditions without ever questioning if they were still valid in a more complex and multi-cultural world. Due to their sacred authority, religious decrees and edicts had rarely been subjected to any real critical review.

The team needed a broader perspective on how various religious organizations perceived what was happening. Consequently, they invited representatives to clarify how different groups around the world were reacting to the object. Randy had asked Father Brian McBride to provide the team with a more mainstream Christian interpretation of the object.

Father McBride, a distinguished Catholic theologian associated with the nearby New Jersey Archdiocese of Newark, was meeting with Sharon and four other researchers when Rob entered the team conference room. The priest's hair was completely grey, yet surprisingly thick for someone who appeared to be in his sixties. Despite the traditional clerical collar, he had a relaxed appearance. He leaned forward slightly as he spoke.

"I have no presumption of understanding this strange series of events. I'd only like to present a few reflections on what it might be." Older than anyone on the research team, Father McBride spoke with a calmness that they greatly appreciated after viewing the histrionics of the televangelists. Rob was immediately impressed with the articulate priest, whose comments flowed easily with a slight Irish brogue.

"Perhaps this destructive object was sent by God as a message to us. Yet what message? And if so, why wouldn't He have made clear what He wants us to do?" The priest explained that this was the gist of the debate occurring in countless mainstream churches. Synagogues, parishes, temples and mosques were all sites of oddly similar discussions.

"But God does not dictate what man should do—His gift of free will allows, even mandates that we must decide for ourselves the right course of action. So why would He send us something that would force us to act in a way to avoid our destruction? Wouldn't we then be acting due to force and not exercising our free will? Civilized humanity dismisses confessions made under torture and discounts statements made by prisoners of war. I believe God would similarly dismiss our actions if they were less than freely made, if they were in fact made under duress. This is a point that many of the more fundamentalist groups find difficult to resolve."

Rob couldn't help but wonder to himself, "But for those who pursued this line of thought, did we really have free will before this object arrived? If we make a decision to believe or do something based on a threat of eternal damnation or eternal reward, are we really acting in a free will situation? Perhaps the degree of free will is negatively correlated to the degree of belief in one receiving a just reward/punishment in an afterlife. This would be very troubling to many of the faithful—the implication that only non-believers, or more accurately, those who didn't believe in an afterlife of either heaven or hell, could actually have 'free will' in this life."

From years of participation on interfaith councils and teaching in several universities, Father McBride was used to working with people of all faiths. He had also dealt with secular thinkers who may or may not have believed in God and he suspected the team of scientists studying the object included an assortment of these viewpoints. He also understood one of their pressing questions: regardless of who created the object, did its presence indicate that a yet-to-be-determined action was required?

The astute priest proceeded with a few thoughts he hoped might be helpful to the team. "As you may be aware, we Christians try to follow the teachings of Jesus. In our attempts to be His disciples, we try to live our lives by acting as He would. In doing so, we eventually realize we must give up our selfish actions and try to be the hands of Christ in this world. We reflect God's love for us whenever we act to help our fellow man, whether that's by helping the disadvantaged, healing the sick or feeding the hungry. We look around and ask what acts of compassion Jesus would perform if He were walking around with us today."

Father McBride continued, "I personally fail to see how this object would aid us in acting as Christ would. So as to who sent this object, it's quite a conundrum. If it is from God, it significantly concerns the very issue of faith itself. One of the core aspects of all religions is belief—we believe in concepts without underlying tangible proof. The Bible is filled with references to the need for us to believe and have faith—Jesus himself states this on many occasions."

"Are you talking about belief in Biblical or modern-day miracles?" asked Rob. "That this same type of belief is needed to deal with unexplained events like the appearance of this object?"

"Not exactly. All of the miracles reported in the Bible occurred long ago, as we're well aware, and none of them can be subjected to any modern verification tests. My point isn't that you must believe in miracles, but that we accept as part of our faith some events that lack solid, confirmable proof of being caused by God. And since we accept these ideas without underlying proof, we're vulnerable to believe in other ideas that lack a verifiable explanation. My point is that if an inexplicable tangible object appears that we don't understand, it's a small step for many of the world's inhabitants to believe that it's a message to us from God."

Sharon interjected, "So are you saying that many religious people are viewing this as a test of their faith? The Bible is filled with stories of God sending plagues to force people to change their ways. Do they think God would halt this object, this modern-day plague, if we take some particular overt action?"

"Possibly. But specifically what action?" The conversation was animated as the priest continued, apparently enjoying the opportunity to talk with the team.

"Is this another test as with Abraham, where he was required to murder his son in order to show devotion to his God? If this is a twenty-first century remake of the same test described in the Old Testament, must we commit to an equivalent act to demonstrate our true devotion? God directed his message to Abraham as a personal command, requiring him to make an individual response. This message seems to be directed to all the inhabitants of the world. What would be the equivalent response for today's advanced world of almost seven billion inhabitants?"

Rob shuddered with a thought. "Some zealous faction could try to destroy a city to demonstrate devotion to their God. Could a hostile theocratic government destroy an entire country that they considered offensive to their worldview? Would they consider an area in the developing world to be a sufficient response to appease their vision of God? Abraham's command was to sacrifice his first-born son. Would that ancient act be more equivalent in today's world to destroying a location more along the lines of Paris or New York?"

The priest continued, "God gave Abraham specific instructions—what are ours? I personally don't believe that God would act in this way, threatening our very existence to elicit an action by us. But based on the news broadcasts of the past several days, it's apparent that millions of the world's citizens are viewing this from their religious perspectives. And there are more than a few fanatical groups claiming a 'sacrifice' will be necessary before this object ceases its relentless growth."

CHAPTER 38
JUNE 21, 3:30 PM

587,202,560 pounds

The press briefing room was packed and uncomfortably warm. The publicized topic for today's briefing was an update on how the world's best scientists thought this object was actually increasing in weight. Rob joined Randy at the podium as they prepared to address the tense gathering. The briefing was stressful for everyone as each reporter struggled to be the first to create the headline story for his respective paper or online audience. However, the primary cause of the enervating stress was the frightening awareness that everyone's life was in ever-increasing jeopardy.

"We're looking at several courses of action, and we haven't given up on searching for a solution." Randy attempted to ratchet down the angst in the room, but he knew better than anyone that there was diminishing room for optimism. His years of experience at least allowed his voice to project an air of calm, belying his inner thoughts.

"We believe whoever or whatever sent this object had a specific purpose in mind. If that purpose was to destroy our world, then we may have no recourse. But if it was to motivate us to a particular action and not actually destroy us, then we still have a chance for survival.

"Our attempts to explain the object's increase in weight have forced us to rethink how our cosmos operates. As we indicated in earlier press briefings, we suspect the increase in mass without a noticeable increase in size is due to its density increasing, similar to what exists throughout the universe within a neutron star or within a black hole. Both of these celestial phenomena are infinitely dense due to extremely high gravitational pressure. Neutron stars are visible, since they emit photons and other particles. Black holes, on the other hand, have so much more gravitational pressure that even light can't escape, leaving nothing visible from the outside."

By kicking off the briefing himself, Randy was attempting to bolster his image as the person in charge of the team. He was very conscious of Rob's public visibility, and for the first time in his career, Randy found himself less threatened by attention to his subordinates. Lacking his usual condescending tone, he willingly turned the briefing over to the team leader who seemed to have the best rapport with the media. "Rob Thornton will now provide a summary of our team's latest conclusions."

Taking one last sip from a glass of water, Rob knew he faced a difficult task: inform the wary journalists about arcane aspects of modern cosmology and simultaneously offer them enough hope for survival. How these journalists represented the planet's prospects to their audiences would be critical to how the world at large would eventually accept the actions the team would soon be proposing. Rob took a deep breath and launched ahead with his prepared speech.

"Astrophysicists are generally in agreement that black holes occur when a massive star burns up its nuclear fuel and gravity forces it to collapse into itself. One of the conundrums in astrophysics is just what happens to the mass that these black holes suck in and compress. We now know that there are millions of black holes scattered throughout the universe, and new ones are continually being formed. Their density is so great that even our concepts of space and time are not relevant within a black hole."

Rob continued, struggling to present their perplexing findings in comprehensible terms. "Does the material eventually get recycled, perhaps somewhere else in the cosmos? Or, could the material even be passed to another point in time? In 1976, the prominent physicist Stephen Hawking concluded that black holes were not entirely "black," and that they actually "evaporate" away. Small amounts of mass could radiate away in the form of photons, neutrinos and other subparticles. Could heavier particles also be transferred, and could this transfer be controlled by a being who actually understood this mechanism?"

The press agents were listening intently, trying to follow the mind-numbing concepts of cosmology, all the while hoping to hear Rob describe any possible way to survive this seemingly fatal object. Rob took another sip of water, trying to ignore the sweltering heat in the room. The air conditioning system apparently could not handle the large number of reporters who packed the room for this mid-afternoon briefing.

"We now theorize the mass that is increasing in the interior of this object is being transferred through a portal that we have not been able to measure or even detect. Whether this portal connects to something similar to a distant black hole in the cosmos, or even to another dimension outside our realm of experience, we can only speculate. In fact, this object could even be the seed of a new black hole being formed."

Still standing next to Rob at the podium, it occurred to Randy that he might need to deflect any later accusations that the team had withheld any information from the journalists. For the sake of providing a complete status on the team's research, Randy jumped back into the presentation with a few comments.

"I'll mention two other theories that our scientists have also proposed. The source of this increasing mass could also be the elusive dark matter that permeates the universe. Our galaxies would fly apart as they spin on their axis without an additional mass that we've not been able to observe. We believe that most of the mass throughout the universe is from this hidden dark matter. This may consist of exotic material, perhaps unknown varieties of heavy subatomic particles that don't combine with the particles that make up the matter we're familiar with. Could this dark matter be somehow compressed and transferred to this object?

"Another possible force that we have considered is dark energy. Ever since astronomers learned that the universe is expanding at an accelerating rate, the belief that there's a type of dark energy has also been proposed. Could this dark energy be used to counterbalance the compressing force of gravity? The intense gravitational force needed to maintain the extreme density of the object might be offset by harnessing a dark energy force that would keep the object from collapsing into itself or instantly drawing in everything in its immediate vicinity like a black hole. This would effectively be a controlled black hole."

Rob was now concerned that any additional comments from Randy would just further confuse the gathered journalists. It was essential to lay the groundwork for what actions they would soon be proposing to deal with the dilemma.

Rob took the lead again and clearly acknowledged the team's lack of progress. "Unfortunately, that's the extent of what we know and what we've theorized. The bottom line is what we've all feared—we're apparently too primitive in our understanding to attempt to halt or even affect the growth of this object. Apparently, stopping this object's expansion is only possible by whomever or whatever sent it."

The team had communicated their feeble understanding of how the object was expanding in weight. Although the explanation was unsatisfying to the media representatives, Randy and Rob had met the briefing agenda. Neither one of them was interested in opening up the meeting to general questions, since they could add no further clarity.

As Randy was about to step down from the podium, he made a final announcement to the press. "We have now halted all efforts to control the object. The entire team is now focused on understanding the message on the cube. We believe that we have a chance to survive if we respond adequately to the message we have been given. We will hold future briefings as soon as we determine the appropriate response."

The journalists were clamoring for further explanations, but Randy was insistent on wrapping up the briefing and getting the team back to work. "We've also scheduled another press briefing for tomorrow at this same hour. At that time we'll include a forecast of the amount of destruction we can expect in the coming days and weeks."

1,174,405,120 pounds

As usual, the daily briefing was lively with the reporters trying to get their questions addressed. Yesterday's session on how the object was increasing in weight had generated even more questions. Rather than answering specific queries, Randy needed to move quickly to present critical information to the media representatives.

"We now have a possible explanation as to why this device is here, which we will get to in a few minutes. First, Dr. Stephan Werner from the Max Planck Institute in Germany will recap our theories of the predicted consequences for the world. As you may recall from one of our first press briefings a few weeks ago, Dr. Werner reviewed a number of issues in modern cosmology. He was the first to recognize the similarity of the object's immense weight to the extreme density present in black holes and neutron stars. Professor Werner has been working with geologists and geophysicists around the world to better predict the effects from the object."

Dr. Werner joined Randy at the podium and immediately launched into an updated summary of the entire team's efforts at predicting the planet's future. He was not one to waste time or words. "The tremors generated by each growth cycle will continue to cause increasing destruction across the planet. Although we can no longer precisely locate the object, we believe it is now within the lower mantle of the Earth's interior, between 1,200 and 1,600 miles from the surface. As expected, the tracking beacon that we attached to the cube while it was still in the lab, failed soon after it descended into the Earth. In spite of this, we can roughly estimate the object's location by the pattern of seismic waves generated at each weight doubling cycle. The same equipment used throughout the world to identify earthquake focal points has been employed to triangulate these geophysical disruptions.

"Since the object sank through the Earth's crust, which is only twenty-five miles thick at this location, the tremors are now producing less ruptures and surface damage in the area surrounding New York. However, now the tremors radiate globally through the interior layers of the planet. Consequently, virtually all areas of the planet are now directly experiencing the tremors, even those almost eight thousand miles apart at opposite sides of the planet."

Dr. Werner clicked a remote transmitter that projected an image on a large screen at the front of the room. The image depicted a cross-section view of the Earth, with the different interior layers highlighted in various colors. One of the team members in the rear of the room dimmed the overhead lights slightly. The projected diagram also identified the depth and degree of liquidity for each layer, some of which were molten and others solid. Several of the news reporters briefly flashed back to childhood images of sitting in a science classroom, but they were undoubtedly paying more attention to this presentation.

As the scientist illuminated parts of the projected image with a green laser-light pointer, he continued. "The tremors radiate at varying speeds through the Earth's interior, through the upper crust layers of bedrock, sand and soil, as well as ocean floors. The tsunamis we are seeing across the world will continue to occur on a daily basis, coinciding with the object's cycles and the resulting after-shocks."

The screen image flashed to a world map. Bold red lines depicted the jagged boundaries of the Earth's eight major tectonic plates. After a few seconds, the projector superimposed another image over the first. Thinner red lines depicted the outlines of another twenty minor plates. The impact on the audience was immediate—every continent and practically every country in the world was physically close to a plate boundary.

"As you can see from the map, the Earth's crust was already covered with cracks between the tectonic plates. Every one of these boundaries represents a weak spot on what we like to think of as terra firma." Dr. Werner paused briefly as the reporters comprehended the truly global nature of this crisis.

"Most of our knowledge of earthquake activity is from studying existing fault lines and continental plate tectonics. Earthquakes have usually occurred at plate boundaries, close to the Earth's surface. Less frequent intraplate earthquakes occur at a much greater depth, propagating seismic waves over a much wider area. Our knowledge from previous seismic activity has proven to be almost useless in predicting the effects of these tremors. We obviously have no history of earthquakes generated by a sudden increase of mass inside the planet.

"To minimize loss of life, we continue to encourage evacuating areas most vulnerable to continued earthquake damage, obviously including all areas below dams, low-lying coastal regions, poorly constructed buildings and areas where hazardous materials are stored or in use." The weary professor continued, as if he were explaining self-evident facts to a mentally challenged audience. "We can also expect more and more fires from broken gas lines and electrical shorts, and a diminished ability to combat fires due to broken water pipes and blocked or damaged access roads."

"I don't get it!" shouted one of the more agitated press agents. "If we're facing doom, why even bother to try and minimize destruction from these daily earthquakes? From what I'm hearing, we'll all be dead within a few weeks no matter what we do."

Professor Werner frowned, not used to having someone interrupt one of his presentations. He recovered his composure quickly, recognizing the distressing effect of what he was describing. He belatedly realized there was an urgent need to identify possibilities for optimism.

"There still is a chance the object might stop increasing in weight when it reaches the densest part of the Earth's core. We have identified several factors that could affect it. The pressure of our planet's mass could offset the growth force, effectively neutralizing it. If the object descends to the center of the Earth, it will be subjected to pressure three million times greater than the pressure at the Earth's surface. It will also be subjected to temperatures up to seven thousand degrees Celsius, which is about as hot as the surface of the sun. Either one of these factors could alter or even halt the object's expansion."

Dr. Werner instantly recognized looks of hope in several of the nearby journalists. Although the professor was no longer optimistic about the world's fate, he was sensitive to the fact that any possibility of surviving would help the journalists continue to fulfill their role. There was definite value in the media promoting a sense of hope to the frightened people around the world. Yet as a scientist, he was uncomfortable with providing what he considered false hope.

Dr. Werner continued, "If the object stops increasing in weight at the Earth's center, this would permanently alter the Earth's equilibrium depending on where the mass finally settled. I should point out that we know relatively little about the interior of the Earth, particularly how the various layers interact. Most likely, the dense object would settle at the center of the Earth but it could possibly stabilize at some other point.

"Another factor that may affect the object is its increasing isolation. As the object descends, every successive foot of rock or magma gives more effective shielding from radiation, including cosmic rays. This is a key reason why scientists construct underground research labs as deep as possible. For example, the former Sudbury mine in Ontario houses a lab that is over a mile beneath the surface, primarily to isolate the lab equipment from such radiation. If an external signal or radiation is being used to control this object, the density of the Earth may isolate it.

"If the object's growth cycles are halted or somehow neutralized, there will be a permanent increased mass for the entire planet, and a corresponding increased gravitational force. This would be survivable, but it would permanently change our world. Our experiments in space exploration have provided us information on how earthbound processes behave differently in an environment with less gravity. We can extrapolate from many of these experiments to predict how life could change on an Earth with an increased gravity force."

Professor Werner paused, not for dramatic effect but in an attempt to pace himself. Although his voice remained strong, the toll of working excessive hours the past few weeks was evident. The dark rings under his eyes and his slightly slumped shoulders reflected how little he had slept over the past few weeks. He diligently continued his briefing.

"One of the most pervasive changes would be to the atmosphere itself, as airborne particles and chemicals stabilize at different heights, affecting radiation barriers and worldwide climate. As the weight of everything increases, so will the force required to fly, to move objects or to launch satellites. Growth patterns will be altered as processes that developed over millions of years in a stable gravitational force are disrupted and forced to adapt.

"Being as realistic as possible, the likelihood of our having to adapt to an altered world due to the object stabilizing is low. So far, we have detected no reduction in the rate of weight gain, despite the increasing pressure as it continues to descend within the Earth's interior. Our computer models project the most likely scenario to be a continuing increase in weight."

Professor Werner hesitated, but only briefly—he was not one to mince words. "If the expansion cycles do not stop, the resulting increase in gravitational force would eventually crush the entire planet into itself, and possibly even draw in any nearby celestial objects. Of course, we would all be dead long before the final implosion, most likely succumbing to the calamitous earthquakes, tsunamis and volcanic eruptions generated by the tectonic plates shifting with the planet's altered equilibrium. This object is now disrupting the internal layers of the planet that have stabilized over billions of years. How long can the planet survive? If the object's weight continues to double at its current rate, we estimate less than two weeks remain before the seismic activity will not be survivable. Immense earthquakes will occur on virtually every portion of the planet's surface."

The room was atypically quiet—even the sound of the fan on the projector was audible. Rob, noting the palpable sense of doom in the conference room, struggled to come up with a closing comment to the briefing. He didn't want to leave the press briefing on such a dismal note, but the world's citizens had to recognize their precarious state or they would not be receptive to the actions the team would soon be recommending. They needed to wrap up this session, and keep the team rolling on dealing with the object's message.

"Our only hope is that we've correctly interpreted the message encoded on the object," offered Rob. "As all of you know from previous briefings, the startling message we discovered on the object has caused us to redirect our efforts from attempting to halt the object's growth cycles. We, as well as others around the world, have been working to comprehend what is specifically expected of us by the object's message: 'Do unto others as you do unto yourselves'. We truly have nothing to lose if we're wrong, but at least a chance of surviving if we're right. At the next press briefing, we'll be presenting our conclusion as to why this object is here. We'll also be outlining our recommended response to the object's message."

1,174,405,120 pounds

Since the media first broadcast the inscription found on the object, a sense of futility had surged throughout the world. The hope that the object had been created by some radical party that could be dealt with was quickly evaporating. The governments of the world could deal with a demand for a ransom or for a specific political action, but now it appeared to many that the inscription was more of a "judgment". Was the message merely a statement of what humanity had failed to do throughout history? And was this failure the reason for humanity's destruction?

As with other periods in history when people faced a high probability of death, there were vastly different reactions. Countless people sought solace with their loved ones, but others resorted to violence against anyone they could blame for the situation. As the tremors grew daily, a number of individuals considered themselves free from the consequences their actions would incur in a normal situation and acted on their formerly suppressed desires. As the number of violent crimes radically increased, it seemed incongruous that attendance and fervor in religious communities likewise increased.

Jonathan Santone, the Channel 4 newsroom anchor, was just beginning a special 9:00 AM broadcast. Reports of earthquake and tsunami devastation had dominated the news for the past week, but within the past few days, the situation had deteriorated in another terrible direction. Civil disturbances were now appearing in several widespread parts of the world. It was frightfully apparent that in many areas, minority groups were being blamed for the world's destruction.

Jonathan Santone's haggard face filled the central LCD screen that was suspended in the lab's main conference room. It was evident the newsroom makeup artist could no longer hide the weariness in Jonathan's face. The sagging lines under each eye were passably covered, but the artist could not disguise the dull, tired eyes. Physical exhaustion from covering the expanding disasters was understandable—very understandable to the research team members who had been living a similarly grueling life for the past few weeks. Rob, Sharon and several other team members halted their discussion to view the live newscast.

"Civil unrest has escalated again in several widespread parts of the world. Today in Uganda, evangelical leaders were calling for the local Hindu and Muslim communities to repent and atone for not living by the dictates of the Bible. Strife between all three of these religious groups has existed in Uganda for many years, but the current earthquake devastation has exacerbated animosity between them.

"In Iran, several highly esteemed mullahs have accelerated their calls for all non-Muslims to recognize the one true faith and convert to Islam. The daily seismic activity has a particular impact on many Muslims, who have always believed the end of the world would occur on what they call the Day of Resurrection. Although exactly when this would take place is not specified, Muhammad himself indicated a number of signs that would occur close to the end times. One of these signs was that 'earthquakes would increase in number.' Perceiving the numerous earthquakes as a fulfillment of Muhammad's predictions, hundreds of thousands, perhaps millions, of frightened individuals are now rushing to convert to Islam.

"The murder of ethnic and religious minority members is suspected by radical groups in several countries in the Mideast and in Africa. Confirmed reports of over two hundred deaths have been received from Pakistan, Iraq and Syria. There is unconfirmed but reasonable evidence that thousands have been killed in northeastern Africa by roving bands of radicals. All these groups apparently believe the daily earthquakes are a punishment from God and that a self-styled 'cleansing' is needed. These zealots believe they are ridding the world of those who disobey and blaspheme their true God."

In addition to the daily tsunamis and earthquakes, another geological crisis was now being reported—the shifting tectonic plates were also triggering major volcanic activity. Many volcanoes that had been dormant for millennia were now active, and new ones were forming along plate boundaries. Preparations were underway to evacuate the entire Yellowstone National Park, due to the alarming fact that the elevation of the giant caldera that underlay most of Yellowstone was rising several inches every day. The magma chamber only a few miles beneath the surface was evidently expanding, causing the land above to dome upwards. Magma and noxious gases had already begun to seep through new fissures at the surface. Geologists speculated that the seepage was relieving some pressure in the underlying magma chamber, but a major eruption could still occur at any time.

Besides the destruction of local areas from flowing magma and noxious fumes, thousands of tons of volcanic ash were entering the atmosphere from volcanic activity in Indonesia. If the eruptions continued or worsened, the circulating ash would block much of the sun's energy from reaching Earth. The particulates in the atmosphere would cause major climate change similar to what had occurred with major eruptions in previous centuries. A supervolcano called Toba erupted in Indonesia around 74,000 years ago. The volcanic winter resulting from the particulates blown into the atmosphere contributed to a major cooling of the planet. According to some DNA researchers, the entire human population was reduced to only a few thousand individuals at that time. The same devastation could occur from the volcanic eruptions now being triggered by the object's expansion. Of course, this problem would only be relevant if the Earth survived the next few weeks.

As each day passed, the increasingly stronger tremors and the rapidly spreading panic had brought most of the world's inhabitants to a very desperate position. They were now eager to grasp at any possible solution, even if they did not agree on the source of the object or fully understand the rationale for a particular solution. From Rob and Sharon's perspective, this new receptiveness provided a glimmer of hope.

CHAPTER 41
JUNE 24, 10:30 AM

2,348,810,240 pounds

"Pascal's Wager!" Rob again had the team's attention, as they gathered in a conference room for another brainstorming session. "Pascal was a brilliant seventeenth century French mathematician, who incidentally is credited with establishing the foundation for decision theory and creating calculating machines. Like most post-Renaissance scientists, he struggled with the compatibility of science and religion, and in an attempt to persuade others to believe in God, established what's now known as 'Pascal's Wager'.

"In essence, the so-called 'wager' was a reason to believe in the existence of God, if traditional arguments proved unconvincing. Since he was part of the Christian world, he described the wager in terms of the Christian faith, although it's applicable to most religions. If the Christian (or Islamic or Judaic or Hindu) theme is true, specifically that God does exist, there is an afterlife and there is a judgment day to determine one's fate in the afterlife, then it's advantageous to be a believer. If after death an afterlife doesn't exist, you've lost nothing. But if it does exist, you'll have benefited by your belief. The potential value of believing is vastly better than the potential loss from not believing."

"Wait a minute. Why are we even talking about some esoteric theological issue?" Randy interjected. "How does this possibly relate to our dilemma?"

Rob continued, undeterred. "I just wanted to make sure we all understand that we're presenting the same argument to the world as Pascal, so it won't be too much of a stretch for the world's citizens to believe us. We humans have a very religious history. Most people, as believers in one religion or another, have already accepted similar logic whether they realize it or not. Now that we face annihilation, we have everything to gain by trying to satisfy the sender of this object, and nothing to lose if we're wrong. Like Pascal, who wasn't attempting to prove the existence of God with his 'wager', we're not establishing who sent this object or why it was sent. Pascal was just pointing out that it was advantageous to believe, just as we'll be promoting actions that we can't yet prove will help, but at this point can't hurt. In fact, we have our very survival to gain if we're correct."

Sharon, who had been silent up to this point but was evidently uncomfortable with the conversation, joined in. "You're right about why many people accept untestable beliefs, but personally I never could accept the 'wager' concept. If an omniscient God does exist, we assume his actions would be just and 'rational' for lack of a better term.

Why would such a God value more highly someone who professed blind belief based on a risk analysis? I'd prefer to think that a just God would more highly value someone who used whatever mental capacity they possessed to question their beliefs in a search for truth. Such a God would likely think less of someone who followed dogma merely to avoid a negative result."

Rob found himself in agreement with Sharon's thinking, but it wasn't relevant to the point he was making. "Yes, there are problems in this religious argument, but the widespread acceptance of 'Pascal's Wager' demonstrates that we may be able to promote a similar 'wager'. It also implies that we can get widespread acceptance of a plan to respond to the object's message."

"All right," Randy interjected. "So let's keep focusing on how to best respond to the message. Whatever recommendations we come up with, we'll need to review them with President Arbust at tomorrow's briefing. Any proposals can also be used to help the UN and other nations promote similar actions."

A radically different perspective was gaining momentum. Rather than attempting to halt the object's growth, efforts to interpret the specific meaning of the message were spreading to conventional groups across the entire world. The United States and the initial research team were no longer waging the only effort to stop the expansion of the object. The focus was now shifting to the world's governments, traditional religious organizations and even multinational businesses and organizations. Any of these groups could evaluate their own activities and determine how they could best demonstrate that they could live without destroying each other or the planet.

Due to daily destruction from seismic tremors, most nations had already halted their aggressive actions toward each other and instead were focusing on survival. Feuds and long-standing disagreements between countries were of relatively minor importance when all nations contended with lethal seismic activity every day.

As soon as the investigation team had forecast the global impact of the object, the United States had uncharacteristically but sensibly involved the world community. The team had invited representatives from a number of countries to the daily briefing of the team's investigation. As it turned out, this had been essential in convincing the entire world of the veracity of the research results, as well as the projected global impact from the object. Distrust among many nations led to their sending scientific and political representatives to observe the object first-hand in the lab before it had sunk into the Earth's crust. Some of these esteemed representatives were now available to assist the team in identifying how best to respond to the object's message.

The original crisis team that analyzed and attempted to understand the device had completed their mission. Those scientists who had exclusively focused on understanding how the object could be expanding in weight were now preparing to leave the team, to return to their homes to face the ever-increasing global threat with their families. Most of the scientific community had painfully concluded that any further analysis would not help stop this doomsday device.

From Randy's viewpoint, there was no doubt about who should provide the core leadership for this next phase of the team's investigation. Rob Thornton's success in locating and decrypting the object's message insured his continuing central role in the reorganized group. After working together for the past several weeks, Randy reluctantly had to admit that Rob was widely accepted as the key expert on the team—it would have been impossible to move the effort forward without him. Likewise, Sharon Catwold's success at keeping the diverse investigators focused on the most productive avenues of research guaranteed her continued central role on the team. Despite the diminished likelihood of the object providing any new weaponry for the Department of Defense, Taylor McCracken's alleged Pentagon relationship ensured his continued participation.

The worldwide destruction continued to worsen every day, providing ever-increasing pressure to determine how best to respond to the object's message. As the modified team resolutely continued their efforts, the U.S. government, overseeing this investigation from the start, was no longer the primary organization trying to resolve the dilemma. Groups around the entire world were intensely struggling to answer the question: What response is expected by whoever sent this object? The disparate groups could initiate changes within their own realm of authority based on how they best interpreted the ancient edict: "Do unto others as you would do unto yourself."

Chapter 42
June 25, 11:00 AM

4,697,620,480 pounds

Most of the scientists who initially worked with the investigation team had now permanently left the lab complex. Of the technical support members on the team, only the engineers performing the ongoing monitoring were still active at the project site. Randy, Rob and Sharon consulted with the original selection committee that had identified the initial members of the team. Given the new direction—responding to the message on the object—the committee identified numerous individuals who could be significant contributors. Randy had persuaded a number of these distinguished persons to join the team that by now had morphed into an eclectic international body.

Since the extent of environmental damage may have been the catalyst for the object's arrival, several leaders of environmental protection organizations were now included in the group. Donald Dellwood was clearly the most widely known figure enlisted. Numerous international organizations had recognized his achievements in highlighting how the global consumption of resources was no longer sustainable, and how it was threatening world stability. Dr. Dellwood had received many awards for his efforts, including the prestigious United Nations Environment Prize. His efforts had been instrumental in relating environmental damage to the resulting negative impact on both far-flung communities and future generations.

Randy also convinced several representatives from the World Health Organization to join the team, providing insight into the most critical health and welfare problems across the world. Mainstream ecumenical councils had also nominated a few additional delegates who were actively contributing suggestions from their different religious perspectives.

Since the worldwide media first reported the strange object, there had been several unsuccessful efforts to convene the UN General Assembly to address the problem. Promoting international cooperation among nations had always been one of the core functions of the UN, particularly when dealing with global problems. Calling the General Assembly to a special session, however, had lagged since it required a majority vote of the UN members. Since many of the members had initially doubted the bizarre news reports, earlier votes had failed to pass.

As the area of earthquake damage extended globally, leaders and scientists of virtually all nations eventually acknowledged that the object was the cause of the seismic events. Once this relationship became widely accepted, the UN Security Council requested a special session of the General Assembly. As mandated in the UN charter, only nine Council members were needed to request an emergency special session, to be held within twenty-four hours of the request. The United States had already cooperated in this move, originally thinking global-wide support might help find a way to destroy the object.

As the UN and other world bodies struggled to find ways to respond to the object's directive, everyone was keenly aware that there was no time to waste. The experts that Randy had assembled needed to develop a unified response that could be used by the dissimilar groups within the world community. Whatever actions they recommended would need to be both reasonable and acceptable to the varied cultures and nations throughout the entire world—a daunting task. Throughout the entire history of humanity, attaining worldwide agreement on significant actions had only rarely been achieved.

As with all diverse gatherings, opinions and priorities were radically different among the team members. In spite of this, all present were cognizant of the immediate need—verify the theory that overt actions would somehow affect the device. Their task was to select an action to implement as soon as possible to test the belief that doing so could actually affect the object.

Randy quickly introduced a few new members to the team, and unnecessarily restated again the urgency they faced. Now acting more as a facilitator for the team discussion, he seemed relieved to turn over the discussion lead to Sharon. Having been involved from the beginning, Sharon was further ahead in her thoughts than the recently included team members. For that matter, her thinking was usually further ahead than that of her peers. She was ready with an initial proposal and lost no time in presenting her opinion.

"What do we do first?" Sharon asked. "If we accept the dictate literally about 'Doing unto others …' my vote is to quickly stop organized violence against each other. What are the most egregious violent actions going on in the world that we could halt very quickly? Declared wars and genocidal efforts seem to be the most obvious choices. We need an urgent cease-fire by all nations engaged in warfare. The UN could orchestrate an agreement by all nations to abide by a global cease-fire and resolutely commit to negotiate their differences peaceably."

The group members debated whether planned warfare could be the reason, or at least one of the reasons, why someone sent the object. Rob provided a few observations that could add support to pushing initially for an anti-violence agreement.

"If we were being observed by an entity, one of the most striking aspects of our planet's civilization would be the degree of violence we commit. Throughout our history, man has continuously resorted to war and even genocide.

"The frequency of war is clearly documented in early Egyptian texts, the Hebrew Bible and ancient Greek literature, and warfare continues today. Homer's ancient story of the Iliad clearly depicts man's preoccupation with violence thousands of years ago. The grotesque realities of war have always been counterbalanced by a glorification and revering of warrior heroes. Apparently, the human condition accommodates being both revolted by violent acts and attracted to the excitement of violent battles.

"Civilization has definitely improved in many regards over the years. Acts considered unconscionable today were commonplace up until just a few centuries ago: barbaric acts used for entertainment, torture as a typical punishment, or homicide to settle disagreements."

Randy interrupted, "Remember, we're trying to identify reasons why the object has been sent to us. From what you've described, it sounds like we've already become a less violent species."

"One would like to think so," Rob responded. "If you counted acts of violence as a percentage of population, past eras were definitely more violent. But the combined effect of our huge global population and our modern weaponry has led to the loss of life in unprecedented numbers.

"We prefer to think of our bloodthirsty history as being in the distant past, in a less civilized era, but that's hardly the case. The twentieth century was the bloodiest in history in terms of numbers of people killed. More than ninety million people were murdered in the past hundred years, and I'm not referring just to battle casualties in warfare. The six million Jews killed by the Nazis is the most infamous travesty, but the Nazis also murdered three million Soviet POWs, two million Poles, half a million Gypsies and others. Many people don't know that even these huge numbers are dwarfed by the twenty million Soviets that perished under Stalin's purges, or the thirty million Chinese who were killed under Mao Zedong, most of whom died during their 'Great Leap Forward'."

Taylor objected, "But those mass murders are still history, at least one or two generations back. Haven't we progressed beyond those horrific days?"

"Not really," countered Rob immediately. "In the 1970's, 25 percent of Cambodia's population, 1.7 million people died from systematic killing, starvation, overwork or disease under the brutal Khmer Rouge. Almost three million people were murdered in Sudan just since the late 1980s, and the killing continues in the Darfur region. Also in the 1990s, the Hutu-led military of Rwanda killed eight hundred thousand of their own country's Tutsi citizens. Genocide is unfortunately a defining and very visible trait of our species."

Rob moved quickly ahead with his proposal. "I agree with Sharon that this could be the most flagrant contradiction to 'do unto others as you would do unto yourself'. Somehow, we need to get the nations of the world to halt genocide and warfare, and get this agreement as quickly as possible. If we've interpreted the object's message correctly, this concrete action could affect the object. It also seems to me the United Nations is the only forum that can quickly coordinate such a global agreement."

As expected, Taylor was the most hostile to this suggestion. If nothing else, he was predictable. "The UN? Good luck in convincing our government to knuckle under to a defective world body. The UN can't even clean up their own scandals. Why don't we just act on our own, and keep our options open?"

Millions of people shared Taylor's negative view of the United Nations, particularly in the United States. The team needed to address these objections if their recommendation was to have any chance of success in convincing others outside the team.

"Every organization has problems," rebutted Rob. "We're not looking for a perfect governing body and we're not expecting to attain a perfect world. Hostile individuals and factions will always exist and humanity will always have to deal with them. Still, we have an urgent need for a world body to minimize hostilities—no individual country can attempt this. Our world is too interconnected and too dependent on other's actions for any nation to act unilaterally. Modern technology and commerce have shrunk our global village to the point where even local conflicts can now have global significance."

Not willing to concede, Taylor shot back. "The UN has never been able to enforce its own resolutions—why expect it to now?"

Rob countered, "Any new resolution banning war would have to be accompanied by an agreement from all countries to abide by any decisions arbitrated through the UN, and also to commit resources to enforce such decisions globally. As with any group, the UN needs adequate resources to enforce its decisions, something that's been lacking in the past. It has to be given both the authority and the means to be assertive in implementing its decisions. At a minimum, a permanent force of professional peacekeepers and relief experts is essential for quick deployment when needed."

After considerable debate, Randy took control of the discussion, "I agree we should push for an anti-warfare policy. There are obviously lots of other things that might have prompted this object being sent—lack of civil rights, poverty, discrimination—but waging a war has to be the most blatant contradiction to the 'do unto others as yourselves' edict."

Randy acknowledged the concerns about relying on the UN to implement a global cease-fire agreement. "This object could have arrived anywhere in the world. I believe it's significant that the sender specifically chose the UN, so it seems reasonable to me that we use the UN to respond to this object. We're all aware the makeup of the UN needs to be updated if it's truly to represent the entire globe. The antiquated post-WWII configuration of the UN perpetuates the inequitable status among the members. It's been over sixty years since its creation, but the real power in the UN Security Council is still limited to the original five victors of World War II. But revamping the UN can occur after we resolve our immediate crisis."

As Randy continued, the nods of concurrence from the team members indicated their unanimous agreement. The group agreed there was little value in continuing the debate—time was running out and the team needed to act on their best available option.

"Let's focus on just this one anti-warfare issue at the briefing with President Arbust this evening." Several core members of the team were scheduled to fly to Washington for a 6 PM Oval Office briefing with the president, the president's key staffers and the UN ambassador.

Over the past week, a groundswell of effort had been slowly rising across the world as individuals and vastly diverse organizations were deciding for themselves how they could best respond to the "do unto others ..." message. Religious assemblies were the quickest to act, calling for tolerance toward numerous "others" who had been marginalized for centuries—minority ethnic groups and members of other religions. Those quickest to move, not surprisingly, were those who interpreted the object's message as a direct commandment from God.

A number of both conservative and liberal Protestant councils quickly issued directives to their members, the Vatican released several papal proclamations and numerous Islamic mullahs issued edicts. Although many of these diverse religions believed that God had dramatically sent this "Final Commandment," their actions were all effectively oriented toward the same goal—treating others as we would treat ourselves.

People around the world were now recognizing that making such decisions was not restricted to large organizations: governments, religious groups and multi-national corporations. Individuals could also modify their everyday actions to be more helpful to less fortunate people. The widespread emergencies from the seismic tremors provided an immediate hands-on opportunity for millions of citizens to help their neighbors. Levels of cooperation across ethnic and religious lines increased everywhere as people struggled to survive against this common threat.

Not needing to convene legislatures, a few autocratic governments had already begun to enforce changes and halt armed conflicts within their own borders. Factions waging internal conflicts in Somalia and Zimbabwe had already suspended their hostilities. Surviving the daily seismic activities had become the highest priority for most people.

Establishing an anti-warfare resolution that the world's nations could support would be a revolutionary event. The UN had independently been struggling for the past several days to determine the best way to respond to the object's message. Along with other international bodies, they had already proposed stopping ongoing wars. But lack of support from the world's only superpower stymied their progress, the one country whose military expenditures exceeded the entire rest of the combined world. The United States government had to take an active role, or any such resolution would be relatively meaningless.

CHAPTER 43
JUNE 25, 6:15 PM

9,395,240,960 pounds

"So I'll be the president who subjugated our nation's laws to the United Nations." President Arbust was disconsolate, as the realization grew that the planet's inhabitants would have to work together as one people, rather than from their own national perspectives. "If we'd known, we could have controlled changes to the whole UN organization, and kept it compliant with our national interests."

Randy stared at his president, the one who appointed him to lead this team, and the one to whom much of the world was still waiting for leadership. The sinking feeling Randy was experiencing was rapidly turning to one of despair. Randy winced from a sudden wave of nausea as he realized the president still didn't get it. The world was about to end, and he was still trying to maintain the nationally-centric policies that had brought the world to this dismal point.

Managing to compose himself, Randy struggled to find words that President Arbust would understand. "But sir, you do realize this is something we can't negotiate—we've been given an ultimatum. If it helps to view it in more familiar terms, we must 'unconditionally surrender'. But we're not surrendering to one of our existing enemies— the entire world must do likewise, and as the world's superpower, we need to lead the way and publicly commit to a new world order."

President Arbust gazed out the large window behind his desk in the Oval Office, sitting in silence. None of the meeting participants wanted to be the first to break the uncomfortable silence in the room. None of the participants was eager to point out what was obvious to everyone in the room, probably even to President Arbust.

Sharon, attempting to remain respectful yet exasperated by wasting precious minutes, took the initiative. "Mr. President? Do you want an estimate of the remaining time till the next growth cycle?" Not very subtle, but she had to prod the president and the meeting forward.

"Sure," the president sighed, not taking his gaze from the window.

"19 hours, Mr. President. The UN body is convening this evening as we speak, and we need to direct our ambassador to support their anti-war accord. If we can act before the next growth cycle, we may be able to avoid another expansion."

Randy tried to reason with the disheartened president. "Even the most ardent nationalists who considered any world body to be anathema are now calling for us to change course. Decades of acting unilaterally and stonewalling international cooperation have only worsened our situation. With all its faults, the UN is the only worldwide body that can coordinate these actions. The fact that the sender selected the UN as the recipient of the directive only strengthens our belief that we need to function through this organization."

The president feared the anti-war accord might be only the first of many major actions to further comply with the object's directive. The team had explained the first global action needed to be something the world could initiate relatively quickly, and the UN's humanitarian council was already well informed where warfare was occurring in dozens of locations across the world. Representatives from these respective nations had all been involved in the UN deliberation.

Over half of the nations currently involved in conflicts had already concurred with the anti-war resolution; most of the rest were waiting for the United States to commit. Besides U.S. military spending exceeding the rest of the entire world's military budgets, the recent policy of taking preemptive action when it perceived a threat to its interests had only demonstrated to the world the arrogance of the U.S. government. The nations were looking for a sea change in attitude from the world's superpower, for a sign that the United States would join the world community as an equal rather than as one that only participates when it could determine the rules. The global anti-war resolution would be a useless measure if the United States did not join in the accord.

After President Arbust dismissed the team, he again polled his trusted advisors for any other method of dealing with the object. But as his staff had been telling him for the past few days, there was no way to control the object. There was no alternative, as President Arbust reluctantly had to admit. The president formally gave his UN Ambassador instructions to endorse the anti-war accord.

The ambassador left to return to New York, in time to join the following morning's general session. The core team members also returned to New York to prepare to monitor the object's next growth cycle, and President Arbust retired with little hope for any sleep.

CHAPTER 44
JUNE 26, 9:00 AM

9,395,240,960 pounds

The General Assembly Hall of the UN was packed as the session was about to begin. Each of the 192 represented countries was allotted six seats—three for their delegates and another three for their alternates. A cacophony of languages filled the impressive room with its unusual concave sides and its beautiful overhead dome. Virtually all of these same delegates had been present when the previous night's session was suspended at 11 PM. Most of the representatives had conferred overnight with their respective governments and were ready to resume the discussion. Debating speakers were queued to address the full assembly, continuing the debate on what actions to implement first. The first spot in the queue had been abruptly reassigned to the U.S. ambassador following a late night phone request from the White House.

The area reserved for media representatives was also overflowing with film crews from major networks around the world. Unlike most United Nations discussions, the global media had been willingly broadcasting this debate for the past several days. Desperate citizens across the world were anxious to see a united response to the object—any response that might somehow halt the daily seismic destruction. Citizens in numerous countries were pressuring their own recalcitrant governments to join the overwhelming majority of countries who favored the anti-war resolution.

As the president of the General Assembly called the session to order promptly at 9 AM, the U.S. ambassador to the United Nations left his official delegate's seat and moved toward the speaker's podium at the front of the General Assembly room. The moderator turned the floor over to the ambassador, who had the full attention of all members. The ambassador wasted no time or words in announcing what the international body eagerly sought.

"Thank you, President of the General Assembly. Thank you, Secretary General. Given the urgency of our situation, I have only a brief statement to offer this morning. The United States unequivocally supports the proposed anti-war resolution and agrees to abide by all UN decisions in arbitrating differences. The U.S. legislature will be convening this afternoon to ratify this agreement."

The applause was immediate and lasted a full minute. The ambassador continued after the clapping died down, "Furthermore, we will be proposing a number of similar peace-oriented resolutions in the immediate future. Thank you."

Once recognized as the moral leader of the world, the United States unfortunately had recently lost that position after a series of ill-conceived foreign policy actions. Much of the world now viewed America with fear rather than respect, and it would undoubtedly take decades to restore the country's image and credibility. This new policy announcement would begin the movement to regain that position.

After having debated the anti-war resolution for the past several days, the General Assembly was able to rapidly conclude the discussion and take a formal vote. Ninety-four percent of the delegates voted in favor of the resolution, including all of the permanent members of the Security Council.

Additional actions would be difficult to initiate if there were no change in the object's growth. The core team would be recommending additional actions anyway, in case the initial UN resolution and scattered worldwide actions were inadequate to affect the object. However, the team knew it would be extremely difficult to promote their theory without tangible results. The upcoming cycle would determine their next move.

By the time the assembly session closed, there were only two hours remaining until the next projected increase in the object's weight.

Chapter 45
June 26, 1:00 PM

9,395,240,960 pounds

"What if we're wrong? What if there's some other explanation for the object?" Sharon could never stop thinking about their dilemma. Even during what might be their last few weeks alive, she heroically stayed focused on their mission—to halt this destructive object.

Sharon had joined Rob in his office to thrash out additional ideas while they waited for the next cycle time, less than an hour away. The smell of coffee never seemed to clear from the room, which was fine with both of them since they considered whatever caffeine boost the copious cups of java provided couldn't hurt. Although the research complex was large and the individual offices were spacious, after the past few weeks the familiar office layout seemed much smaller. For that matter, like the world shrinks around those confronting a potentially fatal situation, all events not relevant to somehow affecting the object were now meaningless to Sharon and Rob.

When working with the entire research team, the two of them spent much of their time just down the hall in a lab conference room. Yet most of their lives for the past few weeks had been spent brainstorming together right in this office. While unspoken, they both recognized a growing bond between them. Both Sharon and Rob wondered if it was solely driven by their shared efforts to first stop, then to understand, and finally to decide how best to respond to the object.

Sharon leaned back in the swivel chair next to Rob's desk and voiced a nagging concern. "What if actions aren't being sought and this object is merely informing us how long we've ignored the message? Essentially, Judgment Day for humans has already occurred and we've failed."

The same troublesome idea had occurred to Rob and he had already given thought to it. "We're working on the assumption that there's a rational reason for this intervention. This might not be valid—there's no logical requirement that any advanced civilization would have to act in ways we think of as rational. For that matter, there's no logical requirement even for a God to act rationally. The ancient Greeks and most early religions viewed their gods as capable of acting very capriciously and irrationally. But almost everything we've discovered since the Age of Enlightenment lends credence to the consistency of causes and effects, at least above the molecular level.

"So I believe there's a definite reason why this message was delivered. The threat initially was very limited and it has progressed steadily in a very measured manner, so I'm convinced we're being given time to act upon it. If the die were already cast, there'd be no need for the delay of these past several weeks. I suspect whoever has the capacity to create this object also has the capability to destroy us immediately if they so desired."

"I suppose you're right. Anyway, it's too frightening to think that someone could just be toying with us, that some advanced civilization could be methodically destroying our world without any opportunity for us to respond," Sharon sighed.

Refocusing on the immediate task, Sharon ended her depressing thoughts by making a suggestion. "Let's head over to the monitoring equipment in the lab—we don't have long to wait for our answer. If we've misunderstood the object's message, we'll know it very soon." They grabbed their half-empty coffee mugs and walked the few steps down the hall to C Lab.

Rob and Sharon knew Randy would be present in the lab, but they were a little surprised to also see at least half of the core team members. Their colleagues were scattered around the room in small groups, either watching the monitoring screens or anxiously discussing other actions the team could have taken. There was a lot of nervous anticipation in the room—what would happen at today's cycle was absolutely critical.

The lab where most of the testing occurred was still the central monitoring site for the underground seismic activity. It was astonishing for Rob and Sharon to realize that it had only been two weeks since the object had descended through the floor. The center of the room where the floor had been severed from the surrounding building structure was essentially the same. The underlying rock strata, which had shifted from seismic activity following earlier growth cycles, had altered the initial hole so that less than a hundred feet were now visible from the surface. Although the descending object had originally formed a deep vertical tunnel in its wake, the shifting layers of strata in the Earth's crust subsequently filled it. The object was still descending within the molten core area, and so far, the intense heat and pressure within the Earth had not affected it.

The lab could only accommodate a small contingent of media reporters, much less than was possible in the larger media conference room. Security had allowed representatives from the six largest media outlets to enter the lab and they had positioned themselves and their cameras in the rear of the lab. Many of the same crew who had been present at earlier expansion cycles were also present to witness today's cycle. Everyone present knew his or her personal risk, but given the situation, there really was nowhere on the planet that was safe from the seismic activity. The underlying rock strata of the New York area actually provided one of the more stable surfaces.

"Just a few more seconds left," Rob thought, although he wasn't sure if he had also said it aloud. The anxiety in the lab was palpable, as millions, perhaps billions of prayers were being said around the world. Those with access to the news media were riveted to their TVs or radios, regardless of the time zone in which they lived. The citizens of the world were about to find out if the actions approved by the UN delegates were on the right track, or if all of their efforts were to no avail.

The room became deathly silent. The cooling fans of the monitoring equipment and the media's telecommunication equipment made the only sound in the room. Rob glanced briefly at Sharon, who was staring intently at an overhead monitor. Everyone's eyes and all the television cameras were focused on the same monitor—the one displaying the remaining time. Only seconds remained.

2 ...
1 ...
0 ...

The monitor displaying the countdown clock froze with only a zero on the display. The panel of surrounding screens all reflected new data within seconds, and most importantly, the graph line on the monitor showing the current mass of the object conspicuously jumped.

"The damn weight is still increasing!" Rob swore to himself.

Desperate sighs could be heard around the room— the team had placed so much hope in having correctly interpreted the message on the object. They had been so confident that the global agreement to halt warfare would convince the sender to stop the object's growth. It had not. The seismic events would soon ripple through the Earth and inform everyone who was not already monitoring the news.

After a few more seconds, another monitor showed the newly calculated mass of the object. Rob's immediate response was a sickening nausea, followed by a growing sense of despair in that it would soon be over for everyone after several more cycles.

Just then, everyone in the room heard Sharon erupt, "Check monitor 3! Look at the magnitude!"

Rob and the others immediately glanced at the third overhead display. The monitor graphed the increased weight of the object from the first observed cycle. Every cycle was exactly twice the size of the previous one. This one was clearly less than double.

The object *had* been affected, for the first time in the past twenty-five cycles.

"We *did* affect it!" Sharon shouted, and the room erupted in cheers. "If it had doubled again, it would be at 18.8 billion pounds—but it's now clearly less. The monitor shows 17.7 billion pounds." One of the lab techs quickly calculated that it had expanded by exactly 88 percent, rather than the 100 percent expansion for every one of the previous cycles.

"We did it! We *are* on the right course!" Randy was exuberant, shouting across the room to Rob and the others. "We were wrong in assuming the object would stop immediately, but it has slowed down. This slowdown is a direct signal that we're on the right track; it's a signal that we need to continue our actions to effect a total halt."

Everyone in the lab was excited, some cheering and some in tears. The merriment was short-lived, however, as they all knew that despite the reduced expansion of the object, massive tremors would soon be destroying many areas around the globe. Since these seismic tremors inevitably would at least shake if not damage local areas as well, most of the press media quickly left the lab. Many of them preferred to wait outdoors until the initial seismic waves subsided.

As they left C Lab, Rob pulled Sharon aside as they walked down the hall back toward his office. He couldn't wait to express a thought that he didn't wish to convey in the lab. In fact, he now realized Sharon was the only person with whom he could share this idea. She was the only one who would understand what he really meant.

"You know, in one respect it's probably best that the object didn't completely stop its expansion. If it had, think how many people would have thought that this one action had adequately satisfied the sender. Any additional actions would have been much more difficult or even impossible to sell if the crisis had been abruptly eliminated."

"You're right. Apparently, it takes a dire situation to get people to agree on any global-wide changes. When I was studying economic issues for the Peace Corp, I recall reading an apt quote from Milton Friedman. 'Only a crisis—actual or perceived—produces real change' because after a crisis '… the politically impossible becomes politically inevitable.' So by only reducing the rate of expansion in weight, the crisis continues. The Earth is still on a certain path to destruction, just at a slower pace.

"We've got to get rolling on pushing the additional changes." As usual, Sharon already had a number of ideas for the next phase of action.

CHAPTER 46
JUNE 27, 9:00 AM

17,663,053,005 pounds

"The United States proposes a resolution for all nations to vastly reduce their military spending. We further propose that all nations commit to destroying their weapons of mass destruction: nuclear, chemical and biological." The U.S. ambassador to the UN was again addressing the General Assembly. The United States, as well as the rest of the world, wanted to move quickly on the momentum established from the previous day.

When the applause finally ended, the U.S. ambassador continued, "Throughout history, humanity has spent a tremendous portion of its resources on military activities. Given the long record of aggressive actions and man's distrust of others, it has always been easy to justify funding both defensive and offensive capabilities. Shifting our expenditures away from military spending will undoubtedly be difficult. Yet given that every nation and every citizen is now facing imminent destruction, it is imperative for all of us to radically shift our national priorities."

The U.S. ambassador had the utmost attention of the delegates, who were eager to hear just how much change America was prepared to make. "After this assembly passed the anti-war resolution yesterday, the object's expansion was reduced for the first time in the past twenty-five expansion cycles. All the nations of the world need to proceed quickly with additional peace-oriented actions to provide further proof that we understand the object's message. Consequently, the United States hereby declares its intention to reduce virtually all of its military activities. We challenge all other nations to join us in this commitment and do likewise." The assembly erupted in applause, providing an immediate indication that they would undoubtedly approve the resolution.

With the bulk of $550 billion that was currently budgeted to the various Department of Defense organizations, and another $160 billion to fund current military operations, there would be vast funds to reallocate. The rest of the world's expenditures on military spending amounted to another $500 billion annually that would likewise need to be reallocated.

The ambassador continued, "If the device completely stops increasing in weight, there will be time to determine how best to absorb the massive economic disruption from such a major shift in spending priorities. It will undoubtedly take years to determine how we can best implement this radical change. Today, the United States is formally announcing that we have begun a review of our entire national agenda, and will be reworking our government's practices in light of this new directive."

In the past, such a radical statement would have been met with utmost skepticism, both in the international community as well as in the fifty states. This time, however, it was widely recognized as the emergence of a new world order. The slowdown in the object's growth was generally accepted as validation that continuing the same approach would actually stop the object's expansion. The citizens of the world, so close to annihilation, were ready to take whatever actions were necessary to survive. The human survival instinct that helped propel man's evolution through millennia was still a fundamental and powerful force.

Back at the lab facility, the team continued brainstorming the next actions to propose. Although the object's growth had slowed after passage of the anti-war resolution, the seismic destruction was still increasing each day, albeit at a reduced rate. There was no respite for the team members who were excruciatingly aware they had to continue to work as rapidly as possible.

The team's immediate task was to identify a list of top priority issues to address. The members realized they were no longer making recommendations solely to the U.S. government, but to all governments, the UN and other worldwide organizations. The team also hoped that many individuals and local groups throughout the world would likewise initiate and support similar recommendations.

After briefly suspending their meeting so the group could watch the televised address at the UN, the entire team was energetically coming to an agreement on their overall approach. Randy summed up their findings. "I want to clarify our strategy so we don't waste any valuable time. As far as determining what further actions would best address the "do unto others as yourself" edict, we agree that anything to be proposed must be evaluated by its long-term impact. Any recommendations have to improve the condition of the planet or its inhabitants without creating further damage."

Taylor had been worrying about how much of the Defense Department budget should remain. Before the team settled on any more recommendations, he wanted to make certain everyone present realized security threats would always exist.

"Even without threats from foreign countries, we still need to provide policing here and abroad. And we still need Homeland Security to continue the battle against terrorists, whether they're home-grown or come from anywhere in the world," said Taylor.

Rob took the lead in the ensuing argument. "Yes, unfortunately we'll always have fanatics pursuing their goals. But this event has drastically affected their recruiting capability and even their objectives. Many radical fanatics have been motivated by a relatively simple concept of what the world should look like—and were confident regarding the specific rules to run their preferred world. This event has introduced a complexity into their world-view that just doesn't fit. They'll be forced to question how this object could possibly occur in their black-and-white view of the world.

"I suspect our Homeland Security will continue to counter rogue terrorist actions, but the organization will most likely transform into a more worldwide Interpol type of agency. The world's citizens will eventually react to terrorist acts in far-flung locales the same as they would to local acts. We need to be just as enraged by a terrorist act killing scores of citizens in Iraq, India or Chechnya as we'd be if it occurred in America."

One of the techs monitoring the object from the lab burst into the conference room. It was just a few minutes past 1:46 PM so there was no question as to what triggered the interruption. The tech blurted out the latest status of the object—its mass had increased again by exactly 88 percent. As the team had expected, the object's mass would continue to increase while they developed the next actions. It also was evident that the deaths and injuries from the seismic tremors would continue to escalate every day.

Acutely aware of the dwindling amount of time, the team strained to keep their personal fears from diverting their concentration. All of the team members silently decided to remain in the conference room for the inevitable tremors that would soon shake the surrounding area. As with the previous few days, the shaking at the lab complex was expected to be minimal due to the solid rock strata underlying that area of New York.

Although they knew it was impossible to know exactly how many more expansion cycles the Earth could withstand, everyone presumed it was only a matter of days, perhaps a week at most. Even if the team worked nonstop, it would take several more days to develop the actions and coordinate them with both the U.S. government and the UN.

Sharon brought the discussion back to the immediate issue with a straightforward question. "So what's our plan?"

Trying not to appear too forceful to the gathered group, Sharon chose her words carefully. "We need to clearly identify the most critical areas where we've failed to 'treat others as ourselves'. We need to create a target list not only for the U.S. government to act on, but for all governments and international organizations to draw from. The governing powers of each country will have to determine what specific steps for them to take, but this list should highlight key areas for them to address. If this device halts completely, the UN and the world's governments will have ample time to continue the dialogue and fine-tune the precise actions."

It was going to be an exhausting day and night of discussion. Although Sharon was unmistakably the crucial one leading the group towards their new objective, she wisely backed off from dominating the meeting. She was sensitive to how quickly a team's momentum could dissolve if any of its members appeared more controlling or ego-driven than results-oriented. History was overflowing with excellent ideas that were never accepted due to an inept or heavy-handed presenter.

Chapter 47
June 27, 6:10 PM

33,206,539,649 pounds

The packed conference room at the lab complex barely held the increased number of representatives on the team. The group had grown to include twenty-six members, all widely recognized experts or leaders in their respective fields. The frequently heated and intense discussions further strained the effectiveness of the air conditioning system during the hot summer afternoon. Randolph Schiller was still the head of the team, but he had learned to take a less authoritative role with the international experts now participating in the group.

After a long day of dialogue, the members had compiled a list of what they viewed as the most critical issues facing humanity. They downgraded scores of other suggested items for future discussion and organized the top recommendations into five clusters. The team decided to define these five clusters in more detail and provide as much justification as possible for why these changes would be the ones most likely to influence the sender of the object.

Group 1: Weapons.

The first group was the easiest to obtain consensus on, as it had previously been widely discussed as a follow up to the anti-war test case. Many of the points had already been debated at the United Nations as the next logical step to the approved anti-war accord. Governments throughout the world were currently determining how to quickly comply with the UN proposal to reduce military expenditures.

Rob reiterated the details that had been hammered out during the earlier team discussions. "Destroy all existing weapons of mass destruction: nuclear, chemical and biological. Proceed as soon as possible with the actual destruction, and accomplish it in the most environmentally safe method. Likewise, cease all development and research related to such weapons. Establish a UN agency to monitor any related research to ensure it's not weapons-related."

"You know what this means," Taylor blurted. "If we get rid of our nuclear weapons, our long-range missiles and our military forces, we'll be vulnerable to any attack. If an advanced civilization did send this object, could they be tricking us into eliminating our weaponry? If we wanted to invade a country, we'd attempt to neutralize any defenses prior to attacking. Maybe someone is using the same approach with us?"

The team was silent for several seconds; Taylor's challenging question was quite disturbing. The researchers had discussed the possibility of an advanced civilization creating the object, but this idea was new—that its arrival was only the forerunner of some greater involvement.

"That's a possibility," Rob conceded. "There's no way we can disprove it. But we can't reject any number of possible explanations for why this object was sent to us. Everyone in this room knows we've given up trying to understand the precise reasons why it's here. All we can do at this point is to try to figure out the best response to the object's edict."

Sharon offered her support for Rob's reiteration of the group's only goal. "The Earth is on a certain path to destruction, and we're talking about only a few days remaining. The creators of this object obviously have the capacity to destroy us at their whim. Our modern weaponry is useless to counteract a force that can produce global seismic events. Our purpose in these meetings is very clear—how do we best respond to the edict?"

"OK, OK. I see your point. But I also see another problem." Taylor threw out one more possibility, a less radical scenario that more than likely would occur. "What if Israel, Pakistan or any other nation refuses to eliminate their own weaponry? What if any country insists on other nations destroying their weapons first?"

Rob was quick to answer, knowing many people would have the same question. "Before this object arrived that would be the expected response. Today, the entire world agrees we must change our long-standing attitudes and any lagging nations will be forced to comply. For the first time in history, the entire world is finally uniting to force any recalcitrant nations to cooperate. The key difference now is that all countries would agree to use the

UN to mediate disputes between nations, and to accept their arbitration even if it were counter to one group's opinion. Essentially, a global rule of law would apply to all countries. Although individual nations may be given unfavorable judgments, all countries could now expect fair and reasonable decisions that would be in the best interest of the entire world."

Compared to the other recommendations, the gathered members found it relatively easy to agree on the issue of banning weapons of mass destruction. The close relationship to the successful antiwar resolution minimized any doubts about it being similarly treated by the sender of the object. The remaining categories required much longer debate to obtain a consensus.

Sharon took the lead on the next category, an area she had personally been involved with for many years.

Group 2: Human Welfare.

"So how should we 'do unto others as we would have them do unto us?' If you were a resident of an impoverished country, what would be your primary need?"

Ever since working with the Peace Corp in Burkina Faso, Sharon had been interested in promoting improvements in undeveloped countries. Her two years of Peace Corp service not only inspired her career choice to develop vaccines for impoverished people, but also drove her interest in studying economic problems in poor countries. Ever since the team had translated the strange message on the cube, Sharon had been intently gathering data to support her proposed response to the directive. She had the undivided attention of everyone in the conference room.

"Three billion people now live on less than two dollars a day—they're essentially off the radar of our modern world. They lack the discretionary income to be a factor in the global economy. The immense economic disparity among the world's citizens has reached the point of being absurd. Together, the United States and Europe annually spend $17 billion just on pet food, while three hundred million children worldwide go to bed hungry and more than 90 percent of them suffer from long-term malnutrition. We also spend $15 billion annually on perfume, while over a billion people lack safe drinking water."

Sharon proceeded to emphasize further the gross disparities around the world. "Nearly a billion people entered the twenty-first century unable to read a book or sign their names. In a number of poor nations, less than half of the children are in primary school.

"What's the best way of assisting these impoverished people to attain at least a minimum standard of living? Fortunately, there's lots of good information available— we only need to look at how social service programs have been addressing this issue for decades. Some programs have been very beneficial while others have been complete failures."

Sharon proceeded to run through a roster of varied humanitarian organizations already in service: WHO, several agencies within the UN, non-profit charities and numerous international humanitarian agencies. These groups had experimented with many types of assistance for years and it was evident that the most successful efforts were those that created self-sustaining improvements either through micro-financing or with basic education.

Randy interjected a longstanding deterrent to humanitarian improvements, an issue that had plagued welfare programs in many areas of the world. "What about corrupt government leaders? It seems to me that many improvement programs have failed simply because of graft. If an impoverished country has corrupt people in leadership positions, why wouldn't those officials thwart any recommendations we make?"

"There's a heightened sense of urgency now," Sharon replied without missing a beat. "Everyone is staring death in the face and everyone's survival is now linked to people around the world altering their actions. If this object's weight doesn't stop increasing, everyone realizes that it will certainly destroy Earth. Government leaders will be either ignored or replaced if their actions conflict with the 'do unto others as yourself' edict. Any skimming or misuse of humanitarian funds would be an obvious violation of the edict that we're trying to satisfy, and would not be tolerated by the people affected or by the rest of the world's citizens."

Not ready to concede, Randy continued. "What about dysfunctional cultural traditions and values? Haven't many programs failed because they conflicted with firmly established beliefs? Beliefs like being able to avoid AIDS through rituals or the tradition that educating females is a waste of time or that the use of birth control is sinful. Why wouldn't these problems continue to block improvements?"

"Again, our desperate situation will lead everyone to rethink established beliefs," said Sharon. "If a tradition conflicts with the 'do unto others as yourself' edict, people will be questioning if this tradition may have contributed to why the object was sent to us. A basic level of education will eventually eliminate patently false beliefs, but deeply ingrained beliefs that are counter-productive will take both money and a lot of time to eradicate, perhaps several generations."

Rob joined in, building on Sharon's remark about the need for money to improve educational programs. "Many of these programs failed in the past due to a lack of funding. With the reallocation of defense spending worldwide, an unprecedented amount of funds will be available that could be redirected. Similarly, an increase in charitable donations from individuals is likely as everyone tries to help 'others as themselves'".

Sharon closed her presentation with one more point. "As the huge disparity in income levels across the world gradually diminishes, much of the traditional hostility and resulting violence will be reduced. Impoverished living conditions have always threatened the overall stability of the Earth's nations. What better recruiting ground for fanatical groups than among impoverished people who see no hope for improvement? The success of the European Union in promoting the growth of its poorer members provides impressive evidence that aiding others can promote overall stability."

Sharon was definitely in her element. After another hour of debate on the details of the proposal, the team was ready to move on to the next category of recommended global actions.

Group 3: Health Care.

Randy Schiller kicked off the next session as the diligent members reconvened following a brief break. A few of the representatives had not met the newest member of the team, so Randy made a brief introduction.

"Dr. Michele Trichet met with a few of you earlier, but for the others, let me present Michele who arrived yesterday morning from Brussels. She's coordinated numerous medical and health programs within WHO for the past several years. As most of you are aware, the World Health Organization is one of the most successful international bodies. Although WHO is an autonomous organization, it's related to the United Nations by intergovernmental agreements. Their global health activities are coordinated with numerous agencies through the Economic and Social Council, one of the key organs of the United Nations."

Ms. Trichet moved to the front of the room, eager to provide her input to the team. Only a few inches short of six feet and with a slender build, the doctor was a striking figure. She had a serious countenance that was undoubtedly the result of working with impoverished nations for decades. In her early fifties and well dressed, there was intensity in her dark brown eyes and in her voice that conveyed a deep enthusiasm for her mission. She recognized this gathering provided a unique opportunity to promote long-needed improvements in global health care.

The global disasters of the past few weeks had placed all non-emergency programs on hold, not only those within WHO, but virtually all similar programs. Practically all of the medical support capability throughout the world had been redirected toward the victims of the earthquake and tsunami generated destruction. As the situation worsened daily, time was obviously precious.

With her strong French accent, Dr. Trichet forcefully addressed the group. "Look at the appalling statistics! Eleven million children under the age of five die each year from preventable diseases. In Africa alone, malaria kills more than a million children every year—that's one child's death every thirty seconds! A malaria vaccine will likely be developed someday, but for now preventive techniques are available that could vastly reduce the number of deaths. Unfortunately, these methods are being implemented too slowly.

"Thirty to forty million cases of measles still occur each year. An effective measles vaccine exists, and at a cost of only fifty cents per child, this vaccine can prevent 750,000 children from dying each year. In order to 'do unto others as ourselves', wouldn't we distribute these extremely low cost vaccines wherever children need them?"

Dr. Trichet continued at the same fast pace, pounding away at the global health problems and the tremendous inequity in the quality of life around the world. "Contaminated water supplies cause about 1/6 of all childhood deaths, most from dehydration. Yet again, a solution is available. Rapid loss of body fluids can be averted by giving oral rehydration salts, which UNICEF currently provides to many at a treatment cost of only six cents. A basic level of health care has to be made available for easily preventable and readily cured ailments.

"The HIV/AIDS pandemic is devastating many areas of the world, particularly sub-Saharan Africa. During

2008, 1.4 million adults and children died of AIDS in this area alone. Besides the obvious suffering for the twenty-two million victims, the pandemic jeopardizes the entire economy of these areas. The reduced labor force, the costs for supporting twelve million AIDS orphans and the stressing of health services are reversing all of the recent progress in advancing these economies."

Energized by this unique opportunity to initiate worldwide changes, Dr. Trichet continued to drill the team on the tragic realities of the modern world. "Malnutrition is the underlying cause of death for over six million children each year. That's twelve children every minute! Every year, more than twenty million low birth weight babies are born in the developing world. From the moment of birth, the scales are tipped against them. They face increased risk of dying in infancy, of stunted physical and cognitive growth during childhood and of reduced working capacity and earnings as adults. When stunting occurs during the first five years of life, the damage to physical and cognitive development is usually irreversible."

Realizing she had to finish this presentation quickly, Dr. Trichet had been ramping up to advance what she considered the most pervasive issue. "We not only need to provide health care assistance to impoverished nations, but we need to address a primary problem: overpopulation. In just the past forty years, we've added three billion people to the Earth! A population of close to seven billion people exacerbates virtually all of the planet's ecological problems. Furthermore, the world's total population is expected to peak at nine billion by 2050. That means the world's resources have to provide food, water and housing for another 1.5 million people every week! Population control has to be a very high priority.

"Every society that's progressed to a 'developed nation' status has reduced their population rate as their living standard increased. Economic policies that encourage increasing population aren't tenable in the modern world. Cultural and religious rules that increase population are likewise no longer justifiable in a world where resources are being rapidly exhausted and the environment is being extremely damaged. Nations with a dearth of natural resources that might support a smaller population aren't viable with populations above that limit. Reducing populations to a more sustainable level will require providing education and economic support to developing countries where most of today's population increases occur.

"Without addressing these basic health care issues, the economies of many of these undeveloped areas will never improve. We need to help them solve these problems, so that they'll gradually be able to support their own level of increased health care."

Rob found himself in total agreement with Dr. Trichet, as he offered a supporting comment. "It's ironic that several leaders in developed countries like Germany and Japan have actually complained about the lower fertility rates their nations have achieved. Sure, there are short-range economic and political challenges from shrinking populations. But these problems are minor compared to the strain on the planet to provide resources for an ever-increasing population. National policies need to be constrained by their global consequences."

As Dr. Trichet finished her presentation, she perceived a general openness among the gathered team. It only took anther two hours for the tired members to agree on which health issues would satisfy best the "do unto others" edict. As Rob, Sharon and the others discussed and ranked the most critical health issues, they were aware that numerous individuals and organizations had been proposing every one of these actions for years. The imminent threat the world was now facing would finally force everyone's attention to these issues.

It was close to 4 AM when the exhausted team members reached consensus on the first three groups of global actions: Weapons, Human Welfare and Health Care. It had been a very long day.

Recognizing their fatigue and the vital need to remain mentally sharp to complete their recommendations, the team decided to break for a few hours. Randy announced they would be reconvening again at 8 AM, only four hours ahead. A few members decided to continue working independently through the break period, but most chose to catch a few hours rest.

Rob returned to his office, slumped into his swivel desk chair and scribbled a few thoughts for the upcoming work session. His thinking gradually turned to Sharon, and within a few more minutes, he had lolled back in his chair to sleep fitfully.

Before leaving the conference room, Sharon reviewed the agenda for the upcoming session with Randy and then headed toward her own office. She walked by Rob's office, expecting to find him working another issue, but was not too surprised to find him already sleeping. Standing in his office doorway, she silently watched him for a few moments and then forced herself to continue to her own office. She reminded herself of the need to keep focused on the object's message—everything else was insignificant until this crisis was over.

CHAPTER 48
JUNE 27, 1:34 PM
HAWAII STANDARD TIME

33,206,539,649 pounds

"We can't outrun it! Quick! Grab the kids and go upstairs!" Holokai's voice was filled with panic as he yelled to his terrified wife. He could see from his front porch the rush of seawater in the distance, swiftly rising up the hillside toward them. The mid-afternoon sun clearly illuminated the disaster, as the seawater now completely submerged the rocky shoreline below. The rapidly rising water had already inundated the few scattered buildings at the edge of Kahakuloa Bay on the Hawaiian island of Maui.

As Maylea carried their frightened three-year-old daughter, Holokai scrambled up the stairs behind them, half dragging their other child, an eight-year-old daughter. Maylea was usually alone at home with the two children during the day, but the seismic activity of the past week had shut down the construction site where Holokai worked. Both parents were in their late twenties, and like many native Hawaiians, often spent their free time together with their children.

"Hurry! Don't stop!" Holokai shouted to his panicked family. They knew about the escalating seismic activity of the past few weeks, but this was the first time it had actually affected their neighborhood. News reports had extensively covered tsunamis that occurred throughout the world, but they hadn't heard about anything of this magnitude. Their small village of Kahakuloa was almost a hundred feet above sea level, on a hillside overlooking the small bay.

Many of the residences and businesses near sea level on the Hawaiian Islands had gradually emptied over the past week, as the residents sought the safety of higher ground. Unlike numerous South Pacific islands and many of the Asian shorelines, all of the Hawaiian Islands had easily accessible higher ground. The Hawaii residents were also fortunate in that they had experience in evacuating shoreline areas for the occasional tsunami.

The emergency warning system had been in effect for the past two hours, the loud sirens and news alerts giving those at sea level an opportunity to move away from the shoreline. An approaching wave was expected to arrive from a detected seismic event in the Aleutians, but the magnitude was not well defined. If the wave continued due south, it would eventually strike the northern coasts of the Hawaiian Islands. Although the most heavily populated areas of Maui were located on the opposite side of the island, the small village of Kahakuloa, unfortunately, was on the northwest tip of Maui.

Over the previous week, the US Geological Survey's Hawaiian Volcano Observatory had been closely monitoring the Kilauea volcano on the Big Island. Lava flows had increased significantly from Kilauea's main crater and several new surface fissures. Rangers at the Hawaii Volcanoes National Park had to evacuate the surrounding area due to the noxious concentrations of sulfur dioxide gas.

Despite the visible volcanic activity, the Hawaiian authorities believed their biggest immediate risk was from tsunamis created by the worldwide earthquake activity. It was well understood that convection currents deep within the Earth cause the tectonic plates to slowly move, building up pressure where the plates meet. When the pressure reaches a critical point, a rapid shifting can occur, causing earthquakes. If a particular movement involves a seafloor and displaces a huge amount of seawater, a tsunami can result, crossing entire oceans to impact shorelines thousands of miles away.

With a six-hour time difference from New York, the residents of Hawaii were now experiencing daily seismic movement as soon as 8:06 every morning. Amazingly, it only took twenty minutes after the object's growth cycle for the first seismic waves to span five thousand miles to the volcanic base of the Hawaiian Islands.

Holokai and his wife huddled with their two young daughters on the top floor of their two-story wood frame home, but that only placed them twelve feet above the ground. There was no time to run the several hundred yards to higher ground. They all stared out the master bedroom window in disbelief as the water continued to rise rapidly toward the bluff.

"What do we do now?" screamed Maylea, as she tightly wrapped her arms around both daughters. "The water's still rising!" Both kids were crying loudly and turned their faces away from the window.

Holokai forced himself to remain calm, at least outwardly to his family. He frantically tried to think of a way to climb onto the roof, which would place them another sixteen feet higher. There was an access panel that led into the attic, but there was no opening from the attic that allowed climbing onto the roof. He was petrified by the horrendous image of his family drowning like frantic rats if they were trapped inside their flooding attic.

The size of the wave was magnified by the water funneling between the immense dome of volcanic rock known as Kahakuloa Head on one side of the bay and the steep cliffs that bordered the other side. The terrified parents could see masses of debris swirling in the frothy water.

Both Maylea and Holokai froze with fear, just staring out the window. Suddenly, the water seemed to stop flooding up the hillside. The churning water grew calm for an instant. Then just as quickly as it rose up the hillside to less than twenty feet from the level of their neighborhood, it began to recede.

"Yes!" Holokai shouted. "The water's stopped rising!"

The whole family was ecstatic—they undoubtedly would have drowned if the seawater had continued to rise. As both the parents and children gradually calmed down, Holokai wondered if the strange object reported in the news could have actually caused this monstrous wave.

Geologists would later identify the source of this particular tsunami to have been a major plate shift beneath the Aleutian Islands, which occurred exactly eighteen minutes after the 1:46 Eastern Time growth cycle. The P waves had traveled at an astonishing average speed of 4.3 miles per second through the Earth's mantle. Since the object had descended deep within the Earth, the increased density of the Earth's interior layers was causing the seismic waves to travel faster than seismic waves closer to the Earth's surface. If the object descended still deeper into the earth's molten core, geologists estimated the increased pressure would cause the seismic waves to travel even faster.

When the first P wave had reached the Aleutian Islands, a massive sea floor shift occurred along the Pacific "Ring of Fire." The resulting tsunami then traveled at an average four hundred miles per hour over the 2,200-mile distance from the Aleutians to Hawaii. The enormous wave collided with the north coast of Maui at 1:34 PM Hawaii Standard Time.

Tomorrow there would most likely be another cycle and even greater shifting of tectonic plates. Depending on the magnitude and location of the next seismic events, even worse tsunamis could occur.

Holokai now had no doubts as to where he must take his family. They would go *mauka*, moving toward the higher mountainous center of the island, and join the thousands already crammed into emergency shelters and temporary tents. All they could do was continue to hope and pray that someone would figure out how to end this destruction—there had to be some way of stopping these horrendous tsunamis.

Chapter 49
June 28, 7:45 AM

33,206,539,649 pounds

Rob and Sharon were running on adrenaline and caffeine. Like the other team members who had briefly slept at the lab complex, or at least had attempted to sleep, they were still exhausted. Those members who had returned to their nearby hotel rooms had even less time to rest, but at least they had an opportunity to shower and change clothes.

Fueled by several large cups of coffee, Rob was animated and clearly optimistic about the upcoming day's meeting. As they waited in the conference room for the rest of the team members to arrive, Rob remarked, "I think today's meeting should go smoothly. Our first agenda item is something everyone in these strategy meetings is already aware of—the huge environmental problems we face. Worldwide, environmental efforts have already increased in recent years—in some areas we only need to accelerate actions."

"That's true," Sharon agreed. "But the environmental problems are immense. Of course, you realize many of the economic improvements we talked about yesterday will cause even more environmental damage. As people improve their standard of living, their consumption of resources will increase, as well as their carbon emissions and all other waste products. We need to figure out how to minimize the negative environmental effects from this added consumption."

"Right. Yet the developing nations don't have to use the same polluting and destructive methods the world has used for centuries. Advanced countries can help them leapfrog obsolete methods and install clean technologies first—a few developing countries have already mandated this approach in at least some areas. Many people would be shocked to learn that China already has more stringent auto pollution standards than the United States."

There were still a few minutes remaining before the scheduled 8 AM meeting, so Rob took advantage of an opportunity to talk alone with Sharon. He still struggled with discussing anything personal with her—the pressure of dealing with the object still overshadowed all other issues, including Rob's emerging feelings toward Sharon. To fill the silence that was starting to seem awkward to Rob, he brought up an emotionally risk-free topic, although he suspected Sharon was already aware of it.

"You know most people think environmentalists are focused on literally saving Earth. But all the different environmental groups aren't actually working to prevent destruction of the planet. They're really only focused on keeping the planet habitable for humans and other species. The Earth has survived numerous cataclysms in its past: asteroid impacts, ice ages, atmosphere and climate disruptions."

Sharon suspected Rob was merely trying to pass the time with idle comments, but joined the conversation anyway. "Right. Those events drastically altered the history of the Earth—one of those cataclysms extinguished up to 90 percent of all species. Yet so far, the planet has always survived and new life forms have gradually evolved."

"And now we have this object," Rob responded. "For the first time, the Earth isn't just facing some of its life forms being eliminated—this object is truly threatening the Earth itself. The environmental changes we propose today may actually help save the planet."

By now almost the entire team had entered the conference room, noticeably tired but also eager to get started. Randy stood at the front of the room while everyone else was settling into their seats, his face reflecting the somber fact that one way or another, their work could only continue a few more days. Without waiting for a few stragglers, Randy kicked off the day's session right on time.

"I don't need to remind anyone of the urgency of today's task—everyone here knows we must complete our recommended list of actions by this afternoon. To expedite working through the next category, Environmental Protection, I've asked Dr. Donald Dellwood to present a starting proposal of key environmental issues and then to lead our discussion."

Everyone in the room was familiar with the esteemed environmental expert since he had been recruited to the team a few days earlier. Before turning over the meeting to Dr. Dellwood, Randy highlighted a critical point to the team. "By the end of this discussion, we need to have a clear answer to the question: How does the mandate to 'do unto others as we would have them do unto us' relate to the environment?"

Group 4: Environmental Protection.

After years of presenting environmental issues to various government and social organizations, Dr. Dellwood was well prepared. He had spent a lifetime trying to generate interest in how modern lifestyles, an unconstrained global economy and the expanding population were jeopardizing the future of humanity. Since the world was now facing potential destruction, he believed humanity was finally eager to hear and act on his recommendations. After working closely with the group for the past few days, everyone on the team viewed Dr. Dellwood as the most enthusiastic member of the team. Even with a full head of silver hair, he appeared younger than his sixty-five years.

Dr. Dellwood began his presentation in an articulate and dynamic voice. "The long-term health of all the world's citizens and the sustainability of the world's economy for future generations are dependent on our stewardship of the environment. All life-sustaining industries such as farming, fishing and water supply require a healthy environment.

"The most important environmental change needed is this—we must factor the hidden costs from damaging or depleting resources into product prices. The world's fragile ecosystems can no longer sustain being raped to maximize short-term gain, whether it's in depleting underground aquifers, decimating fisheries, killing offshore coastlines with fertilizer runoff, escalating global warming by increasing carbon-dioxide emissions, accelerating soil runoff with poor irrigation techniques, allowing toxic contamination, wasting a limited resource, etc. Our reliance on market forces has turned out to be inadequate since it does not address the delayed or hidden costs of a product. A product's cost must incorporate the longer-term costs from escalating pollution or elimination of a non-replaceable resource.

"One example is how a number of crops are produced in the American Midwest. What would be the true cost of a crop if dwindling aquifer costs were included? The Ogallala aquifer underlies portions of eight states, and is key to the high agricultural productivity of our popularly labeled 'world's breadbasket'. Unfortunately, we consume the water at a rate over thirty times what is recharged by rainfall. Although it's taken thousands of years for the water to accumulate, one of the world's largest aquifers will soon be gone. If we estimate, for example, a twenty-five-year remaining supply of water, shouldn't our current cost be increased by amortizing the resulting crop's value over the next twenty-five years? After the aquifer is gone, how much of the crops could be produced by relying solely on rainfall? Could we even afford to import such crops if they were available from another location?"

Due to its politicized nature, Dr. Dellwood had previously decided not to focus at this time on what was probably the best illustration of misdirected environmental policy: encouraging the use of carbon-based fuels as today's cheap source of energy and ignoring the hidden costs. Among the many related costs were increased health problems from polluted air, eventual economic losses from global warming and political risk from continual reliance on a dwindling resource. Scattered efforts had already made major improvements in reducing emissions, but not nearly enough had been implemented at either the international or the U.S. government level.

Many western European governments had very eco-friendly policies, and a few states such as California had enacted legislation to reduce emissions significantly. One innovative "feebates" technique already being legislated was to assess fees on high emission vehicles and use the funds to provide rebates for low emission vehicles.

On a global basis, burning coal produced 40 percent of the greenhouse gases. The technology was available to capture the carbon, but it would lose 25 percent of the energy. Since there was no cost associated with this polluting there was little economic incentive to develop improved carbon collection systems, or for that matter to develop any other less-polluting energy sources. Most of the developed world's modern lifestyle was still powered by an energy technology developed a hundred years earlier—producing electricity in coal-fired power plants. Since coal was still the least expensive fuel, over 1,700 of these plants were spread around the world, all pumping out harmful carbon dioxide.

Dr. Dellwood continued with his presentation. "To be effective, we must develop an 'environmental tax' for products that deplete or somehow diminish our world for future generations. We can't ethically justify actions today when they effectively condemn future generations to a hotter, dryer, stormier and less-livable world. Most economists favor leaving the final decision up to consumers on what to buy or do in a free market. If we factor the cost of pollution and other environmental degradation into a product's cost, competitive market forces will move consumption to environmentally better products. We'd effectively be providing a financial reason to take better care of the environment. For example, if carbon emissions were penalized, wind farms, hybrid cars, fluorescent light bulbs and alternative fuel research all would be more common than they are now."

Ironically, in many cases people were already paying the equivalent of a tax wherever the government provided subsidies to producers. For generations, government-funded irrigation projects have heavily subsidized water use in agriculture. Since the true cost of water was invisible to both the farmer and the consumer, there was little financial incentive to conserve or develop more efficient water-saving techniques, or for the consumer to switch to more economical products.

One of the team members, put off by the economic implications, voiced an objection. "But if we increase the cost of products with an additional tax, wouldn't that unfairly punish lower income buyers, who have barely enough to pay for their needs now?"

The pragmatic Dr. Dellwood responded to what would most likely become a heavily debated topic. "We need to develop a program that equitably takes into account those with minimal incomes. I believe we could support low-income purchasers by either lowering the income tax, providing tax credits or a gradual phasing in of such taxes. This is definitely a very complicated process and we'll need a great deal of research to implement a policy that's both effective and equitable—but at least we can begin the process.

"In brief, we need to recognize the true cost of a product, not just the short-term costs we now identify. To live responsibly and protect our world for future generations, we need to continually take a long-term view of our actions and act with the best long-term results in mind. Since this is a radical and complicated issue, mistakes will undoubtedly occur due to our limited knowledge of the future. But the current practice of ignoring hidden costs has proved to be inadequate."

Objections were being voiced by a number of dissenting members, the most vocal being one of the few remaining research engineers on the team. "We never would have reached our current standard of living if we'd overpriced resources in the past. We've either relied on technology to discover a new resource when one becomes scarce or we've just found new areas in the world to mine or develop. Why can't we continue to invent our way out of these resource shortages? Hydrogen fuel, bio-fuels or more efficient solar energy for example might obviate the problem from diminished fossil fuel deposits."

Dr. Dellwood understood these arguments, having heard them all from the anti-environmental lobbies in the past. "Sure, we can invent our way around many resource shortages, but we no longer have the luxury of ignoring our impact on the planet. The unfettered dumping of toxic waste into our atmosphere, into our oceans and into our soil has brought us to a tenuous position.

"Historically, smaller populations of humans had limited impact on the Earth's ecosystems. In the grand scheme of our environmental problems, the ultimate issue is over-population. With close to seven billion people, we've reached the point where the Earth's fragile ecosystems can no longer absorb the byproducts of our lives."

Several questions from team members were pointing to the one topic Dr. Dellwood had originally planned to defer, but it was apparent that he could no longer avoid the subject of humans being responsible for the rapid rise in global temperatures. Contrary to his earlier decision to sidestep the "hot button" emotional aspect of global warming, Dr. Dellwood now felt he had to address it.

"Take global warming as another example. Historically, global climate changes have occurred slowly, with alternating ice ages and warm periods, usually across thousands of years. Due to the increased production of carbon dioxide since the industrial revolution, we now face a significant risk of rapidly melting ice elevating sea levels in this century, which could inundate coastal dwellings and force the relocation of a billion people. If the rise in sea level occurs over the course of a few centuries, perhaps we can deal with this number of environmental refugees. If it occurs within twenty years, we're facing a global catastrophe of our making, not just for plants and wildlife, but for the human species.

"Sea temperatures have risen dramatically in the past forty years. To illustrate the impact of this warmer seawater, most climatologists now predict that within ten years the Arctic will melt completely in the summer. Although this may drive polar bears into extinction, the loss of this imposing species is trivial when you project the eventual impact of warmer seas on humans.

"The feedback effect of diminished ice, which reflects 80 percent of the sun's heat, is that seawater absorbs 80 percent of the heat, producing further melting and hence further warming. Such an event affects the most distant parts of the world. A few uninhabited islands in the South Pacific have already vanished because of rising sea levels.

"All the oceans of the world are connected by currents in a river-like fashion. These conveyor belts are primary heat transporting mechanisms that affect climates around the world. The warmer temperature in the Antarctic Peninsula has already hastened the melting of ancient ice shelves, enabling the glaciers to more easily surge into the sea. If the West Antarctic Ice Sheet ever surges into the sea, it would raise sea levels by as much as twenty-three feet worldwide. If the Greenland Ice Sheet melted, sea levels would rise another twenty-six feet.

"Today there are over six hundred million people living in threatened coastal areas that are less than thirty-three feet above sea level. Most of these people live in Asia, with the poorer nations of the world most at risk, but the two biggest American cities, Los Angeles and New York, would also be vulnerable. Imagine the economic, social and political disruption of having to relocate hundreds of millions of people."

The next objection was more difficult to deal with. The representative from the UN Office for the Coordination of Humanitarian Affairs countered, "One of the reasons the developed part of the world is more advanced is that their industrialization process has historically disregarded many of its impacts on the environment. Sure, these developed countries can now afford to voluntarily reduce their consumption and protect the environment. But what about the billions of people who are struggling to raise their standard of living? Requiring them to apply a similar environmental tax would not be fair."

Dr. Dellwood recognized the arrogance of expecting every country to act similarly, since the sacrifice made by those in affluent countries would be far less than that of those in undeveloped countries. "Right, a scaled tax would be more appropriate. A scaled approach makes sense not only from an affordability standpoint, but also because developed nations have a disproportionate impact on the environment. Americans alone, with 5 percent of the world's population, generate about 20 percent of human produced greenhouse gases. Much of the pollution in underdeveloped countries is actually due to the consumption demand from advanced countries. Exporting raw minerals and products to wealthy countries frequently leads to damaged environments in poor countries. In a global market, the demand will go wherever a product has the cheapest cost of production, so if one country is willing to sacrifice its environment more than another, that country will end up the most damaged.

"With a global environmental control system, a 'damage' tax can be applied wherever a product is produced to curb the rate of pollution or even depletion of a non-renewable resource. This is particularly critical with activities that affect other countries or even entire regions of the planet, like toxic air pollution or carbon dioxide emissions. The ability of the planet to absorb the ever-increasing quantities of waste has finally been reached, particularly in the atmosphere and water supplies.

"From an environmental perspective, we must view the entire planet as one country and all of the world's people as its citizens. It's imperative that the world have a global environmental protection agency, most likely as part of a reformed UN structure. Obviously, it would have to have adequate capability to enforce its global regulations."

Dr. Dellwood's arguments convincingly showed that the object's mandate included environmental calamities caused by humans, since all such crises directly reduced the quality of life for 'others'. Despite concerns with the complexities, the team agreed that environmental changes needed to be a key part of the overall recommendations.

As the members debated which of the issues to include in their recommendation, everyone was glaringly aware of the next expected expansion cycle. As the time neared 1:46 PM, all eyes and attention focused on the large wall clock at the back of the conference room. No one was surprised when one of the techs monitoring the object appeared a few minutes later with yet another announcement of the object's expansion.

As with previous cycles, mild tremors were soon felt throughout the lab complex as the seismic waves propagated through the Earth's mantle toward the surface. The solid geological base beneath their immediate area would again minimize the local damage, but the increasing size of the tremors would have devastating effects in less stable parts of the world. It would have been difficult for any of the team members to imagine a stronger incentive to rapidly finish their task. Deciding on the best response to the object's message was their only goal.

Continuing to push forward, the team proceeded to address the last category of recommendations. Several team members believed this last area would be the most difficult to implement, but many of the attendees also considered it to be the most significant. Achieving consensus on this last category of recommendations was critical.

Group 5: Tolerance.

Professor Josef Ramon, the head of the Religious Studies Department at NYU, had been an active member of the team for the past two weeks. He had held a number of lively discussions with the researchers as to why so many of the current world trouble spots were so heavily influenced by religious fundamentalism. For this session, Randy had asked him to prepare a briefing on how he thought intolerance toward others could be reduced.

The professor was ready with a specific plan for promoting tolerance, not only toward other religions but also toward all aspects of life. "We must foster tolerance for others' viewpoints, lifestyles, interests and religions. Individuals worldwide need to have the freedom to express their own preferences, as long as it doesn't negatively affect the rest of the global society. To eventually achieve equal rights for citizens across the world, regardless of gender, race or religion, we must first promote an accepting attitude toward other's viewpoints."

The professor launched into his primary recommendation. "One way to improve acceptance of 'others' would be to increase everyone's knowledge of cultures and religions around the world. The more familiar we are with different cultures, the more we can recognize what we have in common and not just focus on our differences.

"We need to launch a world-wide educational program that familiarizes individuals with a 'multi' perspective of world: multiple ethnic groups, multiple religions, multiple customs, multiple mores. The simple fact of realizing there are other religions whose followers are perhaps just as devout as oneself would go a long way toward promoting religious tolerance. I personally believe that educating people in the different religions of the world will directly weaken the appeal of radical religious groups.

"By educating the world's people on how local actions can negatively affect others, we'd be fostering better individual decisions. Exposing everyone to representatives of foreign cultures could be fashioned after the U.S. Peace Corps, recruiting and deploying individuals across the entire world. Expanding educational programs into the most conservative cultures will certainly be difficult, as many of these groups have traditionally prohibited exposure to ideas deemed too radical, too politically dangerous or immoral. We're definitely talking about a very gradual process, one that would undoubtedly require several generations."

One of the UN representatives to the team objected. He considered such viewpoints more of a cultural issue, stating, "Surely you can't expect cultural or ethnic differences to be eliminated merely by a global education effort."

The professor clarified his recommendation with a specific example of intolerance that he felt was destabilizing to the world at large. "Of course I'm not advocating erasing harmless cultural attitudes, just at mitigating intolerant beliefs that promote violence. As an example, look at the religious foundation of Saudi Arabia's culture. Their extremely strict interpretation of Islam is known as Wahhabism, which began 250 years ago with Muhammad ibn Abd al-Wahhab. Saudi Arabia has institutionalized this extreme version of Islam as the state religion and it's actually illegal to publicly practice any other religion. The Saudi authorities firmly believe only Islam should be allowed throughout the entire Arabian Peninsula.

"This attitude is instilled in every generation through their school system. Over one-fourth of the time spent in lower and middle school as well as several hours weekly in high school are devoted to teaching their religion. This focus on religion may appear harmless to some, but unfortunately, their textbooks clearly indoctrinate the children in intolerance.

"Worse still, these same books are supplied to Islamic schools worldwide. Their first grade textbooks state unequivocally that 'Every religion other than Islam is false.' Their ninth grade textbooks assert that '... the struggle between the Muslims and the Jews should continue until the hour of judgment.' And in their twelfth grade textbooks, they teach that 'Jihad in the path of God ... is the summit of Islam.... It is one of the noblest acts, which brings one closer to God, and one of the most magnificent acts of obedience to God.' In the twenty-first century, we can't survive in an interconnected world where such intolerant viewpoints are cultivated.

"Promoting tolerance will be similarly painful for all other individuals or groups who wish to force others to abide by their particular worldview. Anyone that has an inflexible concept of the truth and is driven to convert others to their faith is effectively spreading intolerance. Many of the religious fundamentalists within the United States have a long history of trying to force their views onto their fellow citizens, although they've only rarely resorted to violent means to do so. Yet bigotry and intolerance have frequently led to attacks on the objects of their scorn—the government, abortion clinics, Jewish temples, gays and those of a different race. For these narrow-minded individuals, we're talking about a very difficult change in worldviews."

"Maybe not." Randy realized the team needed to wrap up their recommendations quickly, but he wanted to emphasize why he felt there was room for optimism in getting people to be more tolerant of others. "Where intolerance has been fueled by intractable religious beliefs, we now have a new predicament. Even the most fundamentalist believers now have to wonder if there's a force influencing our world and our individual fates that hasn't previously been recognized. However they resolve these questions, it appears there's less incentive to follow unquestioning dictates that were laid down by our ancestors thousands of years ago. How we fit in the cosmos is definitely more complex than these groups previously thought."

Professor Ramon agreed with Randy's comment. "That's true. Many religious proclamations issued in the past week provide support for your optimism. Several religious bodies have generated more inclusive policies that would have been considered too liberal or even blasphemous only a few weeks ago. Many groups, viewing the object as a message from God, have interpreted the dictate as overshadowing all previous dictates received."

One of the UN representatives on the team, wanting to put an historical perspective on what they were proposing, offered one final comment. "At the UN we have a strong precedent for these five groups of recommendations. All of these proposals have the same intent as the goals that were laid out after WWI in the League of Nations, and again after WWII in creating the United Nations. The Preamble to the UN Charter states that the organization exists '... to reaffirm faith in fundamental human rights, in the dignity and worth of the human person ... to practice tolerance and live together in peace as good neighbors ...' But this time, we're facing a vastly different situation: the threat from this object is mandating total compliance and ongoing enforcement."

Time was running short. It would unquestionably have been better if the team had more time to analyze and prioritize the key challenges and problems throughout the world, but driven by the urgent need to respond, a sub-optimal list would have to do. The team split into subgroups, focused on summarizing and fine-tuning the items into a concise list, and then attached as much supporting data and reference information as they had available. That evening, Randy reviewed the summarized list and added a preface reiterating that it was only intended as a starting point for actions.

Other groups of international representatives would address the details of each recommendation as they were further refined and implemented. Randy forwarded the report to the president on the encrypted communication line as part of the daily status reporting. The encrypting process was now pointless, since the reports were also circulated to a number of global bodies. In fact, the General Assembly of the UN was now the prime audience for these recommendations. The UN assembly had their own committees researching non-stop along similar lines, and they would utilize the team's recommendations.

If the United States acted immediately on the actions, many other nations would quickly follow. Time was critical—for every day it took to initiate the recommendations, another expansion cycle could be expected. Each cycle wreaked ever-increasing panic and destruction throughout the world. Humanity could not survive many more expansions.

Chapter 50
June 29, 11:30 AM

62,428,294,540 pounds

The first wave of cruise missiles struck a military installation two hundred miles due west of Khartoum. The accompanying aerial assault on two additional Sudanese military facilities was over within half an hour, with all attacking aircraft returning safely to their carrier bases in the Indian Ocean. The UN sanctioned military strike was a peculiar but necessary contrast to the global anti-violence efforts.

With a seven-hour time difference from New York, the brief airstrike occurred only a few hours before darkness in Sudan. The mid-90 degree heat was stifling, yet appreciably better than the 113 degrees earlier in the day. The entire country of Sudan and particularly the Darfur region had been plagued with a series of tragic conflicts for decades, leading to hundreds of thousands of its citizens being killed or persecuted. Ethnic and religious warfare had been the norm for many years.

Due to the daily seismic destruction and almost universal efforts to treat "others" better, scattered violence between opposing factions had considerably diminished around the world. Sudan's government was a notable exception in that it was actually ramping up genocidal actions against its own citizens. The dominant leaders in the military government interpreted the arrival of the object as a religious mandate to rid the world of infidels. To the radical Islamic leaders in Khartoum, this clearly meant that the Christians, animists and other non-Muslims living in Sudan had to be eliminated—not just driven from their homelands into refugee camps in neighboring countries, but murdered as quickly as possible. The government was even willing to kill other Muslims who did not share their own brand of extremism. This was pure genocide not unlike the Nazi extermination programs in the mid-twentieth century.

The African Union had formally agreed to intervene and stop the slaughter, yet the Union was in a quandary since they were also attempting to cooperate with the entire global community to cease all violent actions. The crux of the issue debated within the African Union and in UN committees was an ancient dilemma: how should one deal with an intractable opponent who uses force? Can one condone or perform violence in order to rid the world of violence?

A small percentage of the human race had always fallen in the sociopath category, capable of unwarranted violence against others. Whether this percentage diminished in societies that were more "civilized" or more "open" was debatable. Prior to the Nazi extermination program, much of the human race viewed Germany as one of the most advanced cultures in the western world.

Although there were numerous factors that encouraged a country such as Sudan toward genocidal acts, two key aspects were leadership and accountability. Sociopathic individuals in positions of authority always had tremendous influence on others' thoughts and actions. In Sudan, these individuals had absolute power and were not accountable to any higher authority. This was a striking contrast to democratic governments, where the leaders ideally were held accountable to all segments of the population. With adequate checks and balances, representation that was more diverse usually lead to decisions that were more moderate. In Sudan, there was nothing to constrain the criminal actions of those in power.

The African Union represented fifty-three countries across the African continent. When the Union asked for military assistance from the UN to halt the genocidal actions, they were establishing the first test case for a new world order: when could violence be justified in a world seeking to eliminate violence? Authorizing the attack on the Sudanese military installation underscored the continuing need to deal with sociopathic governments and individuals. In a rare demonstration of cooperation, even the Arab League endorsed the action against the predominantly Islamic government of Sudan. This decision served notice to any government or tribal leader that if they continued to use violence, they themselves would be eliminated by this new world order.

The survival of the world was at stake, and globally arbitrated and sanctioned violence would be used wherever needed. The cooperating governments of the world were intent on demonstrating they were serious about eliminating intolerance, including the use of lethal force when necessary. Inherent in this logic was the belief that reasoned decisions by the majority would have more validity than decisions by any individual or minority. This would not always be true, but after seven thousand years of experimenting with ways to organize societies, this was the best system devised to-date.

Chapter 51
June 30, 7:30 AM

117,365,193,736 pounds

It was astounding how rapidly the attitudes and actions of people were changing. Figuring out how to comply with the object's mandate dominated the thoughts of billions of citizens throughout the world, and as it turned out, the most egregious situations were in fact the simplest and quickest to stop. Wars between countries had ceased almost immediately after the UN antiwar resolution had passed. Literally thousands of less dramatic actions were being planned to improve the treatment of 'others' throughout the world.

Practically all actions were based on efforts that had already been identified and attempted in earlier times. Countless organizations had been promoting economic and welfare changes for decades, and individuals concerned with environmental protection had been identifying the destructive effects of human activity for years. Likewise, social support agencies had been attempting to improve the lot of the world's most downtrodden citizens and many religions had promoted the concept of tolerance for millennia. For the first time in human history, these varied groups now found an extremely receptive audience.

It became apparent that practically all of the major issues addressed were highly interrelated—each problem area contributed to worsening the other problems. As an example, overpopulation had led to environmental degradation, which exacerbated resource shortages and reduced economic development. These problems had further reduced health services and educational opportunities, and in many cases had increased political unrest. Yet voluntary population control was impossible without adequate education and without raising living standards.

Piecemeal approaches had not been successful in altering the systemic causes of global problems. For any reform program to be successful in the long term, it was evident that all of the problem areas must be addressed together. Consequently, the U.S. legislature, other governments and the UN were viewing all five areas of recommendations promoted by the team as integral parts of a unified package.

The U.S. Senate convened a special session at 7:30 AM, fully aware that it would be meeting only six hours before the next cycle of weight expansion. The reduced rate of weight increase that had immediately followed the antiwar resolution had given new hope to humanity, and there was an urgency to initiate as many additional changes as possible. A resolution had been drafted for both houses of Congress to affirm the five areas of change that the team had recommended. If the object ceased its growth, congressional committees would have time to develop the implementation details over the next few years. The resolution being debated and voted would establish a formal American commitment to a radically different national policy.

Unlike exaggerated or bogus promises often made in Washington and other political arenas, dealing with this object involved sincere actions. Little thought was given to reneging on commitments if the object permanently ceased its expansion. If whoever or whatever sent the object could stop its growth at any given time, it was probable that it could just as easily be restarted.

Despite the life-and-death ramifications of passing the resolution, four senators actually attempted to water down the policy. The bipartisan majority easily overrode the four dissenters who apparently wanted to see more proof of the connection between the actions taken and the object's reduced rate of expansion. A portion of the general population undoubtedly had the same concern, but as the debate progressed, it was apparent the majority of senators felt otherwise.

Even if many of the senators were not convinced of a direct connection, they at least recognized there was nothing to lose since the planet was quickly heading toward destruction, possibly within just a few more days. Importantly, a significant portion of the population also recognized that if the planet survived, the recommended changes would effectively produce a vastly better world.

Aware of the limited time before the next expansion cycle, both houses of the U.S. Congress met simultaneously. As the senators and representatives debated direct challenges to all five areas of recommendations, the most argumentative discussions occurred in the House of Representatives. As the morning hours rapidly passed, all debate hastily concluded since the members of both houses of Congress realized there was no other way to affect the object. The atypical swiftness was aided by the simple fact that all legislators earnestly wanted to vacate the 150-year-old U.S. Capitol building before the expected 1:46 PM expansion cycle.

As soon as the Senate bill passed, the House of Representatives quickly reached consensus and passed the recommendations with a vast majority. The United States had formally gone on record with the most fundamental and sweeping policy change in its history.

Throughout the world, other countries were forming similar policies as rapidly as possible, knowing the next cycle was due within hours. Many nations used the same five groups of recommendations as a starting point for changing their own national agendas, expanding the list with locally specific actions to foster greater tolerance for others.

A global revamping was also occurring at a personal level, as citizens sought individually to satisfy the mandate to "do unto others." People around the world had finally recognized the protection of the planet for all of the world's inhabitants and for future generations as a moral issue. Suggestions were rapidly circulating as to how individuals could adjust their consumption patterns to reduce negative impacts on the environment. Small everyday actions like minimizing energy consumption and recycling had the capacity to significantly affect the environment if practiced by large populations. These ordinary acts were constructive steps that individuals could immediately perform regardless of what higher-level government actions were implemented.

Media commentators were suggesting longer-term changes that could eventually be implemented by an enlightened populace if the planet survived the immediate threat. One recurring topic was how to power cars with less fossil fuel, stressing the fact that the United States with less than 5 percent of the world's population consumed 43 percent of the world's gasoline. The commentators debated how the government could implement improvements by requiring higher miles per gallon for vehicles, encouraging development of hybrid and alternative fuel vehicles with tax incentives and funding an infrastructure to deliver alternative fuels.

Although only a few hours remained before the next cycle, governments around the world were driven by the lead of other nations and by their own activist citizens to continue legislating improvements. Countries were desperate to respond to the object's message and they were actively working to change their national agendas.

Late that morning, the UN General Assembly efforts to create a roster of recommendations was a dramatic event, resulting in the most globally unified position that had ever been attained in the history of the world. The General Assembly Hall was again packed to capacity as delegates filled all eighteen hundred seats, scores of individuals lined up against the side walls and accredited news reporters crowded into the balcony. With an unobstructed view of the packed hall, television and film crews filled the broadcasting booths and transmitted every minute of the crucial session to their audiences.

The UN resolution about to be voted incorporated all five areas that the team had recommended and that the U.S. Congress had already approved. The UN version also incorporated numerous related recommendations that the UN sub-committees had hammered out over the past several days. The critical voting was about to begin.

Just behind the speakers' rostrum, an electronic board displayed the votes next to the name of each Member State. Delegates only needed to press a button at their desk to record their decision: a green button to designate support for the resolution, a red button to vote against the resolution and a yellow button to abstain.

Although only a two-thirds majority was required to approve the resolution, virtually every member country pressed its green button, thereby giving a mandate to the UN to enact the progressive recommendations. Only three countries voted in opposition to the resolution. North Korea continued to act bizarrely, in total disregard for the world's future. It was rumored a coup was underway in that country, with a more rational leadership about to take control. Two African countries also opposed the mandate, both headed by obdurate dictators who were still convinced the United States was orchestrating the event and creating the seismic activities in an attempt to take over the entire world. They were about to be forced into the new world community by their neighboring countries and their own citizens.

As the electronic board displayed the final vote results, the resolution passed the General Assembly 189 to 3 with no abstentions. The Assembly Hall immediately erupted in cheers and the delegates were still applauding as the Security Council members hastened to leave the hall to convene their own follow-up meeting. According to the UN charter, the General Assembly could only adopt recommendations, not make binding decisions. Only the Security Council was authorized to approve any resolution that included the use of force, but since all the Council members voted in favor, the subsequent Security Council session quickly authorized the resolution.

Only one hour remained before the next cycle.

Chapter 52
June 30, 1:00 PM

117,365,193,736 pounds

The world's citizens were anxiously waiting. At each of the last four expansion cycles, the object had increased in mass by 88 percent, causing greater seismic destruction every day. If the next cycle expanded at the same rate, there would be the most devastating seismic activity ever known. If it turned out that this next cycle was survivable, it was certain that only a few more cycles would remain before there would be no one left to observe the planet's eventual fate.

Billions of people around the world struggled with deciding how to spend what could be their last hour alive. Other than workers in the most critical emergency services, virtually everyone who had a family retreated to be with their loved ones. Those without families sought solace with their friends—it would be better to have someone to commiserate with or to celebrate with if the world's actions were successful in finally halting the growth cycles. Everyone was desperately hoping that the additional actions would sufficiently demonstrate understanding of the object's message.

The core team had gathered in the lab's monitoring room, for what might be the last time. Rob watched Sharon as she checked the various monitors. If the object continued to increase in weight, the seismic waves would again gradually propagate through the Earth's interior to affect the entire globe. The satellite communication system, however, would immediately broadcast the results to the world. Just like having advance warning of an approaching tsunami, they would have advance knowledge of the approaching seismic waves. But unlike a tsunami, in this case there would be no safe place to flee.

Twenty-five minutes to go.

Rob was oddly more perceptive to his surroundings than he could ever remember. He silently asked himself, "So is this the heightened sensitivity when one faces impending death?"

There was nothing to do at this point but ponder recent events. Standing behind Sharon, Rob noticed for the first time the fine downy hairs on her neck as she scanned the monitors. "What an odd thing to observe at this time," he thought to himself. Despite only minimal sleep for the past several weeks, she still looked as beautiful as ever, maybe more so. He knew they both really connected, and he hoped she also felt that if they survived this ordeal, they needed to see a lot more of each other.

"Twenty minutes, Sharon. Not that much time to reflect on life, but maybe that's just as well. I really think we solved the puzzling message and have gotten the world redirected to a better future. But if we're wrong, I guess this is as good a place as any to spend our last minutes."

Rob hesitated, but recognized this was no time for being indirect. "I'm glad we're here together. There's no one I'd rather experience these next few minutes with." He smiled, pleased with himself that he had finally acknowledged how his feelings had grown over the past weeks. But he also was very curious as to how she would respond. He waited.

After a few long seconds, Rob wondered if perhaps Sharon hadn't heard him. Or worse, maybe the inept wording of his feelings had somehow offended her.

"Yes" she finally answered. She continued looking ahead as if at one of the monitors, but she was just carefully choosing her next words.

"I really wish we could have met earlier, when we could have focused on each other rather than this object. After working together so closely on this team, I can't imagine losing touch if we survive this crisis. When I've gotten stressed out over the past weeks dealing with this dilemma, my first response was always to persevere to get us out of this mess. And for what? To save the world? To make the world a better place for future generations? Sure, but what brought me the most peace was to fantasize that surviving would allow us to share our remaining time together. Yes."

Five minutes remaining.

At that moment around the planet, billions of people were fervently praying that they might survive, that the object's growth would finally halt. Another billion were disconsolate with grief, a few committing suicide to end the stress, and many venting their anger at a likely abbreviated lifespan. Another billion were trying to escape their terrifying thoughts by anesthetizing themselves through drinking, drugs or even sex. The remaining billions just anxiously waited, reflecting on how they had spent their lives, and how they would spend their remaining years if they were spared.

Ten seconds remaining.

Rob wrapped his arm around Sharon, as they stood together in the silent lab. Their minds were racing, filled with rapid-fire images from the past. Significant events were oddly intermixed with seemingly trivial occurrences— vivid memories from early childhood flashed between scenes of recent meetings with other team members. All of these disparate events now seemed so intricately related.

Five seconds remaining.

They both closed their eyes, attempting to ratchet down their intense mental state as they silently counted off the last few seconds.

Silence.

They both quickly scanned the various monitors. Other than the countdown clock, absolutely nothing had changed on any of the screens. The first signals should have registered instantly. The growth cycles for all of the past generations had never varied even by a millisecond from the previous cycle.

"YES!" Rob and Sharon both shouted, jubilant with relief. Everywhere in the lab complex, people were yelling with joy.

It worked; the object had finally stopped expanding. Completely. Everyone in the lab was ecstatic—they were not going to die from this object. The team also realized they had successfully determined the correct response to the object's message.

Randy shouted across the room, his voice booming with excitement. "Finally! We did it!" Randy was not only celebrating their escape from death, but also that his persistent optimism on the project had been vindicated and his long string of career successes was still unbroken.

Taylor was also ecstatic, realizing his suspicions of a foreign conspiracy were unfounded. He figured there could still be some surprises waiting, but at least the immediate crisis had now ended. He no longer saw any need to relay information to his Pentagon contact—the government would see the news broadcasts the same as everyone else.

Rob and Sharon were euphoric that they would be surviving and they would be experiencing the future together. They embraced each other as the noise from the rest of the team mounted around them.

"Rob, let's head over to the pressroom and join the party," Sharon shouted. The two most critical monitors in the lab had been simultaneously displayed in the nearby pressroom—the clock counting down to the expansion time and the weight of the object. As soon as they left C Lab, they could already hear the shouts of elation and relief from those in the pressroom. The media reps that had agreed to remain during this latest and potentially most lethal expansion cycle were jubilantly broadcasting the results.

As the spectacular news quickly spread, spontaneous celebrations erupted throughout the entire world. Virtually all of the world's citizens had been expectantly waiting for the results and lost no time in celebrating.

People on every continent, spread across every time zone, were simultaneously reveling in a renewed opportunity to live.

Tens of thousands of ecstatic people soon formed crowds in city centers, town plazas, churches and mosques. The crowds grew larger and larger as virtually everyone wanted to join with others to share the excitement. Confetti fell like a heavy rain in New York's Times Square and throughout the financial district as the revelers screamed and shouted to each other. Noisemakers of every conceivable type filled the air in cities across Asia and India. In the streets of Europe and South America, oceans of people danced to any available music. There was a carnival atmosphere as celebrants packed into London's Trafalgar Square, the National Mall in Washington D.C., Moscow's Red Square and dozens of other historic sites. This was truly a planet-wide celebration with billions of people also offering prayers of thanks from their homes and from their local churches. The world's citizens knew they had not only survived, but now they faced an immensely better future for the planet and all its inhabitants.

EPILOGUE

Although minor changes to the planet's gravitational field and equilibrium had occurred, stopping the object's growth secured the Earth's future. The increased mass of the Earth served as a permanent reminder to future generations of the planet's narrow escape from destruction. For the next several weeks, there were minor seismic aftershocks that caused an ever-diminishing amount of damage. The usual stress buildup between the planet's tectonic plates had been eased by the intense month of seismic activity, eliminating all earthquakes for the next several decades. As the glacial pace of plate movement continued, the frequency of earthquakes would gradually return to a normal level.

Despite the diversity in beliefs and values among the different cultures of the world, a planet-wide ethic gradually developed that held every person of equal value, regardless of their nationality, ethnicity or religion. This pervasive belief provided common ground for cooperation and for negotiating differences. By including planetary ethics in global education programs, the values that were initially compelled by the doomsday object were absorbed and passed on to future generations. Social justice issues remained paramount in this new world order, and national interests were eventually subjugated to global interests.

By taking a long-term view toward protecting the planet's ecosystems, people throughout the world developed an appreciation for less consumptive living. Acquisitive lifestyles that disregarded the environment became less common, and in fact were associated with an obsolete era. Reducing one's consumption was no longer considered strictly an environmental matter but rather a moral issue. How could one morally produce unnecessary pollution or consume a limited resource if it negatively affected individuals elsewhere on the planet? How could one morally continue to abuse the environment when everyone's children or grandchildren would have to pay the price?

As dissimilar groups have always interpreted events differently, the various religions incorporated this event into their respective theologies. The fundamentalist Christian organizations treated the delivered message as another of God's commandments. The more liberal Christian groups further split their organizations based on their understanding of why God had sent this object to the world. Islamists viewed it as a prophet-less message from God, allowing them to retain their view of Muhammad as the last prophet.

Among the non-religious, agnostics were content with merely adding another mystery to ponder. Atheists had no difficulty viewing the object as a message from a benevolent alien civilization. Over the following years, the experience provided a greater enticement to expand the search for other life forms in the cosmos.

A completely unexpected outcome was the rapidly growing body of followers that formed a new religious movement structured around the object, and who used images of the cube as their icons, supplicating the God who sent it. The cube's message was their only scripture, resulting in the most egalitarian and liberal religion ever founded.

With the clarity of hindsight, humanity realized the object's arrival was *not* a terrible scourge of destruction for the planet, but in reality a priceless gift showing the people of the world how to avoid their self-destruction. Despite the preponderance of evidence, the human race had failed to recognize that virtually every natural system on the planet was threatened. This object was sent to unite the people of the world against a common threat and offer them a last opportunity to avoid destroying themselves. It provided the disparate peoples of the world with urgent motivation to examine how they were leading themselves toward mass extinction not only from advanced weapons, but also from environmental destruction and intolerance. Prior to the object's arrival, the Earth had already been on a doomsday path. The real threat to humanity had actually been escalating for centuries—the instrument of destruction was themselves.

There were no further communications from the sender, nor were any necessary since individuals now realized that their future was tightly bound to the planet's health and to the kinship of all people. Decisions in business, government and personal lives would henceforth be guided by their long-term impact on the planet and its inhabitants. Humans at last viewed themselves more humbly as part of the Earth's ecosystems, and not as the rulers of the planet. This awareness enabled the world's citizens to halt their path toward self-destruction and embark on a promising future for humanity.